Time to Go Home

By

Jennifer Baylor

D1235951

ISBN: 1-4033-5764-1 (e-book)
ISBN: 1-4033-5765-X (Paperback)

This book is printed on acid free paper.

1stBooks – rev. 9/24/02

Chapter One

The sun sat high in the sky on this mid summer day. The heat so intense that even the dirt clods exploded when stepped on. Dust rose up from the ground caused by the hooves of the horse nervously stamping the ground in wait. Sweat soaked both the animal and it's trainer in the heat. It was too hot in the day to be saddle breaking. If they waited any longer the horse would forget what it has learned up to this point. She checked her watch and looked down the long drive. The boys were late. She made the decision to go on ahead with just Katie's help. The girl was strong for her seventeen years. If anything went wrong she could handle it. She stepped up to the horse and gently placed the saddle on to it's back. He suddenly flinched at the unfamiliar weight. Katie crooned to soothe the animal while she kept her hold tightly on the reins. Her boss tightened the cinch and buckled the strap quickly.

"Aren't you goin' wait on Huck and Dale?" Katie asked.

"It's too hot to be waitin' on those two to show up." The woman stepped back from the horse pulling her hat down tighter on her head. "Don't waste your time waitin' on any man when you can do it yourself and probably get it down a lot quicker and more efficient." Riley looked over the saddle at her and grinned. Experience is the

1

greatest instructor in life. And she pitied the man that taught Katie Wilson the lessons she needed to learn. The thought made her chuckle to herself.

"Good luck." Katie replied heading towards the gate to where she climbed up and sat on the top to watch. A nice and safe distance. Riley stroked the horse's neck. She would never rush a horse before saddle breaking. Let him get used to the feel of the saddle. When you build a trust with an animal if it gets broke at anytime a trainer will never regain it back. She respected these animals and they sensed it. This particular one was going to give her a fight of his life to save his independence. There have been only two horses Riley couldn't handle and that was years ago when she first started training. A few tricks she learned along the way. That was the reason Huck always insisted that him or Dale were present when she broke a horse. The horse that ran her into the fence leaving a seven-inch splintered wood piece in her upper thigh, was the last animal that got the best of her.

Riley stood back and cautiously placed her boot into the stirrup. The horse jerked sideways and took off just as her bottom touched the saddle. The first trick was to anticipate it's every move. He gave her a hard ride kicking his hind legs up attempting to throw the weight off his back. She bared down hard with her legs to gain control and find the horse's rhythm. The whole corral turning into a cloud of dust in the process. Katie sat perched on top of the gate holding her breath as she watched.

The old Chevy truck made it's way over the old rickety bridge going towards the barn. Both men got out and headed towards the corral at a slow jog. "How long has she been at it?" Dale asked as he climbed up to sit next to Katie.

"Just started. She got tired of waitin' on you all." She stated never once taking her eyes off the horse and rider. Huck pushed his hat back to let what breeze there was cool his head and watched. "One of these days her stubborn streak is goin' to get the best of her."

"How many times has she done this?" Dale asked as he climbed over the fence to the other side.

"About forty." Huck answered. "What the hell you gettin' at?"

"She knows what she's doin'. And watch your mouth." Dale glanced at Katie.

"Like I've never heard it before." Katie grinned. She had been around the boys enough to hear all the words she wasn't suppose to hear.

A car turned down the county road gong slow as it climbed up and over the hills. "There is the church so it's the next road to the right."

"I see a dirt road. Does that count?"

"Who knows. Are you sure you wrote the directions down correctly E.G.?" The other woman asked as she glanced from the paper to the dirt road ahead.

"The store clerk back in Springdale said Riley's place was way out. Who in their right mind could find a place so far away from even the simplest of life?" Both women looked at each other knowing Riley as well as they did. The car made the turn on the dirt road slowly trying not to create alot of dust unsuccessfully. "Whoa, will you look at that view!" E.G. exclaimed. "These hills are almost mountains." Her companion just sat looking out the window without expression. To her this whole trip to Boonsville was a waste of time. She didn't even know why she had agreed to go with E.G. in the first place. A few miles down the road a mailbox came into view behind a clump of weeds and wild flowers. The car turned left into the drive. The rest of the ride was silent as both took in the scenery around them. They had only seen landscapes like this in paintings or postcards. Never before in person.

Springdale was known for the beauty of the hills and the shops around town which still kept it's nineteenth century decor. Craft stores, leather goods, pottery, all made from the hands of the artist in the county. There was also a barn converted into an art gallery that had those paintings of the hills full of color and abundance. The tourism of Bradford County was outrageous during the fall. The winter had it's skiers hitting the slopes after the first good snow fall and during the summer months which were the slowest there was the state park just up the road. The main attraction was evident but the towns around Springdale no one cared to venture out to. A few explored but no one cared about the legends in the holler. The ridge above the valley between the hills had enough history running through it's core to fill books on end. No one cared about the little towns like Stanford. A Bed and Breakfast, a Mercantile, and a feed

3

store which was still run by the same family for over a hundred or so years. A Christian Church sat in the middle of the town to which all the residents attended some not so regularly. Stanford is the defination of small town.

The car came to the bridge in the drive over the creek and stopped. E.G. maneuvered the vehicle slowly over the wooden planks wondering if the bridge would hold them. The farmhouse appeared up ahead. A two-story whitewash slightly elevated with a huge porch that went the total length of the house. She parked the car near the other vehicles near the barn. Both women got out of the car speechless as their attention focused on the woman behind the fence thrashing about in circles on top of a horse. "Oh my God, she is taking this cowboy thing too serious." Lynn exclaimed.

"Pull down, pull his head down." Huck gritted through his teeth. Katie had turned to look over at the two women coming towards them from a car. They had the strangest looks on their faces. The shorter one wore a baseball cap and shorts while the other looked as though she just emerged from the pages of a fashion magazine.

The horse and rider whirled by kicking up dust. The heat was getting to the animal as his fight began to slow. Sensing the change Riley pulled down hard causing the bit of the bridle to go deeper into his mouth. The horse reared up for one last fight but the rider was more experienced keeping a firm grip. Riley could feel the muscles in her arms strain as she fought for control. One last attempt the horse reared up, she held tight. He came down hard on front legs and she loosened her grip. The horse too a side step and he broke out into a canter riding around the fence line. Control was accomplished, as the wild animal was now a tamed but still spirited horse. Riley gradually slowed him down by bringing him towards the center of the corral.

Sweat had foamed at the horse's sides flying off with every twist and turn he'd made. Riley couldn't tell if she was soaked from her sweat or the horse's. She reined in feeling his responses to the command. Either he was taking the direction or just plain worn out. The latter seemed more practical considering his temperament.

"Atta boy." She spoke stroking his neck. "You still got you spirit. I doubt you'll let anyone take that away." She replied as she slowly dismounted. He was still jumpy and would probably stay that way for awhile. Once down on firm ground her legs felt shaky. She saw Huck walking towards them.

"Don't go blaming' me for being late. Dale was out checking his traps." He took the reins from her. Huck Hopkins, Dale Benton, Jesse Monroe and Riley Jones inseperatable friends during high school. A week after graduation Riley left for the military and Jesse got on the bus to Nashville, Tennessee. A few years ago Riley just showed up one day at the Feed and Seed inquiring about the boys. Said she bought her grandpa's farm and was going to make a run at it. The boys helped her get started on the horse boarding business, which at some point not planned turned into a training facility also. It didn't take along for her reputation to get around and the business began to grow. She was a natural around animals. Either you had the instinct or you didn't. Riley had it.

This particular horse belonged to a Banker in Albany, the state capital and largest city in the state. He had purchased this horse for his daughter. The banker had a summer home near the resivour in the next county. Every weekend he'd bring his daughter out to the ranch and Riley would go over the training with her. The weekends were busy in the sense the owner's would come to spend time with their animals. Some wouldn't but every horse in her charge got adequate attention and exercise. At times her own horse Cherokee stayed in the pasture as she and Katie would ride. The boys would borrow mounts anytime they went up into the holler. People knew their horse was in the best care at Riley's ranch. She had cleared many trails up in the woods for people to ride let them explore the hills on their own. They'd ask how far they could go into the hills and she just told them until they ran out of trees.

The humidity was so thick this time of day it made her irritable. "Whatever." She took the bandanna off around her neck and wiped at her face and neck heading towards the water trough. "I had no qualms about this one. He was an easy ride." She glanced over by the gate and suddenly stopped in her tracks. Those women talking to Dale and Katie. It couldn't be she thought to herself. Her legs felt like rubber but she managed to get to the trough and dip the bandanna in the cool water. This was the visit she never expected. She wasn't exactly prepared for. The years of trying to put that part of her life so far back in her mind she was beginning to forget. Now they show up bringing it all to the surface again.

E.G. Thomas and Lynn Carlton stood right before her as she opened the gate. Riley placed the smile on her face. "What in the hell brings you two down to Stanford?" She asked in greeting.

"The star's map to the boonies." The tall woman retorted. Not missing a beat checking her old acquaintance out from the cowboy boots on up the jean clad legs and what used to be a white sleeveless T-shirt now was smudged with dirt and sweat. The cowboy hat completed the picture of the Marlboro Man in her mind.

"Nice to see you again Lynn." Riley bit her cheek. Lynn Carlton never was nor will ever be her favorite person but she was E.G.'s girlfriend and she had to respect that.

"I thought it was time to come find you. No one has heard from you in a long time." E.G. looked around. "So this is what you do for a living? Ride bucking horses?" She grinned. It was nice seeing her friend from so long ago. "I thought my job was dangerous."

"What's your job?" Katie asked out of turn. She could tell these women were different from those in Bradford County. They had an intriguing sense about themselves especially the tall one Riley had referred to as Lynn.

"A police officer in Albany." E.G. looked over at the teenager.

"We have two of those here. That is if you can call them that." She chuckled.

"Suppose you met my hired hand who needs to helping with Diablo." Katie was a good kid and totally a teenager. Riley depended on her help more than Katie knew.

"Come on I'll go with you." Dale replied leading her over to the corral.

"I never get to stay around for the good stuff." She pouted.

"I know. Me neither." Dale smiled down at her.

"Cute kid." Lynn lowered her sunglasses as they walked away. Riley just smiled politely towards her.

"Man you got one hell of a place here. The view of the hills is exhilarating." E.G. was mesmerized. She had always loved coming to Bradford County just for what she saw from where she stood. "The house reminds me of that one show during the seventies when we were kids."

"Which one Little House on the Prairie or the Waltons?" Lynn looked every bit bored just standing there in the middle of a barnyard. Riley just didn't have it in herself to warm up to her personality and really didn't care to try.

"Let's go up to the house. I could use something to drink." Riley took off her gloves noticing the dirt clinging to her. She sure didn't smell any better either.

"I'm sure you have indoor facilities." Lynn inquired in her snobbish tone. Even thought she was here purely for E.G. The day was too hot to be hanging around a farm with all it's farm smells.

"Tell me again what rock you found her under." Riley asked under her breath just loud enough for E.G. to hear. Once they reached the back door into the kitchen Riley directed Lynn to the bathroom just under the stairs on the landing. "There's beer, soda, and ice tea in the fridge help yourself. I'll have a beer." She went to the sink to wash some of the dirt off her. "I love training horses but it sure doesn't leave you smelling too good at the end of the day." she replied soaping up.

E.G. opened a couple of beers sitting Riley's down on the counter next to the towel. She also pulled out a folded envelope out of her back pocket and handed it to Riley. She looked at her name written on the front. Her stomach turned as she recognized the handwriting. "How is she?" Riley asked staring at the envelope as a new set of buried memories began to surface.

"Doing quite well for herself. She has literally turned the art gallery around. I don't even think you would recognize it." E.G. was beginning to feel like a traitor to her friend. Riley and her go way back even before she joined the police department and both women were working at a small computer software firm in Albany. If she remembered right Riley had just been discharged from the military and this was her first civilian job. She lasted almost a year typing in data before she started working for a home improvement/remodeling company. The work seemed to fit her but her involvement with Tess McGuire was ruining her. She was going through an identity thing and one day Riley just up and left town. No one knew for the longest time where she had gone off too including Tess. One day Riley had called her at home and told E.G. about her grandpa's passing and she had purchased his farm. They kept in touch by phone but soon careers overtook them both and today E.G. had decided to see for herself how her friend was doing. Lynn had mentioned the trip to Tess at the gallery. Lynn worked for her and had become close friends. She had seen the spark in her friend's eyes when she had mentioned Riley's name. Lynn wasted not time convincing E.G. that these two women were meant to be together. E.G. had seen it first hand when she picked Lynn up from work the previous night. Tess and her had a chance to talk as E.G. waited for Lynn. It didn't take any words to see the woman wasn't over her feelings for Riley. And from the reaction of knowing who the letter was from E.G. knew her friend was far from healing.

"So this is what brought you down here. To deliver this letter." Riley challenged.

"No. That was last minute. I had planned on bringing Lynn to Springdale because she had never been. If I had known how close you were I would of come down a long time before now." She leaned against the counter next to Riley taking a long swig of beer. The coldness hit her throat and she felt the intense sensation. Riley just looked at her from the side. E.G. would have to do better than that scenario.

"Yea, right." She chuckled before becoming more serious. She could just imagine what was in that envelope and for some reason she wasn't in a hurry to find out. "I have done nothing for the last three years but try to justify my life in Albany. I stopped trying. It's no use. That was just a part of who I was but not who I am now. I couldn't give her what she wanted. I'm not the party going, gallery opening gala, or who is who in the art world and did you know… Uh huh. Look around you. This is who I am. There is no point in even considering anything else."

"Who are you trying to convince? I understood what Albany was doing to you so it's not me you need to convince. I think you owe her that much. Look, she's taking the first step." E.G. walked over to the steps to the landing to see if Lynn was coming. "Just hear her out and give it some thought."

"Like I haven't been thinking about it everyday since I left." She commented before finishing off her beer. Just then Lynn walked around towards the kitchen taking in every detail of the decor. She hadn't spent all her life around art not to notice the finds Riley filled her rooms with.

"Where on earth did you get taste?" She asked as she briskly walked across the landing. "This is just so…God, what's the words I'm looking for?" She asked mostly to herself. Riley glanced at E.G. with a look she always gave of despair. What was it that her old friend saw in her and kept it going for all these years? Had to be love.

"This house was my Grandpa's. So most of the furniture is his. I've picked up a few pieces here and there at auctions." Riley remembered the decision to just leave the house as it was. A reminder of her grandfather and of the childhood she had. "There's a lot of history in this house and the land around it. Grandpa's deed dated back to 1845 when his grandfather built the house for his wife and family. It's really interesting if you have time to dig deep into it." Lynn turned around suddenly interested.

"You can trace your ancestry that far back?" She asked.

"People from these parts stay put a lot longer than those in the city. A few will stray off looking for excitement that only a city can give them. Fewer will come back" She couldn't help but smile. That was nicely put. She made her point to Lynn. And it was taken from the response in return.

"I know an art gallery owner who would love to fill this house with treasures." Lynn smirked and E.G. took the distraction for their exit.

"We had best be going. I promise Lynn a tour of Springdale and it's getting late." For the life of her she couldn't figure out why these two could not get along. A talk she would have on their way back to Albany.

Riley totally ignored Lynn's comment and turned to E.G. who was glaring at her companion. "I'm glad you all came down. Next time let me know and I can make plans for a longer visit." She walked both to the door and followed them out to their car. E.G. turned and took Riley's hand giving it a squeeze

"You can come up to Albany sometime. It wouldn't kill you."

"Think not?" she grinned. "Be careful going back. If it's any consolation I will give your advice some thought so you won't feel like you wasted a trip."

9

"It wasn't wasted. I got to see Riley Jones ride a bucking horse." E.G. winked.

"Be careful."

"Yea, you too." Riley leaned down to look at Lynn in the passenger seat. "Nice seeing you again."

"I find that hard to believe but thank you." She replied. E.G. started the car and slowly backed out to turn around. Riley waved once before going towards the barn to finish a day's work. The visit wasn't as bad as she anticipated. E.G. never would put any pressure on her. She understood. She may not agree but she understood.

The rest of the day she tended to the horses and managed to weed the garden. Katie and the boys left about an hour after her company. She wondered if they could tell just how eccentric her friends were. Maybe Huck could. His senses were very acute. His reputation as a hunter and tracker was the best in the southern part of the state. Dale and him spent most of their time at the lake. She preferred the creek that ran through her property for cooling off. This wouldn't be a bad evening to go for a swim. The temperature hadn't dropped any. There was too much that needed tending to around the house before she would allow that luxury.

The sun was beginning to hang low in the sky when the last of the weeds had been thrown away. The chickens were fed and the horses too now the laundry needed taken off the line and folded. Once everything was done it was her time and that would be spent soaking in the tub for a prolonged period of time. On the way up tohouse she remembered the letter she laid on the kitchen counter. She picked it up before going into the bathroom. Her heart began to beat a little faster but she waited until she was in the bath to opened it.

The water was so cool against her skin she gasped. Relaxing had never been one of her strong points but after today she needed it. She took the envelope off the towel and looked closely at the delicate handwriting. Tess McGuire had never been called delicate before but her handwriting had a certain class to it. She hesitated before opening it. Did she really want to know what was inside? As far as Riley was concerned she didn't have anyone to answer to. Curiosity got the best of her and she carefully took the letter out and began reading. How typical the letter was typed. Nothing personal about it. The only thing she got from the contents was the fact Tess wanted an explanation for her sudden departure. The years of anger had long ago vanished. She was trying to put her life back on track and needed closure. In her opinion she felt that Riley owed her that much. Funny that was exactly what E.G. had told her. Riley had to laugh on that one. She owed Tess. How ironic that Tess didn't have a clue to why their relationship ended so abruptly. Was she that naive or had she been so busy with her career in the gallery that she was actually clueless. Riley dropped the letter on the floor and totally submerged herself in the water. Allowing the coolness to go over her head. She barely heard her name when she resurfaced. She looked at the half open door. The voice was familiar.

"Is that you Lucas?" She shouted as she hurriedly rinsed off the soap and reached for a towel.

"I just came by to give the Williamson's horse her shots. Mind if I just go on out to the barn? I really didn't mean to disturb you." He stood at the bottom of the landing near the kitchen.

"Go on out. I'll be there in a few minutes." She replied.

"Take your time, don't rush on my account." He stated. It was all he could think to say. He hadn't realized she was in the bathtub when he knocked several times on the back door. It was late in the evening for house calls but he waited to come out to Riley's for the last appointment. That way he could visit with her and not feel rushed about it.

Riley hurriedly put on a pair of jeans and a T-shirt before combing out her hair. This is what took so long. Her hair had grown past the middle of her back and she mostly wore it in a braid. She couldn't tell how long it had been since she cut her hair. The longer it got the more tangles it had to comb out. Of course now that she was in a hurry it wouldn't be manageable. It would just have to hang wet. She grabbed her boots near the door and headed out to the barn.

The light was on in the barn0 and the one in the stall shone over Doc Garvey as he finished giving Wind her shots. She walked in. "How late do you work every night?" She asked as not to startle him while he had the needle out.

"I've really been swamped at the office and with house calls. I'm sorry for coming out so late." He apologized.

"Oh I didn't mean it that way. I'm up late. I always welcome company." She stated thinking this must be her day. Normally days would go by before she saw anyone other than the boys or Katie. Sometimes her friend Logan would come out but with the coffeehouse doing good business that was a scarce visit. She liked Doc Garvey. He was a whiz with the horses. Every one of them trusted his touch even Cherokee.

"I shouldn't of walked in your house like that. I knocked but you didn't hear me." He put the medicine back into his bag.

"You have to stop apologizing. I was just taking a bath." She repied. "I broke in Diablo this afternoon and I needed a good soak." She tried making conversation.

"I don't know how you do it." He shook his head all the while smiling down at her. Riley could tell the local veterinarian had a huge crush on her. Logan told her that a long time ago. She was just now noticing it herself. She tried not to encourage the feelings but was finding it more difficult not too.

"It's a job." She shrugged.

He decided to change the subject before something slipped. He glanced at her standing over by the stall door. Her damp hair falling over her shoulders. He probably stared more than he should but he had never seen her with her hair down before. Riley Jones was a mystery to the whole town. People knew her family but could not figure out why she would move back at such a young age and live by herself on a ranch. Any man in town would be honored to have her as his wife. The sight of her in a pair of worn Levi's was enough to buckle any man at the knees. He had to admit on more than one occasion he had found excuses to come out to her place. "I take it you will be in the rodeo competition next weekend."

"Wouldn't miss it. I heard Cole is bringing in some prime stock. Huck said he's been all over the northern part of Wyoming and southern Montana gathering what wild horses he could find. It would be hard to pass up a chance at owning one of those animals."

"Isn't that how you got Cherokee?" He remembered.

"I won him two years ago." She smiled back at him.

"I was wondering if you had plans to go to the dance this Saturday night?" He found himself asking on impulse and wouldn't dare look at her directly. She might think him silly and laugh at him. At their ages people didn't actually go out on dates, or did they?

Riley felt the smile at the corners of her mouth widen. She realized this was not at all easy for him. "Lucas Garvey are you asking me out on a date?" She couldn't help it. This was all too cute. He caught the twinkle in her eye. "It's been a long time since I've been out on a date." Longer than she should admit.

Lucas knew she was teasing him and he took it all in fun. "Should I take that as a yes?" He looked at her quizzically.

She nodded in response. "That would be a yes."

He couldn't believe his ears. She said yes. "I'll pick you up at six thirty on Saturday."

"I'll be ready." She watched as he closed the latch on his medicine bag and walked towards the door.

"All right Riley I will see you then." He waved and walked to the driver's side of his truck. She could see he was still smiling as she watched him back up and drive off down the driveway. Riley walked up to the front porch and decided to sit outside for awhile. She really didn't think too much about going out with Lucas. He was nice looking and very sweet. Everything a woman would want in a man. But the one thing she knew she could never give him or any man back was the same feelings he had for her. And she wasn't going to lie to anyone nor herself.

There were times when life here in the country got lonely to the point it almost drove her crazy. But to give any part of this life up for a relationship was a definite no. That would never be an option. The purpose of her and Logan getting involved in antiques was to fill her days during the winter months. Riley would spend hours in her makeshift workshop off the south end of the barn restoring some kind of antique. Logan had kept her busy when they worked on redecorating the coffeehouse to the rustic look the tourist seemed to be attracted to.

The porchswing creaked as Riley absentmindedly moved her legs back and forth creating a rhythm. Now she was second guessing whether to accept Lucas' offer. This might be leading him on to something she would have to confront in the end. It was only a dance and not a commitment. She thought of the letter she hastily placed on the table beside her bed when she was rushing to get dressed. This could complicated things for her. If Tess got the notion she would come down looking for her answers. Tess seemed to get what she wanted and at times at any cost. The years that Riley took to build her reputation as a strong businesswoman was begining to pay off. Trust and hard work made her what she was today. Granted most of the town knew her grandpa and she'd remember the talks he had about this person and that when she would come for a visit. Some of those stories she still remembered. A few she started herself. This ranch was the best thing to happen to her.

Tess wouldn't understand that kind of bond. Her world was bound around art and socialites. She wouldn't understand the real people. The ones who physically labored for a living. Now Tess was wanting more of her. Why couldn't she just let it rest? Even though Riley didn't leave an explanation surely Tess wasn't that dense. That weekend they planned especially for themselves so they could talk and reconnect. Both realized there was a strain to the relationship and Riley was taking the initiative towards putting them back on track. The next thing she knew Lynn was giving her a message that Tess had to unexpectedly leave town but world be returning in a few days. Tess was treating her like some client and not like the other half of their relationship. Riley knew then nothing was going to repair the damage. It was hopeless to try. She packed her things in the truck and headed south. No one knew where she had gone and that was fine by her. She could get her fresh start and not have that kind of hassle to deal with in the process. Riley had decided if Tess' career was more important then so be it. If it wasn't for the perks that came with being a police officer E.G. would of never found her either. But E.G. had kept up her end of the friendship and kept Riley's whereabouts a secret. Until now, maybe she did owe Tess some kind of explanation. Let her know how willing Riley had been to salvage their love while Tess threw it in the back seat like discarded trash. Either way there was a decision to make.

Promptly at six thirty on Saturday Lucas was on the front porch knocking on the screen door. Riley turned off the kitchen light making sure she remembered to shut everything off. He stood and watched her through the screen as she made her way towards him. He couldn't help but swallow hard when he saw her in a loose fitting sleeveless gauze shirt, old Levi's and boots. Her hair was down but pulled back from her face. Riley walked towards him carrying a dish.

He found it hard to look away and not just plain gawk at her. "Right on time and I'm all ready." She managed past him as he shut the door after her.

"You look very nice." He let out his breath hoping she didn't catch on to his stupidity. "It's supposed to be getting cooler out." He should just give it up he thought as they walked down the walk to his truck.

"Let's hope so." She placed the desert on the floorboard and climbed in the cab. Lucas started to go around to hold the door but she was already half way in.

"Smells good." He stated. Riley didn't know if he meant the desert at her feet or herself personally. He was looking quite good tonight she noticed. His beard was trimmed and his hair looked as though he ran a comb through it. Working outside without a hat most of the day left him looking disheveled most of the time she saw him. She never liked wearing hats either but in winter it was necessary.

"It's apple crisp." She replied shifting herself a little going around a curve. "My own recipe so make sure you get a piece." She looked over at him. She hoped he wasn't thinking too hard on that last statement. "A secret ingredient was added."

"Whiskey?" he turned to look at her. Something he found quite easy to do.

"Old Barton, Kentucky's finest bourbon this side of the Ohio." She stated like a commercial. 'Can't even buy it this far north."

"How did you get it?"

"Dale and I went to Lexington about a month ago to look at this thoroughbred. That is some kind of training I wouldn't mind getting into. The horses don't seem to throw you as much." They both laughed. "My Grandpa used to drink only Ol' Barton's. I on the other hand prefer not too. But it's an added flavor in cooking." Maybe she was rambling on too much. It was just hard for her to fully concede she was on a date with not only this man but any man.

"I'm sure there will be liquor floating around there tonight. That is if Chuck is around." In reference to the town character Chuckie Allen.

The Bed and Breakfast was lit to the sky with gas lamps and a few strands of Christmas lights from last year. The outside deck was filled with tables of food, and the gardens were lit up for people to see

15

to walk as they made the way to the barn where the music was coming from.

"Smell all that food." Lucas commented as he sniffed the air around him.

"Yoo hoo! Riley Jones!" Riley turned around when she heard her name to see Mrs. Tucker come from behind the desert table. "Here let me have that dish of yours." She took it and placed it on the table with the other dishes. "Let me guess. Apple crisp." She grinned.

"Like every social." Riley commented.

"Hmmm, did you put your secret ingredient in?"

"Now it wouldn't taste the same without it."

"Oh what to do about you." The older woman chuckled and for the first time noticed Doc Garvey standing with Riley. This was interesting she thought to herself making a mental note to tell Gracie.

They walked down to the garden taking the path out to the barn. The Inn's building used to be the town's hotel constructed in the 1850's. The barn used to be the livery stable in the same years. Through time each owner had successfully kept it's washed out clapboard look preserving the history behind each wall. The barn was converted into a dance hall although most of the people preferred to the cool night air. Bales of straw had been placed along the dance area for those to rest between dances. A refreshment table was set up near the back. A convenient place to spike it and go unnoticed. Lights had been strung up making the place clearly out of a Norman Rockwell painting. Riley looked around and found her friend Logan with her husband Clark near the door. She waved them over. "Close the coffee shop up early?" Riey asked. The band was just warming up so they had to speak loudly in between tuning up instruments and checking the microphones.

"I had too, everyone in town is here tonight. The tourist are either in Springdale or at home." Logan grinned when she noticed who had accompanied Riley. Clark took the opportunity to talk shop with Lucas. "So anything knew goin on?" She emphasized tilting her head towards the men.

It took a minute for Riley to get her meaning. "Oh no, don't start anything there Logan. He was out at the ranch a couple days ago and just happened to ask me to go tonight. There is nothing too see into. Trust me on this."

"Whatever, it's good to see you out with someone other than me or the boys." She replied. Riley was her closest friend and vic versa. They had spent nearly a year putting the cafe together. Antique stores, estate auctions, and miles of traveling the back roads in the southern part of the state. It was two summers ago that they virtually lived at the shop working on the wood floors or walls. Refinishing tables, chairs, and church pews converted into booths. One night at Riley's workshop too many beers were opened and Logan's persistence finally got rewarded. A few questions here and there and Riley had opened up about her life in Albany. This included the few months she spent with Tess McGuire. She really wasn't shocked although appearance wise her friend looked nothing like the stereotypical lesbian that everyone thinks of when they hear the word. The years of knowing Riley and the friends they become made her realized through mannerisms, and the esteem she held for herself that Riley acted more masculine. The truth be told it really didn't matter to her one way or the other. Clark didn't even know because this was something just between friends.

"I do have other friends and Lucas just so happens to be one of them." Riley retorted in jest.

"I heard a couple of those friends paid you a visit the other day." Logan reveled in the look Riley gave her.

How on earth did she know that? Riley looked at her in disbelief.

"Your visitors stopped in at the Marathon station in Springdale asking for directions and Mrs. Simms was in paying for gas at the time.

"Ahh, it makes sense." Riley glanced over at Lucas still engaged in conversation but looked her way and returned the smile. "They were on a mission of sorts in delivering a letter for me." She stepped over to the punch bowl and took a glass smelling before she tasted it.

"Too late. Chuckie made it to the punch bowl before anyone else could." She wrinkled her nose. She could smell it from where she stood. "So who was the letter from? Was it her?" She asked. The story was getting intriguing. Riley nodded in response and took a sip of the punch and feeling it burn as it hit the back of her throat. He must of poured the whole bottle into the bowl. Surely there was a virgin bowl sitting around somewhere. "What are you going to do?"

17

"I don't know yet. She can be very persistent which I can't have her coming down here. That part of my life is over." Not even Logan believed that remark. "She wouldn't cause a scene or anything. That is not her style. I just don't want her invading my life." Not like when she invaded her dreams at night, Riley thought to herself.

"That's understandable but I know you and if you're ever going to have a chance at happiness you'll have to find those answers." Logan dipped herself a cup of the fire water punch.

"What answers?" Riley was confused at what she meant.

"Is that part of your life really over? You can dress a skunk up all fancy but when it comes right down to it, he is still a skunk." Logan started to laugh. "Okay maybe I should of thought of a different metaphor but I already had two glasses of this before you all got here."

That was all Riley needed to spit out her drink in laughter. The thing was Logan was right. It doesn't matter how you phrase it, obviously. The band struck a chord to get everyone's attention and Lucas found his way back over by his date. They welcomed everyone to the Summer Festival Dance and thanked Don and Mary Stolfer for letting the festivities take place at the Inn. A round of applause went up. The chords to the first song started and everyone headed out to stomp their feet. Clark grabbed Logan as Lucas offered his arm to the two stepping tune of a Bill Monroe song. Around and around they went as the beat sped up. Riley felt it hard to resist the urge to lead but trying to keep up with her partner. Lucas was quick on his feet.

One song led into the next until a slow waltz was chosen to let everyone catch their breaths and cool off a bit. Lucas took her into his arms pulling her close up against his chest. She could feel the hard muscle under his shirt as her hands moved along his shoulder. Their bodies moved against each other in rhythm. She closed her eyes letting the song take her far from reality.

The dance went late into the night as some of the older people began to call it a evening and head home. The ladies of the church and social counsels all gathered on the garden porch supervising the dishes so everyone got their pans and casserole bowls back. Every now and then someone would spot Chuckie or one of his cohorts going up to the punch bowl to relieve a pint of the chosen liquor. The effects were starting to wear on the group, as the line dancing became

18

more of a do-si-do than a heel to toe. Even though tomorrow was Sunday everyone had to get up early either to go to worship or to feed their stock. A perfect evening and Riley didn't want it to end.

The ride home was less tense as the conversation was on Huck bringing Sara Benson one of Logan's waitrress' at the coffee shop. Riley and Dale figured out he was sweet on her for quite some time. Both thought he'd be to shy to do anything about it. Tonight Huck proved them wrong. For the first time in years he looked like he was really enjoying himself. Huck took things way too seriously and had a hard time loosening up. Even in high school he was the same. Dale on the other hand took life for face value and tried his best to slide by it all. The women were on to his charms and some even tried to get him tied down. He played their games until things become too serious and then he was out the door. Riley had hopes for both of them but she figured they both would retire up into the hills and live the rest of their lives off the land. Martha Cowen had been doing it since she was a young bride.

Lucas parked the truck next to Riley's in her drive. He kept the engine running but turned to her. "Don't move." He instructed and got out of the truck coming around to her side. "Both times tonight you never gave me the chance to show my manners."

Riley smiled as she accepted the gesture. "I guess I'm not used to this kind of treatment." That wasn't a misstatement on the truth. She pulled her key out from her jean pocket placing the dish down on the table between the rocking chairs on the porch so she could unlock the door. "I really had a nice time tonight. It's been quite awhile since I have been on a date. How did I act?"

"Like a pro." He cleared his throat and suddenly looked serious. "Maybe you would like to go out for dinner some night?" He saw from her expression he'd taken her by surprise.

"Maybe I would." She managed a smile. She did enjoy his company. Lucas took a step closer and placed his hands on her waist. She lifted her face up towards him and his lips gently found hers. She put her arm around his neck drawing him closer. Then something snapped inside her and she gently pulled away. He took it as a sign of going to far too soon and released his hold.

"I'll call you." He backed up towards the steps careful not to go making a fool of himself.

19

"Goodnight." She opened the door and waited until she heard the tires on his truck backing up. Oh my God, Riley thought to herself. He had mad her feel suddenly alive again. The wall she spent years and years to build up around her heart was being chipped away slowly. She still had time to stop it. But did she want too?

Riley went to her room and turned on the lamp by the bed. She spotted the letter and opened it up rereading the words over again like she had done every night since it was delivered. Could Lucas make her love again? Or would he end up hurt in the end? With so many secrets in her past how could she completely bury all of them and what if one day all the secrets came out? Could he live with knowing the truth? The time had come to put her past where it belonged. But was she strong enough to face Tess? She put the letter back propped up by the lamp and taking off her clothes she crawled into bed. Too many questions to deal with and she was too tired to figure them all out tonight.

The sun was barely up before Riley had completed feeding the horses and the chickens. Katie was just coming up the drive while she dressed from her shower. She backed away from the window to sit down and put her boots on. Today she was going to face her demons in Albany. The last two nights had been spent sleepless as old memories stirred old feelings that she needs to lay to rest. Then maybe she could get some.

The back door slammed announcing Katie's arrival. Always coming in befoe starting on the chores to get a glass of orange juice. She figured Riley had been up way earlier since a good part of the work was done.

"Mornin'." Katie greeted looking over the door of the refrigerator as Riley came down the steps into the kitchen. "See you survived Saturday night."

"And what would make you doubt I wouldn't." Riley poured herself a glass of the juice.

"Doc Garvey might of kept you out really late." Katie teased. She could get away with a lot but it was fun to just see how for she could push her boss. From the look that Riley shot her way she was getting close to that 'no go' zone as she referred to it.

"What is that supposed to mean young lady? And I am emphasizing young." She retorted back.

"Everyone in town is talking about you and Doc Garvey and that was long before the sun came up yesterday." Katie had heard a few remarks at the dance from some of the ladies around the food tables. She and her friend Jane from school hung out with a few guys from the FFA club. Not a whole lot of teenagers tend to come to festival functions but the Summer Dance was not one to miss. It gave them something else to do rather than going to Springdale. Even she had spotted the couple out dancing and could see Doc swooning all over Riley. The person getting the swoon was always the last to figure it out.

Riley just looked at her. "One day since the dance and I'm gossip." She decided to change the subject. "I'm going out of town this morning. I've already fed and watered the stock. If you can wash down the Harrison's mare I would really appreciate it. I got a message his daughter might be down in the week to ride."

"Not a problem. Where you headed to?" She asked.

"To see a friend. I should be back before noon." Riley glanced at the clock. She had best be getting on the road before she ran into the morning rush hour traffic.

"Are you taking the jalopy?"

"I don't have a choice. It'll make it." She had confidence in the engine as long as she didn't push it too hard. The truck was a 1952 Ford pickup but the engine was fairly new. The fact was she was in no hurry for the confrontation she was about to have.

Within the hour the jalopy pulled onto the interstate heading north. Miles behind her she seemed to relax. Thoughts kept her occupied and before long the signs announcing Albany came into view. The lane for North Albany was getting backed up with slow moving cars. The air inside the truck was stifling as the morning grew hot. Riley could feel the sweat on her back making her T-shirt stick to her skin. The truck was made long before air conditioning was installed in transportation. The windows and sixty miles an hour was all she had.

The 65th Street exit came up and she veered off towards the right. The whole street was lined with expensive sport cars like BMWs, Jaguars, and SUVs. Florence Street was just up ahead if she remembered correctly. Slowing down Riley made a left turn. The building was just up ahead on the right side of the street. Luckily she found a parking spot at a meter just a few feet down from the door. She got out and stared down the street. The building looked the same except for a few minor paint jobs around the door and window. She dug out the change for the meter. It was now or never she thought taking a deep breath before walking the short distance to the door. Her stomach twisted in knots when the bell on the door went off announcing there was a customer. The reply came from up the stairs in the loft.

"I'll be with you in a moment." Riley didn't answer but began checking the place out. Tess had really put a lot of work and money into the gallery. The paintings were of a higher quality than she remembered. She took in the decor not realizing her back was turned.

Tess had just put the latest treasured find away for the opening of next months showing. An artist she found in upstate New York last month. He work was superb by high standards and no one was even getting a peek at this work. She started down the stairs locating the customer that came in stopping in her tracks. It was unmistakable. The cowboy boots, Levi jeans and t-shirt. Her heart began to beat faster. What was she doing here? Lynn had told her bits and pieces about their visit and how Riley wasn't interested in drudging up her past. If she wasn't interested then why was she standing in the gallery?

Tess continued down the stairs taking in the noticeable changes in her ex. Like the length of her hair that was pulled back into a long braid. Being outdoors not only lightened the blond color but left a nice healthy looking tan on her skin. Tess had to struggle with her composure. "That's a piece from a local artist. The title is "Midnight Walk'. Catchy isn't it?" Tess replied as she closed in on the distance between them. She watched closely for reactions as Riley looked over at her.

The black slacks and sleeveless black blouse complimenting every curve of Tess' body. This was the style that only Ms. McGuire could get away with. Riley was thinking to herself. The straight black hair hung loosely to her shoulders in long layers. Riley didn't have to touch it to know its silkiness. The woman herself was a piece of art.

"Hey Tess." Riley seemed barely audible as she spoke. The sight of Tess in all her beauty recaptured her senses.

"Riley." Tess more or less stated with a tinge of anger around the edges. "I'm surprised to see you." That was an understatement.

Riley managed a smile. "Well there are a lot of things one never thinks she might do." She glanced around the room. "For instance you've done wonders with the gallery."

Tess watched for any signs of the true meaning but found none. Riley was known for doing the unexpected so she should have been prepared. Lynn had told her of the changes in her but she was not quite prepared to see for herself. Riley's body looked as though a sculptor had chiseled out the muscle leaving a dark tanned finish. "The farm life seems to agree with you." Tess commented. She was losing her senses but she had to gain control of the situation.

Riley just nodded and took a few steps towards her. Those crystal blue eyes could still make her quiver. She tried to shake it off. "Your letter was delivered." She heard herself start. She had to get this over with and may as well not beat around the bush about it.

"My letter? What are you talking about?" Tess looked at her not understanding what she meant.

Riley look back just as confused. She reached into her back pocket and unfolded the envelope with her name written in Tess' handwriting. But from her reaction Tess didn't seem to have a clue what Riley meant. "This one." She handed it to Tess.

Tess looked at the front before opening it to read. Riley watched as her forehead creased in confusion as she read. She waited until Tess was finished. "Well?"

Tess looked up into those green eyes that haunted her thoughts and realized they had both been duped by Lynn and E.G. "I'm not the one who wrote this. Although there are some interesting points that could use an answer." Tess handed it back to Riley.

"Shit." Riley exclaimed as she wadded the letter up. "This was E.G.'s doing wasn't it?" The embarrassment and anger building at the thought she had be cohurst into making this visit.

"I'm sure she had help from Lynn." Tess couldn't help being ammused. Although she didn't agree with their tatics she understood why they went to those lengths. Tess held Riley's stare. There was something quite different behind those eyes. "Were you that unhappy with me?"

Riley blinked breaking the moment she walked over to one of the displays and tried gathering her thoughts. "The whole situation wasn't so much about if I was happy with you or not. Hell, we barely knew each other. You were in Chicago, LA or Seattle or some other place other than here with me. This city was getting to me and you had no clue." Riley felt a twinge of resentment keeping the conversation civial.

"I admit my career took on more importance in my life but you knew what art meant to me." Tess stated the fact that Riley knew from the start.

"I remembered what being an artist meant to you not what being a shrewd business woman meant. And I took the time for you Tess. You didn't take the time to find out what meant to me. My goals and dreams." She felt the heat rise in her neck. Tess looked at her like for the first time. Riley was right in a way. But Riley never voiced her ambitions. She just seemed as satisfied being who she was. "We were falling apart just after we got together. I don't think it was meant to happen. Take this visit any way you wish but I am sorry for leaving the way I did. Mostly I'm sorry that our lives together didn't work out." She started to turn around to leave when she felt Tess grab her arm. Riley looked down into her eyes. Tess reached up and gently touched Riley's face feeling the electric current race through her skin to her heart.

"I never meant to hurt you or us." Tess' eyes bore into the depths of Riley's. She could almost feel the pain herself. "I've missed you so much." She whispered. Familiar feelings of arousal and passion swept over them both.

Riley saw a glimmer of a tear at the corner of Tess' eye. She could feel her own behind her eyelids. Oh God, how she wanted to touch those lips with her own. To feel the softness, taste the sweetness of the inside of Tess' mouth once again. To her surprise Riley stepped back. "I can't do this." She stated breathlessly.

"Why Riley? What was so wrong that we couldn't fix together?" Tess looked defeated. "You just packed up and left. You took the easy way out."

Riley stood by the door looking out the window at the city. Tess' words stinging with hurt. "Don't you think I tried?" She turned around to face her to see Tess' reaction. Instead she saw a tear fall that was quickly wiped away with a swipe of a hand.

Tess was losing her battle to keep control. "Why did you come here today?" She asked as she crossed her arms. "I mean you thought I had written that letter so why did you come up here?" She was persistant for an answer.

"You didn't write the letter so I guess that changes my reason." Riley retorted back.

"No Riley. You came to see me." Tess stated. "I know your reason and just because I didn't write that letter doesn't change a thing."

Riley placed her hand on the doorknob. It was time to leave. Their conversation wasn't what either expected the day the met again. Riley had no clue why she came to see Tess. Other than the desire she had to see her again. Tess saw it the moment she looked into Riley's eyes. She had too. Riley knew where Tess was concerned she was transparent.

"Don't take the easy way out again Riley. Let's talk this out." Tess took the inititive by offering both another solution.

Riley ran her hand through her bangs in frustration. Tess didn't realize all that she was asking of Riley. She faced Tess looking into those eyes. She became more beautiful with age. "I don't know. I'm sorry Tess." Riley opened the door and left fighting the temptation to look back.

When she reached the jalopy she unlocked the door and got in. Riley sat for a moment thinking it shouldn't end this way. For some reason E.G. and Lynn wanted them to meet face to face. This wasn't E.G.'s style unless for desperate reasons. This was not exactly how she anticipated their meeting. Riley definitely didn't expect the reactions Tess seemed to bring out in her. She started up the engine and pulled out onto the street not seeing Tess in the window as she drove by.

Tess went back to her desk and fought the urge to scream. She went about it all wrong. What was it about Riley she couldn't get over? She had a point admitting how little they knew of each other. Rae was right about the whole situation. Tess couldn't let go to find

25

the closure she needed. It was the main factor in putting an end to hers and Rae's relationship. Rae was also correct about the inability of Tess to admit that something in her life had failed. She needed to let go of the feelings she had for an ex-lover who one day up and left her. Tess wouldn't admit to any of this until recently.

This visit had not gone the way she had thought their first meeting would be. Riley still thinks of her as the money driven business woman that she was years ago. Everything in her life had changed. She missed being the creative artist she once was. Something else Riley had known. The business was becoming cut throat and if you couldn't keep up then you were weeded out. Mistakes were made and Tess' was in giving up being the artist. She had passed on many offers to leave Albany for the larger galleries in more populated cities. Tess didn't want to leave Albany, not just yet. The time had come when being shrewd was tiresome. If any was the time to make things right in her past this was it.

Riley heard the horn behind her as she snapped back into reality. Up yours too you frickin' moron. She found herself thinking as the sport utility vehicle passed her and the driver shot her the bird.

Chapter Two

Four years earlier Riley had quit the software company she had worked since her discharge from the Air Force. She had answered an ad in an employment magazine for construction help for a home improvement and remodeling company. The work was plentiful, just as every business owner on the northside of Albany were wanting new looks to their old historical buildings. That was the case at the Florence Street Art Gallery. The day Riley and the rest of the crew had the blueprints to start working on a loft in the art gallery. This was supposed to be the offices of the gallery to allow the first floor open for exhibits.

Fernando Lopez was the owner and director of the facility. He was as gay as gay came. It wasn't long before Riley started a friendship with the Latino. He was a hilarious human being. The parties he would talk about while she hung drywall kept her in stitches most of the time. The people who worked for him were nice enough but very professional snob attitudes.

A few days into the job Riley was in the loft framing the wall to separate the offices. She could hear Fernando on the stairs trying to talk above the noise around him. Riley was pounding nails and Marty was sawing boards to fit in the frame.

27

"Up here is where I'm putting the offices I think. The reception area here. No. I don't know decisions." Fernando rambled on in his exasperated broken English. Riley was amused just listening. Riley looked over at Fernando and saw the most beautiful woman she had ever seen standing next to the little Latino listening politely. The woman glanced over where Riley was and their eyes met and it was as though a brick had hit Riley smack dab on her head. She couldn't remember how long they stood staring at each other when Fernando stopped talking. The woman suddenly looked away and made what looked like a comment to him. Riley felt her stomach tingle and made herself go back to hammering. She bent down to get another piece of wood when she saw the two approach out of the corner of her eye.

"Riley, you must meet my friend from many years ago. Tess McGuire this is Riley Jones the he-man of all trades." He stood back subtly when Tess offered her hand. Riley took her glove off and took the smooth but yet firm grip.

"Nice to meet you." Tess replied holding Riley's hand a little longer than custom allowed. "You have done wonders with this place."

Riley felt herself swallow hard before thanking her. Her eyes looked back appreciatively. What Riley didn't see was the look on Fernando's face as he stood back and watch the attraction between the two women. He had known Tess McGuire for years and was trying to persuade her to help him build the reputation of the art gallery. She had driven down from Chicago as a favor to look around and see exactly what she had to work with. He also knew she had recently ended a relationship with an artist who used Tess' connections to find work in New York City then ended up ending their relationship soon after. Tess was not as upset as one would of thought. But from the look she gave his handyman he could see the spark in her eye once again. Tess was interested and it was up to him to throw these two together. Then she could concentrate on the gallery. He definitely had his work cut out. Or maybe not.

"And this is Marty." Fernando included the short middle age man coming up from behind him. Marty was you typical easy to get along Italian man. He had two teenage girls and a wife to whom he had been married too for almost twenty years. Marty loved to tease

Fernando and behind his back the comments he made were not only hilarious but also true. Marty just nodded in greeting and took the pieces of wood over to Riley.

Riley found she could not keep her eyes off of that woman as they walked away. She also noticed the glances this woman threw her way. Tess followed Fernando around taking notes every now and then. The rest of the crew downstairs were beginning to put the equipment up. Riley stayed in the loft as she was putting the finishing touches after she got all the drywall hung and seamed. It was going on five o'clock when she emerged from the bathroom after washing the day's filth off her. Marty was the only one left as the rest of the guys took off already.

"Tomorrow we should be ready for the trim." He stated as she put her tool belt down out of the way.

"Great. I also want to start the varnish on those beams. That'll take most of the morning and I can help with the trim. This is really going to look awesome when it's finished." Riley smiled. There was nothing like stepping back and taking a good look at a finished job. There were even times she was amazed at the transformation a room took with a little of this and that.

"I have to admit this job is the best yet." Marty slapped her on the back affectionately. They were doing their best work and it showed. "I have to go. The wife is fixing a huge meal tonight. The girls don't have to be anywhere, which is rare we even have sit down dinners anymore. When are you getting yourself hitched?"

"I'm really over that Marty. Guess it's just not in the cards for me." She winked.

"Yea, okay, and whatever. See you at seven tomorrow." He remarked as he went down the stairs. Riley put a few more tools out of the way in case anyone came up here they wouldn't hurt themselves before heading down the stairs.

"See you in the mornin' Fernando." She shouted as she went to the door.

"Wait. My God you women are in hurry so much." She heard Fernando voice coming from the back of the studio where his office was located for the time being. The broken English he spoke humored her. Riley stood where she was until he came out of his

29

office. "I'm having a what you call a get together this weekend and you are coming." He stated so matter of factly.

"I am? What makes you think so?" She asked. She didn't have any plans for the weekend unless E.G. had made some to include her. "Is this one of your famous parties you've been tellin' me about?"

"You really have to work on your English girlfriend. You sound like you're from the sticks or the boonies. I like that word boonies." Fernando stood with his hand on his hip.

Who needs to work on who's English? She thought to herself. "Fernando, I am from the boonies." She chuckled.

"Anyway you need culture. Do you clean up well?" He asked almost throwing Riley into hysterics.

"I guess you're going to have to wait and see." She grinned mischievously. "Unless this is formal. I don't do formal."

"Wear your Levi's. Your ass looks so good in Levi's." He waved his hand in the air to announce he was finished with the conversation. Riley just laughed. This could be a fun time.

Fernando wasted no time going back to his office not even trying to hide the smirk on his face. Tess was waiting to going over some marketing tactics with him. He had heard Marty leave and rushed to catch Riley before she left. Tess had been his friend through thick and thin and he wanted to do something nice for her. What she didn't know was what he had in mind. "Sorry, some last minute changes in the loft." He sat down next to her. "Where were we?"

Tess just looked at him slyly. She could tell when Fernando had something up his sleeve. And from the look on his face it was big. She also learned long ago to just let him have his fun. There wouldn't be much she could do to stop him. Once Fernando was on a mission he lost all reason.

The next day Riley kept a look out for Fernando's friend from yesterday. All last night she couldn't stop thinking about the look the woman had given Riley. She didn't appear to be a lesbian but not all women fit the stereotype. E.G. on the other hand had not only looked like a dyke but she did nothing to hide it. In her case Riley was just who she was. A country girl with an education and the need for fulfillment in her life. Ever since her discharge from the service it was as though she was out there searching for something and so far has never found it. In time she thought she would have it all. But for right now the dark haired woman who held her hand longer than she should have never came back. The story of her life. Maybe she would in a roundabout way try to get information about her from Fernando. Tomorrow at his party she might have a chance.

Saturday afternoon E.G. came over when she was getting ready for the big evening. "What are you wearing?" She asked as she helped herself to a beer in the refrigerator.

"It's not like I have many choices." Riley came out of the bathroom. She had decided to wear her shoulder length hair down and put on a white tank top to which she would wear a black jacket over it. The nights were getting a bit chilly and Riley really hated wearing long sleeves under a jacket.

"Cotton, one hundred percent cotton is all of your wardrobe. You really need to go shopping." E.G. went through the clothes in Riley's closet. "You're so butch."

"Dah!" Riley gave the 'I'm with stupid' look.

"You don't exactly look it but you sure do live it." E.G. commented as she gave up trying to dress her friend suitably. "So where is this dude's house?"

"About two blocks down from the gallery. He is so hilarious. You have to meet him sometime." She had already told her the story on Fernando. "I'll check it out and if it gets uncomfortable I'll just say I had made other plans and leave. Where you hangin' out tonight?"

"I don't know maybe go down to the Ten and see what's going on there. Meet a woman and take her home for uncensored sex. Nothing out of the ordinary." She teased.

The idea of going to the bar seemed a lot better than spending the night at home.

"Maybe I'll stop by if I ditch early." Riley checked herself in the mirror. She was beginning to put on a little weight she could tell around her middle. If she held in her stomach and stood up straight it wasn't noticeable. Mental note to keep stomach in all night. "How exciting is an evening with a group of gay men going to be?"

"Ah, but you don't know there could be gay women there also." She now wished she had invited herself. No, the bar would be more interesting.

"How do I look?" She stood back for E.G.'s inspection.

"Looks pretty damn good to me."

31

"You wish." Riley gave her a little shove as she went by. "May as well get this over with."

"Have fun. See you about ten o'clock?" E.G. teased. Riley just waved as she shut the door. She had remembered her keys. E.G was more like a sister than friend to her. She had been trying for months to get on at the police department. Right now they weren't hiring and every day E.G. put in at the software company she prayed it was her last.

Riley parked out on the street at the address Fernando had given her. She looked around to make sure she had the right house. It was a brick bungalow with a wide front porch with French doors making the look of the home modern but keeping it's historical background. She was always looking for different ways of accenting a home with just something as simple as a door. It depended on the look you wanted to express.

Riley rang the doorbell and waited only a few seconds before the man himself opened the door exclaiming her arrival. "Everybody this is my handyman Riley Jones." He turned to her, "And Riley this is everybody." He rushed to the first person and introduced each person greeted her warmly. "Oh and you remember Tess from the other day." Riley felt her stomach suddenly cave in as she turned around towards the dining room where Tess was leaning against the wall looking right at her. Both women nodded and smiled in acknowledgment. Fernando wasted no time in entertaining. "Now come wet the whistle as you Americans say." He replied. Riley wondered where on earth this man learned to speak English. It was probably from a rest stop in Kentucky.

"I'll just have a beer." She replied.

"Of course." Fernando smiled up at her branishing his perfect pearly whites leading her into the kitchen.

Riley didn't know if he was making a statement or just being his charming self. She did make note the gender of the room was equal women and men. "I hope you like imported cause that is all I have. I refuse to be domesticated in any way or reason."

"Don't listen to him. He is very domesticated for a woman." Riley turned again to find Tess coming into the kitchen. She wore a white silk sleeveless shirt tucked into a pair of tight fitting black jeans. A single gold chain hung from her neck. Her black hair was styled in the latest fashion of long layers with a teased curl to it. It was her eyes though. Riley could get completely lost in the clear, crystal blue pools. Tess looked as though she had Greek in her.

"I can tell." Riley noted the apron laying on the counter near the stove. From the first moment she saw Tess walk over, Riley's mind just went a total blank. The palms of her hands were sweaty. How long had it been since anyone had effected her this way? There was no doubt this woman was a lesbian. "So I guess you know Fernando pretty well."

"Oh, and what a trip it's been." Tess smiled. Riley took notice of how her upper lip thinned out when she smiled and it sent jolts through her body. "We met at an art gallery in Chicago. He was so ecentric I fell madly in love." She took a sip of wine from her glass waiting for some sign of visual reaction from this woman. Normally she didn't go for the construction worker type but there was something so very different about this one. The other day while Riley worked Tess saw a subtle side to her with each stroke of the hammer. She was very drawn to her physically. Fernando was right about the way Riley's ass looked in those Levi's. The attraction was mutual Tess could tell by the way Riley acted. She seemed nervous. Tess was used to that and it made the chase more challenging.

"I can see the attraction." Riley gave her a look that said more.

"And it's mutual." Tess could also play the game. Before Riley could reply Fernando came up to them.

"You seem to be getting to know one of other. Has Tess filled you in on the life of hers?" He took a bottle of wine from the rack on the counter. "Party is in here girls."

Riley started to follow when she leaned over and whispered for only Tess to hear. "Have you ever tried to teach him English?" That brought a laugh from Tess.

"I tried once and it was such a chore I gave up before we could begin."

"Oh." Riley grinned.

Most of the evening everyone sat around telling stories, drinking wine and filling up on Fernando's finger food. Riley never once felt out of place within the conversation as she had traveled extensively herself as with everyone here. What they didn't know was the military provided Rileyr with all these places. She just didn't think it was necessary to share her whole life story with people she just met. Michael was Fernando's significant other and Rita was Richard's wife. He was an artist who Fernando was featuring in his gallery once the remodeling was finished. Everyone was very interesting to just sit and listen to. Every now and then Riley would catch Tess looking at her from the sofa. She would return the look holding it for awhile longer.

It was going on ten thirty when Riley decided she shouldn't wear out her welcome. She got up to take her glass to the kitchen where Fernando had disappeared. "Thank you for inviting me but I really need to be going." She informed him.

"Oh it is still early." He looked fretful that she almost decided to stay but she really didn't want to seem over indulging. "Okay, wait a minute. Stay here." He said flamboyantly leaving the kitchen. Riley just stared after him. He was a nut. And she wasn't stupid. She knew ten minutes into the evening she was being set up. It felt flattering. The next minute Fernando was ushering Tess into the kitchen. Riley chugged the rest of her luke warm beer and couldn't believe the little Latino was that forward in shoving this woman at her.

"Tess here has not seen what a beautiful city we have. You take her and show her. I promised you culture so now you go." Fernando waved his hand at them both. Even Tess had a disbelief expression on her face. Before they could reply he was announcing their departure to the rest of the guest. Out on the porch the night air felt good. Tess looked up at her as they went down the steps. She had to be honest with this woman. She doesn't know Fernando like she did.

"You don't have to do this." Tess realized she should have warned her sooner.

"Oh no. I hope I didn't give that impression." Riley slowed her pace. There was a bar up the street that had a patio she thought they would stop in. "Has Fernando always pushed you onto people?"

"Oh yea. He is an impatient gay Puerto Rican and at times it's a lethal mix." She replied. She felt Riley's hand slide into hers as they walked. Tess smiled to herself at the gesture, which she welcomed. They found a table outside at Tess' insistence. The candle on the table gave off little light. For awhile they sat and got to know a little about each other. Tess felt so completely comfortable with this

woman who appeared so down to earth. Riley was also quiet in the
sense she seemed reserved. That could be a sign of once being hurt.
The music came from the open doors providing a good background
for the night.

Riley found herself relaxing by leaning back in the chair and
closing her eyes when she heard the first few lines of Clapton's "You
Look Wonderful Tonight". Nothing could be so perfect. "This is the
greatest song of all time." She sighed.

"Kind of sets the mood for the evening." Tess leaned on her
elbows and looked right into Riley's green eyes when she said it.
This was an evening she didn't want to end. The attraction was so
strong. Riley reached across the table and took one of Tess' hands in
hers. She let her eyes roam up the smooth skin of her arm to the soft
area laying between her shoulder and neck. Riley shuddered slightly
at the thought of her lips touching those areas. What she didn't
expect was the reaction she received from Tess who felt the look bore
into her with intense heat. Both were so turned on.

In a throaty whisper Tess asked if Riley was ready to go. The
song played on into the night as they left for Riley's apartment. They
decided to walk since it was a short distance neither wanted to take
the time to get into a car.

It was all Riley could do to control herself when they ran up the
steps to her door. She put the key in the lock and opened it. As soon
as Tess walked in she turned and took Riley into her arms kissing her
long and passionately. Riley shut the door and led Tess into the
bedroom. Clothes started coming off falling where they landed.
Riley laid Tess back on the bed taking in the beauty of her nakedness.
The long legs, slim hips and full breast with pink nipples taunt with
the need to be touched. Riley hovered above her as she gently
nibbled at Tess' lips teasing her. Their tongues began to explore the
depths of warm moistness. Tess biting lightly on Riley's lower lip
sending wave after wave of pleasure through her body. Riley ran her
hands the whole length of Tess's body cupping her breast she teased
the nipple with first her thumb and then her tongue. Tess arched her
back groaning in the pleasure it brought. Riley gently parted Tess'
legs with her hand until her fingers found the wetness between the
folds of flesh, which she immediately began a steady rhythm of
caressing until Tess was writhering under her touch. She replaced her

fingers with her mouth hearing a gasp as she let her tounge bring this exotic woman to an exploding orgasm.

Riley fell on top of Tess who wasted no time in wanting to return the pleasure. She rolled Riley onto her back kissing her deeply. She could taste herself on Riley's mouth getting herself even more aroused. Riley gasped for breath once Tess' lips touched the inside of her leg. Her hands entwined in Tess' hair feeling the pressure of her mouth. Their passion grew to heights neither had ever attempted to go before. Each wanting more and more until they lay exhausted. Beads of sweat ran off their skin as they tried steady their breathing. Riley felt like she had just ran around the city a few times. This woman was beyond her wildest dreams.

Tess propped herself up on her elbow and leaned over Riley. Gently she pushed back the strands of wet hair from her forehead. Riley looked intently at her. Tess was so intoxicating. "I had never done this before." Tess looked at her unbelieving at the comment. Surely Riley didn't mean she had never made love to a woman before. "I mean just meeting someone and taking her to bed." Riley caught on to the look.

"Oh. I thought you meant...but we met on Thursday and this is Saturday. So we just didn't meet." Tess grinned. It had been so long since anyone had touched her the way this woman laying next to her has. She didn't even care to remember who that could of been.

"You do have a point." Riley remarked. She ran her hand up Tess' arm towards her neck cupping her hand behind Tess' head and drawing her down onto Riley's parted lips.

The Florence Street Art Gallery had its after the remodeling grand opening featuring Richard's most recent work. The studio looked great with the modern decor of white walls and lots of lighting. The sculptures were placed on cubes at different heights in the center of the room allowing the walls to be open for people to look freely at the paintings. Friends of Fernando who he dutifully employed for this evening were passing around champagne. The exhibit was a hit. The contemporary pieces mingling in the modern graphic of society. Riley kind of stood out of the way and enjoyed watching the people as they interacted.

"Are you having a good time?" Riley turned to see Tess standing behind her.

"Yes. I think some of these people are a work of art themselves." She pointed towards two men over by the Avenue display. "Now there would be an interesting story."

"I see what you mean." Tess put her arm through Riley's. A bold gesture. "You know we could leave at any time. I'm sure Fernando wouldn't even see us slip out." She whispered close to Riley's ear. It had been five weeks since Tess accepted Fernando's offer to help manage the gallery and moved in with Riley. The relationship was still so new and very physical to the point it was so hard keeping their hands off each other. An innocent touch here or there would send vibrant chills through their bodies. Riley was falling in love but she couldn't bring herself to tell her. Tess was so much more experienced. The years in the Air Force never allowed Riley to explore her sexuality although she knew there was something different about her. The fear of anyone finding out was way before the Don't Ask Don't Tell law. There were no rights for gays and lesbians. Tess had more years of experience. The day would soon come and both would know when the time was right in confessing their love.

Riley wanted nothing more than to go home and lay in Tess' arms. "Sounds good." She placed her empty wineglass on the tray of a passing waiter.

Later that night as they lay awake in bed Tess told her Fernando was considering on semi retirement and wanted her to take more control of the gallery. One of the benefits was he would let her have the rooms in the loft for her own personal living space. Riley was flabbergasted which turned to disappointment at the thought of Tess leaving. She swallowed hard.

"So does this mean you'll be moving out?" Riley couldn't keep the edge back from her voice. She had enjoyed Tess being there every night and waking up next to her every morning. She didn't want it to end. Tess looked at her funny.

"I want you to come with me." Tess bit her lower lip hoping Riley would say yes. She wouldn't even consider it if Riley refused to move. She accepted Fernando's offer on a whim. Her feelings for Riley had grown intensely. If she knew exactly what love was she would say it was happening between them both. Every woman she has had a relationship with in the past seemed to want more than what Tess could give. Her reputation was solely based on her business tactics and not on her own art. Riley gave her that inspiration to want to pick up her sculpting tools and actually use them again.

Riley didn't even have to think about it. "What? And give up this luxurious space I have so built into a home?" She asked playfully.

Tess grinned knowing good and well this place was not only small for two people but was in need of alot of work. "Does that mean yes?" Tess snuggled closer and started planting little wet kisses down Riley's neck making the decision easier to make.

"Yes. Yes...oh my god YES!" She screamed faking an orgasm.

"Ssh...You're going to wake your neighbors." Tess giggled and started tickling her lover and Riley tried to do the same. Both were wrestling around on the bed in fits of laughter.

Several more weeks went by and both women moved their belongings into the loft of the gallery. Riley installed more counter space making the whole front area their living area. Their bedroom was decorated by using light colors and several bookshelves filled with books. The other room was used as a small studio for Tess for when she started sculpting again. She had been so busy with the move and now with the gallery's increasing demand in the art world took up most of her time. Riley hadn't been getting home until after seven on most evenings. The company had expanded and some days she found herself going to other cities around Albany. They made good use of the time they had together.

Riley had a job in Springdale one week and decided to spend a few days with her grandpa. She had seen a few people from high school and was caught up on everyone's life. She had ran into Jesse Monroe's mother at the diner. Jesse and her were inseparable growing up. She told her Jesse was working as a studio musician in Nashville. Riley thought then her best friend's dream was just around the corner. What had Riley done with her life? She asked herself more than once that day.

When Riley returned to Albany and back to the routine of every day she began to feel like something was pushing her. She just didn't know in what direction. Tess threw herself into her work. Even though her office was just downstairs there were nights she didn't come to bed until late in the night. Riley would have been asleep for hours. Then the trips to New York, Detroit or Chicago for exhibitions and always in search of the new talent. Riley had her job and couldn't get the time off to go with her on these trips. The nights were so long without Tess laying next to her. They were spending more and more time apart and even when they were together there seemed to be a strain coming between them.

Riley had been prepared for Tess to come home from one of her trips and announce she had met someone else. It was something Riley wished would never happen but there has to be a certain amount of protection you can give your heart so it won't break as hard. This was one of those times. But Tess never did make that announcement. Instead they would go to bed and make love until the early hours of the morning. Making up for lost time. Always in bed was the honesty and trust. It was out of the bed that worried her. The more Riley looked at how different their lives were the more convinced this relationship was not going to last. Tess was sophistication as to where she was down to earth. There would come a time when both would clash. She couldn't see Tess planting a garden or spreading manure as much as she could see herself at any more art exhibitions. Something was going to change. She could feel it in the air.

That time came a few days after Tess returned from New Orleans a day earlier than planned. Riley didn't get home until late and Tess had been waiting on her. They got into a huge argument about where she had been. Riley trying to convince her there she wasn't seeing anyone else. The whole accusation was ridiculous as far as Riley was concerned. Who was sharing Tess' bed on her out of town trips? For all Riley knew she had other women. Riley would never know.

Tess was irrational and informed Riley of her position in this relationship. It was finally out how Tess really felt. She was the superior partner in the relationship leaving Riley subserviant. Either way that was how Riley took the comment.

"What the hell do you mean by my position? I was not aware we had roles." Riley shouted back at her when Tess went into the bedroom.

"You know what I'm talking about." She yelled back in response.

"Because I don't make the kind of money you do? Or is it my family wasn't rich enough to live in your circle." She was hurt. This was just the kind of shit she had been thinking about. Tess stormed back into the living room.

"That was uncalled for." Her voice wavered. "You are never here even when you are physically." She lowered her voice to a normal level.

"Don't give me that shit. You're the one who is never home. How can you work on a relationship Tess when you're a thousand fucking miles away?" Riley took a deep breath. She was right and Tess knew it.

"Fuck it." Riley stormed out of the gallery.

The night air had a chill reminding Riley how mad she was when she left forgetting to grab a jacket. She walked along the canal looking at the moon's reflection in the water below. There were days she wanted to go back to the life she had as a girl. Things were not so complicated then. She loved Tess with all her heart. But they were too different. The sex was immaculate but you don't build a relationship on just that alone. She was ashamed to admit it but that was all that was left of their relationship. The sex. There were no more quiet evenings sitting together on the couch watching a movie or the long walks along this very spot just talking and touching. There was no time for them to really get to know each other as people. The fact was all they were together was lovers. Plain and not so simple.

Riley threw a rock into the water and watched the rings form around the surface. It was over. She knew at that moment their time had been spent. Riley turned around and walked back towards the gallery. She wondered if Tess had figured out as much.

Chapter Three

The cameras were set up behind the roped off area near the old stockyard railroad tracks. Huge lights faced a wall bearing the name of the Wilburn Brothers, former owners of the establishment. This is the part of Nashville a tourist will never care to see. The yard closed many years ago leaving the area vacant for vagrants and of course the drug dealers and users. Every large city had that part of town kept from the vacation brochures about their fine city. This morning a music video was being filmed. A song about the new becoming old and all you can count on in life is the change. A ballad that needed the scene of the solitude and desertion that the industrial district had. All the equipment being set up to accommodate the direction. A huge sound system was placed on a temporary platform a good distance from the cameras. The song will be played as the singer mouthed the words, and acted the part as the production company captured it all on film.

"My God your hair has all this natural curl. I know plenty of women that would kill for this kind of texture. But the color is off." The set hairdresser fussed over the mass of long reddish blond curls. There was nothing wrong with the color of her hair other than maybe a high light. The color and curls were natural whether this guy chose

41

to believe it or not. "Who has done you hair, girlfriend? Hmm…" He asked. The trailer door opened and a man wearing a black cowboy hat entered. Both looked up.

"Jackson, I'm glad you're here." The woman started to get up from the chair but the hairdresser wouldn't let go of her hair. He had a schedule to keep.

"Honey, you're not finished." He stated. These musicians were pretty much the same. He hated the work but the it paid his bills and it's not like Nashville was a Los Angeles.

"Derik, this is a black and white video. What does it matter what my hair color is? No one is going to see it." Jesse Monroe asked sarcastically taking a last look in the mirror.

"Oh, get out of here. I am tired of you already." He began to shoo her away like a pesty nat.

"Whatever." She retorted in humor and took the opportunity to escape before he changed his mind. She took Jackson's arm and led him outside.

"What the hell was that all about?" He asked trying to supress the urge to chuckle.

"I don't trust him with my hair. He had this look in his eye like I should be a red head or some other awful style." Jesse made a face at her friend and lead guitar player in the band. "If he wasn't done with his fussing trust me he wouldn't of let me go so easily." They stepped over cables as they walked over to where the director was waiting.

"Where's Toni at? I figured she would like to see this." He looked around maybe seeing her around the sound stage.

"You would think so, since she co-wrote the song." Jesse kept one eye to the ground so she wouldn't trip over any wires and make a fool of herself as she tried her best not to look nervous as she was. The truth was it had been a couple of days since she saw her roommate. Toni had a job in Memphis at Sun Records to run the sound board for a new blues artist. The record label loaned her out. Toni said she'd be back in time for the shooting but so far no one has seen nor heard from her. This song was as much Toni's as it was the rest of theirs.

"She'll show at the last minute like always." Jackson only half believed his own words. Toni was dragging Jesse and the band down. Ever since Nadine Nash the reining Queen of Country Music walked into the Blue Ridge recording studio a few weeks ago shocking everyone including Maynard Williams the main boss. Nadine got her start in the business by singing the folk ballads that put her on both the country music charts as well as the pop charts during the early seventies. Her high pitch bluesey tales of the hard life living up in the mountains of Tennessee. The strong willed women standing up to and falling behind their men. The years had been good to her in this business but Nadine wanted to get back to the songs and style that made her what she was today. Blue Ridge recording studio was just the studio she was looking for. The building was as old as Nashville and would project the sound she was looking for. The songs recorded from her first album where the studio walls were lined with old mattresses to keep the sound from bouncing back. Although Blue Ridge was a bit more sophisticated without the bedding hanging but it still projected the sound she was looking for. It was the talent she found within the confines of the studio made her wonder why this small group of musicians hadn't been discovered before now. The business never sought out the real talent unless they were on the club circuit.

Jesse Monroe had been Nadine's pet project. The first time she heard Jesse belt out a song with her husky voice combined with Nadine's higher tone made for a smooth sounding duet. Nadine was many things but stupid wasn't one of them. She knew what she had found in this young woman. The band was just as good. A person could tell the years these musicians spent together through their sound. It was as if each one knew the other one's next move. By the end of the session Nadine's label had bought out these musician's contracts and had them signed with RCA Records. Jesse, Toni, Jackson, Bobby Jim nor Joey expected to be on their way up Music Row that day they went into work. It was true that when you least expect something then it happens. Maybe the quickness contributed to how Jesse was feeling. Even today filming her first video it still didn't seem real to her.

"Miss Monroe." Jesse heard her name and turned to see a short man waving his hands frantically at her. He was the assistant to the director. "Jason would like to go over a few things with you." He replied standing back to look her over. "I love the style." He was referring to the black cowboy boots, worn jeans with the black shirt tucked in. Her blondish red hair bouncing in the breeze as she walked. The weather was overcast with the sky in the distance turning a dark blue with the threat of rain. The director was anxious to get started before the storm came.

"Okay people, let us get everything ready and checked. Fifteen minutes." The director shouted to those standing about waiting for his direction. The assistant went scrambling trying to get everything perfect. He turned around noticing Jesse and Jackson for the first time. "Ha, the star." Jason replied. "How are you feeling?"

"Fine." Jesse stated taking in the sight around her.

"Good, I see you read the script." He referred to the paper rolled up in her hand. "We're going to start with you over by the warehouse." He pointed to the Wilburn Brothers building. "Walk up to this side on your cue which is just after the first chorus, then I want you to stop here." He pointed to the spot of intent. "Just sing along with the song, the sound stage will be blaring just pretend we're are not here. That's the acting part." He winked. "Any questions?"

Jesse took a look at the course she was to follow. She just had to literally walk down the street singing the words to her song. How hard could that be? She stood at her mark and waited. "Lights, sound and go in three. Are you ready Jesse?"

Jesse waved in agreement. Then the first chord of the song hit the speakers. She lowered her head in concentration letting the music sink into her mind and block out everything else around her. She didn't have her mandolin to occupy her hands. Her thoughts drifted back to Toni and the night they sat in the studio writing this song. A twinge hit her stomach. It was her nerves working on her she thought. The cue came and Jesse started the walk. She opened her mouth and sang as if she was the only person there at the stockyards. She stopped at the Wilburn Building letting the wind take her hair to one side as she glanced down the railroad tracks as if she was expecting a train to come by. The music ended abruptly pulling her back into reality. This was too easy she thought to herself.

Jesse stood there waiting for the next direction. The director and the short funny talking man stood huddled near a monitor. The director shaking his head. "I don't believe it. Never has happened tome before. It's perfect. Now let's get the cameras set up by the tracks and get the band in the next shot." Jason waved at Jesse to come over. "Jesse Monroe a director's dream." He praised her.

Jackson was standing near the monitor and saw the screen. "Shit girl you are a natural." He exclaimed.

"How's that? I didn't do anything he didn't tell me to do." Jesse commented. This was a lot easier than writing the song.

"Oh, I think you might have done somethin' cause it only took one shoot. Ate up." Jackson playfully shoved at her but she was too quick. They walked over to where the next scene was to be shot. The guys were in the rest of the shoot until the sky showed signs of dumping rain at any moment. Forcing the production to close down for the day. The director got alot of good footage of the upcoming storm to use. Once he knew how he would edit the film. Jason was known for his creativity. He could work them in. The crew invited everyone out for a few beers. Jesse went out of the chance Toni might be at Bogg's.

The rain was coming down hard by the time Jesse made it home and parked her jeep up near the backstairs that led up to her and Toni's apartment. Their landlords Mr. and Mrs. Kelly had already gone to bed. Jesse noticed their lights were off. Usually if she came home and saw Mrs. Kelly on the front porch she would join her for a while. Times like those made her home sick. She made it to the hall and unlocked the door.

The answering machine's light was flashing. She pressed the play button and headed back to the bathroom to run a hot bath. She listened to the messages and none were from Toni. Where in the hell was she? She asked herself for the hundredth time that day. Once the hot water began to relax her muscles and let her mind drift back to the beginning

The bus from Indiana dropped the eighteen year old girl off at the bus terminal in downtown Nashville. There were people all around waiting for departures and arrivals. Jesse remembered what her mother told her about how people lurk in the shadows just waiting for young girls like herself just off the bus with no where to go. She took her bag and her mandolin case and walked out of the station as if she had a place to go at eighteen.

Miss Maybell's Diner on the corner of Eighth and Broadway had a sign in the window advertising for a waitress. This was something

Jesse could do to make a living. Back home Joyce Sanders worked at the Stanford Inn waiting on the tables and she made good money especially during the tourist season. Jesse built up her confidence and walked in the finely lit dining area. A heavyset woman sat on a stool behind the counter near the register. Their eyes met and Jesse discreetly placed her bags down and straightened her posture.

"I would like to apply for the position you're advertising for." She stated matter of factly and very nervously. The woman just glared at her before answering with her own question in the roughest southern drawl she ever heard.

"How old are you?" Before Jesse could answer she waved her hand in the air. "Like the hell it matters. You got experience waitin' tables?" The woman smiled making her eye makeup almost crack.

Jesse looked at the woman and blinked. Then she nodded. She couldn't think at that moment. This woman scared her to death but she needed work and a place to stay. She had enough money to last maybe a week in a motel if she stretched it. The lie worked since she found herself in the back of the diner with the rest of the girls. That's when she met Toni Griffin.

Toni arrived two weeks prior from Whitley, Texas. She had been working at the diner for a full week and lived in a run down motel room not too far from the diner. She greeted Jesse with open enthusiasm and they soon became not only fast friends but roommates as well. They figured two incomes were better than one. Toni had the knack of getting people to not only like her but also eating right out of her hand. Maybell Baker was her hardest customer to win over but in time she did it. A natural talent dealing with customers and people. Toni took Jesse under her wing so to speak and shown her the ins and outs of Music Row. They went to the seedy taverns and walked alone at night near the Ryman Auditorium sharing their dreams and never once giving up.

When Toni landed a job at a recording studio as an assistant sound engineer it wasn't long before she had Jesse a job as a studio mandolin player. Bluegrass musicians or singers making a demo tape to take around town to the record labels are the artist that mainly used the studio. The money was better than waiting tables but not by much. After the first year the sessions became more frequent and Jesse managed to put money aside. The first time the other musicians heard her play Jesse had secured a position amongst the band. Jackson Taylor played acoustic guitar, Bobby Jim who had higher aspirations as a rock and roll drummer had some how managed to put that desire to his style creating a certain quarter beat. Joey Clark was from the Appalachian Mountains when at twelve he picked up his first violin or fiddle as it was known. His appearance alone gave way to the kind of sheltered background he grew up in. Mountain people never seemed to adjust to the city life but Joey had dreams of his own that carried him to Nashville. No one came to Music City without one. The band lacked a bassist but Toni was able to compensate by increasing the bass through the sound board. A closeness soon developed between the musicians and spent alot of time after hours writing and laying tracks to their own material. When the time came they were ready. And that time was the day Nadine Nash arrived unexpectedly at Blue Ridge Studios.

Jesse ran more hot water as her mind stayed in the past. She had never had a friend such as Toni since Riley Jones from back home. She hadn't even thought of Riley in ages. Whatever became of her she wondered? The last she heard her mother commented that Riley had bought her grandfather's farm after he died. Had it been close to ten years since graduation and they went their separate ways? Now her dream was coming true. Jesse wondered if Riley's had also. She caught herself nodding off and decided to call it a night and go to sleep. Maybe Toni would come home tomorrow. She thought to herself as she dragged herself out of the tub.

The days start early in the music business. This morning Jesse looked in Toni's room finding it as it had been for the last few days. Maybe this time she had cause to worry. Jesse decided to call Blue Ridge and got the phone number to Sun Records in Memphis. After a couple of calls she was placed on hold by two different people. Both of who never even heard of Toni Griffin therefore they kept transferring her to another department. The third person answered.

"I'm trying to reach Toni Griffin. She is a sound engineer." Jesse was interrupted by the person on the other end.

"I am sorry no one by that name works here." The woman replied drawling out her syllables...

"I know that, she is on loan from Blue Ridge Records in Nashville." Jesse was gradually getting frustrated.

47

"Let me check with the sound room. Can you hold?" Without a reply Jesse was placed on hold again. A few seconds later she returned. "Ma'am, this Miss Griffin was a no show on Saturday. Anythin' else I can help you with?"

"No, thank you for checking." She placed the receiver down. Toni didn't go to Memphis so where did she go? Jesse began thinking. Maybe she went home. No, she would have told her if she planned on leaving. As of late she had been seen with the type of people she herself wouldn't go near let alone associate with. Jesse wasn't stupid and she knew her friend was getting high just about every day, which was the reason she ditched work. Usually Toni let her know when she wasn't coming home for a few days. A consideration they had between them. She did the sound mixes for Nadine's bluegrass album and got her praise but then something changed. Toni would show up for work strung out. When Jesse tried to talk to her about it and the turn their careers were taking Toni jumped down her throat. She informed her she already had a mother and didn't come this far to look for another. This wasn't the girl Jesse met years ago when they both were young and naive. Something was bothering Toni and she refused to open up about it. There wasn't much else Jesse could do. She finished her coffee in thought. The last time she saw Toni was Friday night at Bogg's Tavern. Jesse didn't stay too long. Toni said she was leaving that night for Memphis. Jesse's gut feeling told her something had gone wrong. She looked at her watch before grabbing her keys off the counter. The first place she would look would be the tavern.

Traffic was light as the rush hour was over until late afternoon. Jesse pulled her jeep to the curb in front of the door. A run down building kind of set off from the alley right next to it. The back door actually opened to the small lane where the trash bins were. At times it was used as a back entrance. Years ago this place was the most popular bar on the Row. The Grand Ol' Opry's cast sometimes made their way down to Bogg's to have a few drinks after the show. The stars never made it past Tootisie's except for an occasional rough neck. The day Kris Kristofferson and Willie Nelson walked through the door was the day Carl's reputation grew. Now no one came in except for the locals and old timers who'd set around and tell the stories of their past. How they almost made it on the Opry stage or the record deal that went bad at the last minute. The best excuse was their agent took the money they made or a song was stolen. Some were true and some become the truth through many times telling. The front windows were open letting in the brightest light in the place. There were a couple of men sitting at the bar. It had been a long time since Jesse had been in here during the day light hours.

"Hey Jesse." The bartender looked a bit surprised. "Ain't it early for you to be comin' in?"

"I'm not here to drink. Have you seen Toni around lately?" She asked watching his expression change.

"Not since Friday night." He thought for a second. "She left with some dude. I wouldn't of thought much if Toni hadn't of paid the tab before she left. She paid that guy's also. Said you all sold a record."

"What did this guy look like?" Jesse asked. She might of seen him that night.

"Rough neck, real quiet like most of the guys that come in here from the waterfront. The darkest eyes you ever want to look into. You know the type." He wiped at the bar as he thought about it.

"Has he been in since?" She was getting somewhere.

"Have you turned cop?" Carl smiled. "You ought to ask Wynette. She knows more about the customers than I do. I just make the drinks. If I see Toni I'll tell her to get her ass home."

"Thanks Carl." She turned to leave. Where to next? Would she have to report Toni missing? It had been over twenty four hours.

"Moleson." The sound of the man's voice made her stop near the door. The grungey looking old man sitting at the end of the bar got her attention. "Hank Moleson. Also known as the Mole."

"Excuse me?" Jesse stepped over next to his stool.

"That's who your friend left with." He stated matter of fact and never looking directly at her.

"Did you see my friend with this man?" Jesse was cautious.

"She got black hair and wears a jean jacket with a patch on the sleeve? You don't have to answer I already know it." He took a long pull of his beer. "Your friend is hangin' out with bad news. Best be warnin' her. That is when you find her."

"Why are you tellin' me this? She asked. Carl didn't even seem to know who this man either. But he listened intently. He'd had his share of psycho customers and this coot seemed to fit the bill.

49

"I might have a score to settle." He remarked reaching for his wallet he paid for the beer.

"How do I know what you're saying is true then?" Jesse was becoming a bit leery of this man.

"You don't." He looked directly into her eyes. "You can take this information however you want. I just have a feeling this guy is involved. My guess is your friend is into heroin or she wouldn't be seen with the likes of him."

Jesse just stareed in disbelief. He knew too much about Toni not to of seen her with this man. "Thanks."

"For what? I don't remember having a conversation with you." He looked at her hard before walking out the door.

Jesse took the hint and started to leave herself. "Be careful Jesse. Be real careful." Carl warned her. She knew what she had to do.

First shift was just finishing getting debriefed in the Detective room of the Nashville Police Department. The latest case had all of the evidence of a serial killer. Ten days and three bodies found in different locations along the Columbia River. All three bodies apparently took a lethal dose of heroin. This particular heroin was laced with strychnine, which caused the closing of the air passage resulting in death. They were probably so high they didn't even realize they couldn't breathe. The latest victim was lying in the morgue undergoing an autopsy. The coroner and the police detectives knew the outcome of the report.

Detective Wesley Carson sat at his desk studying the file of the first two victims. He noticed the time between ingestion and the time of approximate death added up to just a few minutes apart.

"What kind of sicko would lace this shit with strychnine?" Wes spouted off more to his own benefit than if anyone else was listening. It amazed him how crime keeps getting sicker and sicker. For what reason would there be in benefiting to watch someone die of such a hideous crime? But this case wasn't the worst he had seen.

"Some psycho path." His partner answered. Wes looked up to see a uniform officer approaching their desks. A woman followed close behind him.

"You all might want to take this one." He handed the detective a report. Missing person just what they needed. Detective Carson offered the woman the chair next to his desk. He took a few minutes to glance over the paperwork to familiarize her complaint.

"Ms. Monroe what makes you think your friend is missing and just not off on a weekend trip?" A standard question.

Jesse sat looking at him in almost unbelief. She had just answered a battery of questions with the other cop and now she had to go all through it again with this one. She couldn't keep the annoyance out of her voice.

"No one has seen her since Friday night. She didn't show up for a job in Memphis, which I have already checked. She hasn't called and I just found out she left with this man Hank Moleson. No one has seen or heard from her since." Jesse was nearing the point of desperation. The look of recognition from the mention of Moleson's name came across both detective's faces. The detective's tone took on a more serious note.

"We know about this guy." Det. Carson leaned back in his chair. "This man gave you a positive description?"

"Yes and of Toni. He definitely had seen them both together at the same time since he describe the jacket she always wore. And was wearing that night. He was very animate about the conversation we didn't have. I doubt you'll find him." This whole situation seemed like an awful charade of some sort. Jesse was becoming uncomfortable.

"We need to take this from the beginning." Wes turned in his chair to look directly at her. This woman didn't appear to be the squeamish type and he could sense her annoyance. "We have a body that just came in from the streets down at the morgue. I'd like to start there." He noticed her face went white at the thought. She probably hadn't even thought her friend might be dead. "Hank Moleson's reputation as a dealer is making me assume your friend was involved with drugs. Right now we have a situation involving some tainted heroin. We had three bodies brought in. Two males and a female, all without identification. If you don't mind the morgue is just downstairs."

Jesse got up and reluctantly followed the detective towards the elevator. Once they made it to the basement and through the double doors marked County Morgue. Jesse didn't know how to react if Toni was in there. Oh God, please don't let her be in there, she prayed to

51

herself. The detective talked a few minutes with the coroner and then they took her into a room with drawers along each side of the walls. The coroner went up to one in the middle and pulled it open revealing a body with a sheet covering it. He waited until the detective nodded.

The sheet was pulled back to expose the pale face of a lifeless woman. Jesse felt her stomach tighten when she took a step closer. The long dark hair was a tangled mess as if it had been wet and never combed out. Her eyes were closed in a deep sleep and her skin so cool to her touch. Tears stung at the corners of her eyes and Jesse stepped back turing away quickly. She swallowed hard. "It's her. Toni Griffin." She replied in a whisper and left the room.

"Thanks John." Wesley motioned for the coroner to put the sheet back. Identification had been made. He followed the woman out and caught up with her at the elevator. He saw the tears streaming down her face but she tried desperately to wipe away. "Are you all right? I mean I know this is a shock to find your friend in there." He felt concern for this woman.

"She threw it all away. I can't believe it." Jesse stated more to herself.

"I'll need to get some more information about this man who told you about Hank Moleson. I'll get a mug shot for you to look at and see if you can identify him." Once back on the third floor Wes gave the thumbs up signal to his partner and began the questioning.

Jesse arrived home just before dark and went up the stairs to her apartment noticing the Kelly's were still up and watching television. She could see the blue glow from the bottom window. Unlocking the door she went in. The apartment seemed different to her now than when she left this morning. She dropped onto the couch placing her hands over her face and letting the emotions take over. Jesse cried like she had never cried before. There was no stopping. The tears just kept coming with the memories of Toni in her mind. Jesse would have to call her family back in Texas cause the body had to be removed tomorrow from the morgue.

The bottle of bourbon hidden under the sink would help she thought as she got up to get it. After two shots Jesse took the glass and frantically threw it against the wall. Anger started to swell up inside. "How dare you do this to yourself. How dare you do this to your family." She shouted sinking to her knees in tears. "How dare you do this to me, Toni?" She found herself laying exhausted on the floor in the kitchen and cried.

Chapter Four

The last of the horses were herded out to the pasture. Susan Whitman had driven up from the lake to ride her horse. She was about the same age as Katie but the differences in the two were as night and day. This was her second ride since Riley broke the animal. The more time Susan spent with her horse the less time Riley would so the animal will learn to trust its owner. Katie saddled up one of the other horses and both were going to ride out to the pond. Riley told them before they left that she'd be going into town this evening. That was meant for Katie not to go too far into the holler. Before she would be going anywhere the hayracks needed filling and the stalls raked out.

Miss Mayme's Coffee Shop is the heart and soul of Stanford. There's Cooter's Bar, which was just down the street for those who preferred something a bit stronger than coffee. The Milburn's who owned the diner for years decided one day to sell the diner and buy a Winnebego and travel the country in the joys of their retirement. Logan Ross saw the for sale sign in the front window one morning and by agter noon she had herself convinced this could be the investment she was looking for. The business was there. All that was needed was the time and energy put into making a go of it. The outside was deceiving with the look of a run down shack. The building had never been painted showing its original wood. A step throught the door and it was a different story. Three months of going to real estate auctions around the tri county area to find the authentic pieces. The booths were church pews from the very first Baptist Church in Greenville. A fire in 1982 had destroyed a big part of the structure and for years it stood abandoned. Another church was built closer to Stanford for the congregation. Every kid growing up in the area visited the old building and knew the history behind it's torn walls. Logan had spent a lot of time as a girl in that old church and thought about it when she bought the diner. The thick, solid oak bar and stools were found at a sale of an old tavern in Louisville, Kentucky. The walls were of old barn wood found along the country roads in southern Indiana. Riley had the capability to negotiate with the stubbornness of owners, which were mostly elderly. One afternoon Logan had found herself picking tomatoes for an old lady in exchange for all the wood they could salvage from the barn half falling down from years of weather and exposure. The woman couldn't get around much even to her garden and Riley never could say no to anyone especially the seniors. Many long nights of hard work and the decision to change the menu to cappuccinos, lattes, regular coffee and flavored and to serve deli sandwiches and soups. The diner's business had slowed considerably and she figured it was on the change of times. People were eating smarter. For those who wanted a meal there were the Inn and Cooter's for greasy food. The doors hadn't been open for long before she had to hire a wait staff and someone to work in the kitchen. On the weekends she would hire a guitarist to play for the evening crowd. The fall always brought the people in from all over to spend the day amongst the fall foliage. The vibrant colors along the hills were breathtaking. People from all over the state came just to go for drives or to the State Park for picnics. It was a simpler life than what they were used to although the locals didn't mind too much since tourism brought in money for the businesses in town. The Inn can do it's year's business just in the fall months to support the business for the rest of the year. The atmosphere was just laid back. No one was in a hurry to get to anywhere.

The old Ford pulled in next to a couple of cars in front of Miss Mayme's. Riley shut the door and noticed Logan's Jjeep parked along the side of the building. Sara Benson waved as she noticed Riley come in. Sara was a recent graduate from the university in Greenville. Her future was unclear, as she was reluctant to leave Stanford.

She had worked at the cafe for living expenses while she was going through school. Milly Thatcher a high school student who worked in the kitchen and handled customers at the bar on slow days. Patsy Moore worked the morning shift and was a housewife who needed something to fill her time while her boys were in school during the day. Miss Mayme's had instantly become the hot spot for the high school kids after school. Fashion magazines were never far from Mill's reach nor her opinions about this and that and who was seeing whom. Logan had a good versatile staff to run the place and never a worry about the business when she wasn't around. She still did the bookkeeping for the farm and that's where she spent most evenings at the dining room table.

Riley walked up to the counter and sat down. "Hey Sara. Is Logan around?"

"She went next door to get a few things. She should be back any minute. Can I get you anything?" She closed the magazine she was looking at.

"A coke." Riley replied and glanced around the room. No one she knew. The place wasn't busy at all. It was still early in the week. The cow bell went off above the door when Logan walked in carrying a couple bags of groceries.

"Hey, Riley." She greeted heading back of the counter towards the kitchen and yells over her shoulder. "What brings you into town?"

"Want to go over to Cooter's?" Riley shouted once the door swung close. Then just as quickly swung back open.

"Sure could use one." Logan looked at Riley more closely. There was something going on with her. Within a few minutes they were on their way accross the street.

The bar had a few more customers than the coffeehouse. The jukebox was wailing out a country song as the two women walked through the the swinging doors. "Now there's a tit and a tat." Both saw Chuckie down at the end of the bar with a huge toothless grin on his whiskered face. "Come park your skinny lil' asses over 'ere." He slurred.

"Not tonight Chuckie." Logan replied as she found them a table near the door. He grabbed Riley's arm as she passed. "Ain't that ol' tomato 'posed to be making coffee?" He busted out laughing drunk as a skunk. Riley squeezed his hand but ignored his comments. Chuckie was known for his rude and crude comments. She sat down at the table opposite Logan.

"What a day. We did close to five hundred dollars for lunch today. I have no idea where the people are coming in from. But I'm not going to argue with it." Logan replied as the waitress brought their beers. "So, what really brings you into town?"

"Guess I was gettin' a bit antsy at the ranch. Katie and Susan Whitman went for a ride. The chores were all done and I just didn't feel like stayin' at home."

"Have you heard from Lucas?" She asked bluntly.

Riley found it hard to look her in the eye. "He's left a couple messages. I can't think about him yet." She ran her hands through her hair. A habit she did when frustrated.

Logan took it a step further. "Have you heard from Tess?" She noticed the tenseness come over her friend.

"I went to see her a couple days ago. It wasn't quite the meeting I expected." She tipped up the bottle of beer and welcomed the burn on the back of her throat as it went down quickly.

"What did you expect?"

"Just to tell her I was sorry I left the way I did. I felt we never had a chance in the first place...all that shit." She took a deep breath. "I took off like a scared silly jack rabbit. You would of loved it." She managed a smile.

"Why don't you just give in?" Logan took her by surprise. "You know you want to. I can see it in your eyes. You can't keep denying who you are, Riley." A person has to accept who they are before anyone else will.

"Bull shit. I've done it for years. As long as I keep busy the time goes by faster and I forget." Riley believed her own lie for all it was worth.

"But you're not busy all the time. What then?" She was right and Riley knew it. "You lived an open life in Albany and I can understand your hesitation down here. But you have the right to be happy like anyone else. Lucas wouldn't be the one to fill your needs as a woman."

"I have a business to protect. Can you imagine what would happen to it if these people knew I was a lesbian? I have spent a lot of time building what I have now not to just lose it all on rumors, beliefs, or lies. I have seen it happen before where families disown their children or siblings all on the justification of the Bible. People judge you Logan whether or not it's right or wrong."

"I think you underestimate this town. These people know you from the caliber of a person you are." Logan got the waitress' attention for another round. "I will give you the fact that the church social won't be knocking on your door for your membership but you don't have it now anyway. Why does anyone have to know?" She was standing high on the soapbox now. "Clark and I don't go around tellin' people what we do in our bedroom. Trust me if they knew..." She laughed.

"I knew you were the vixen type." Riley teased. "Actually I really don't want to know that."

"Exactly my point. People don't want to know those things. I'm sure you wouldn't take an ad out in the paper announcing your sexuality so who the hell cares what you do in your own home. Hell, I bet alot of folks has made the comment anyhow. Face it you're a knock out and you are single, never been married and these folks talk. I bet it would surprise less than you think."

"Don't forget Lucas is involved now." Riley placed her bottle down.

"Lucas has taken you out once not big deal." Logan brushed it off.

"He kissed me."

"Okay, he might be an obstacle but not a big one." She leaned slightly over the table. "Did you like it?"

Riley shrugged. "It has been a long time since anyone had put their arms around me and kiss me."

"Did you kiss him back?"

"Dah, of course I did. I got swept up in the moment." The image of her and Lucas came into her mind. "I can't hurt him. He is too nice of a man."

"Then you better nip it now before it gets too complicated for you in the long run."

"I've been avoiding his calls hoping he will just give up."

"He's a man and he ain't going to give nothin' up. Look at Chuckie." She nodded towards the old man. "He's over sixty, drunk all the time, but he is still tryin'." They both laughed at the thought of anyone being intimate with him. "Have you signed up for the rodeo yet?" Logan changed the subject.

"Went in this morning and signed up. It's going to be something this year. Ralph Moore's son Beau is back this summer from college and he has been doing junior rodeoing in Oklahoma. He is going to be the one to beat."

"Uh oh, I wonder if Milly knows he's back. She was a croonin' all over him last year. That girl must be a handful of worry for her parents." Logan commented.

"She will have some competition this year. Katie went with me to the fairgrounds and caught her an eye full. She went completely silent. That tells you something when Katie doesn't have a thing to say." Riley smiled. The two beers were starting to take effect on her. One more ought to do her in. "Wilbur said Mr. Bancroft is bringing in quite a herd from Wyoming, wild mustangs."

"Think you got a chance?" Logan asked. Riley was a good rider and had won the competition before. Ed Bancroft had a huge horse ranch just outside of Stanford. Once a year he went out west to purchase a herd of wild horses and brought them back to Bradford County for the annual rodeo for the riders to break in the horses. For two weeks prior his ranch hands trained the animals on halter and the weight of the saddle so at the rodeo all the contestants had to do was break them in. He gets a good herd to sell and the winner gets a pick of the horse he/she chooses. The town makes money as well as the 4-H and Horse and Pony clubs who sponsor it. The whole county looks forward to the event.

"Wilbur also said Ed brought back a hellion this year. A lead stallion. Huge animal and mean. He'd just as soon take a bite out of you than let you ride. It'll take a skilled rider to even get into the

59

saddle." Riley was beginning to get excited when she talked about horses.

"Be careful. I know you'd love to have that one in your barn." You didn't have to look hard to notice the gleam in her eye. Riley wanted that horse in a bad way. The rest of the evening they made plans to go antiquing after the weekend of the rodeo. Riley wanted to look around for a few things for the house and Logan was always interested in a find for the coffeehouse. The night grew late as they both went to their vehicles for the short trip home.

Logan thought about the dilemma Riley had created for herself and wondered if the advice she gave her friend was true to the fact. The one thing she knew is both Riley and Tess needed what they never had, closure. Riley did have a point about how the town would feel having a lesbian in their mist. But Riley didn't know that everyone has questioned her before. Logan heard the gossip going around her coffeehouse. Everyone tended to laugh it off. Riley has always been secretive about her life in Albany not a lot of people even knew she was in the military. They knew her grandpa and respected him and it just trickled down to Riley and her family. What was a good looking woman such as Riley doing single? Was she married before and just didn't want to talk about it? Give them a few dates with her and they'd have her barefoot and pregnant in no time. Logan had heard it all before where her friend was concerned. Riley's secret would remain as so.

The sun had been up for hours as Tess sat at her desk getting things ready for her trip. Lynn had just come in and was up in the loft getting coffee. She had done nothing all week but think about Riley's visit. The feeling came from deep down. Today she would find out. This time she couldn't run away. It wasn't easy getting the directions to her ranch out of E.G. but once Lynn interfered, the process was easier. She checked the directions one last time before putting them away in her bag. Lynn came down the stairs carrying two cups of coffee.

"Are you positive you're ready to do this?" She asked setting the cup in front of Tess.

"Now or never." Tess stated matter of factly. Lynn worked part time as an assistant in the gallery. Tess never considered her a confidant but she knew of E.G.'s friendship with Riley and they went way back. She also knew that Riley never cared a whole lot for Lynn. But E.G. had befriended Tess a long time ago just after Riley left. "You have my cell phone number if anything comes up that you can not handle. Although I don't know what that would be." Tess gathered up her things and headed for the door. "How long did you say the drive would take?"

"About two hours if you don't get lost." Lynn smiled.

"See you tomorrow." Tess left and didn't see the look Lynn gave her. She herself knew Tess wouldn't be back for a few days at the least. There was always the possibility Riley really didn't want anything to do with Tess and it would take a little longer. She looked out the window as Tess' black jaguar pulled out onto the street and down the block. This would be interesting either way and she wished she could be a fly on that wall.

Hot dogs, cotton candy, soda to wash it all down with and everyone's favorite elephant ears were all for sale in the booths set up along the backside of the bleachers. People started mingling about. There was still about an hour to go before the start of the rodeo festivities. Everyone wanted to get a good seat. The Horse and Pony Club was putting on their barrel racing contest and Katie was entered. The parade was scheduled to start in a few minutes. The county 4-H queen would make her entrance first and then the contestants would be announced.

Riley checked in with the judges just after ten o'clock and received her number to which Huck had pinned on her back and she obliged him as well. "456, hmmm, think that's a lucky group of numbers for some one as spry as yourself?" Riley turned to face the honeriest excuse for a human being that ever sat foot in Bradford County.

"Harlan McCoy. When in the hell did you get out of prison?" She asked with a hint of teasing sarcasm in her voice.

"I ain't never been in prison and you knowed that." He joked back. "Unless this is what you call this place." Harlan shook Huck's hand. "Been a long time buddy."

"When did you get into town?" Huck asked trying to ignore Riley. Harlan was a childhood friend of his and Dale's. He was a couple of years ahead of them both in school and he was sure Riley didn't forget that she dated him for a couple of months. For some reason it just didn't work out. With respect for his craft Harlan knew all there could be known about horses. Years ago he took off and bought himself a spread in Montana and no one in this town had seen him since.

"We got in on Thursday. I brought my wife and kids." He glanced over at Riley. She really was looking good these days. The years had been kind to her. "Why hasn't any young stud come along and dragged you to the hitchin' post." He grinned.

Riley just rolled her eyes. "I have to go tag my saddle. Nice seeing you again Harlan. I can tell you haven't changed." She walked off towards the barn door hearing his laughter as she went. She could feel his eyes on her back.

"I got a feelin' why no fella has lassoed her in. Stubborn streak in her a mile wide."

"That's right you two did go out in high school. I forgot." Huck chuckled. "You still pinin' after ol' Rley?"

"Shit, with an ass like hers you'd be stupid if you didn't at least try. Who'd of thought she'd grow up and be filled out like that." He whistled under his breath. "You'd be lyin' if yourself hadn't thought it." Except Huck knew better. Riley had long ago confided in him about her sexuality. A topic he didn't clearly understand but he loved Riley as his friend. Always had and always will. And he knew the feeling was mutual.

"After this is over we'll go down to Coot's for a beer." Huck replied as both men headed towards the judge's table.

The Jaguar pulled into the parking lot of the fairgrounds raising a lot of dust behind. It seemed the whole town was parked in the fields around the grandstand. Tess had never in her life seen so many pickup trucks in one place, she noted. She looked around until she spotted the old green jalopy Riley was in last week over by the barns. Luck seemed to hovering above when she decided to stop in that store to see if she was heading the right way. She went through the screen door and was sent back in time. Wood planks, a few shelves filled with cans and jars of homemade jams and jellies. The coke cooler in the back and the computerized register gave away this was the twentieth century. The girl behind the counter seemed like she would rather be some place else. When Tess asked how to get out to Riley's house the girl informed her that everyone including Riley were out at the fairgrounds for the rodeo. She gave her the directions then whistled when she saw Tess get into the black Jaguar. She understood the reaction. Everyone in this town seemed to drive pickup trucks. Tess paid for her ticket and then followed a group of women towards the bleachers all the while looking out to see if she could spot Riley.

The crack of the PA system boomed from the speakers. "Ladies and gentlemen, welcome to the annual Bradford County Horse Breakin' Rodeo!!!" The announcer paused for the scattered applause and cheers. Everyone sat waiting for the festivities to start. "This year we have the finest horses yet. The riders all drew straws and the line up for the saddle ride is Dan Morgan. Second goes to Huck Hopkins. Third to Miss Riley Jones and pullin' up the rear is Beau Moore. Beau has been on the junior rodeo circuit all summer. This ought to be a show worth your money." The audience applauded and cheered as the show began.

The walk up the wooden bleachers wasn't as easy as Tess thought. The old weathered planks had seen their better days. Like in the 1930's, she thought to herself as she found a seat close to the end of the row near the gate. When she heard Riley's name announced she stopped suddenly in her tracks. Riley was a contestant in this horse thing? E.G. nor Lynn had told her everything about their visit. A line of quarter horses came prancing out into the arena circling around the barrels at high speed. A commotion from behind the bleachers drew her attention. Three men in cowboy hats were trying to shove an ill-tempered horse into the chute. The horse appeared to be outsmarting them because he wasn't budging. Riley had to be back there near the barn if she was one of the riders. Tess leaned over the rail trying to spot her. Everyone was wearing cowboy hats down low on their heads making it hard to see their faces. This wasn't going to be easy.

Logan walked over to the barn going towards the corral that kept the wild horses. She wanted to get a look at the herd for herself and see if the rumors were true. She spotted a man over near the corral fence. Logan didn't recognize him from around this area so he must be one of Bancroft's men. The rumors were true those horses looked to be a fine herd. Wild Mustangs, the finest of all the breeds, in her opinion. It didn't take long to locate the stallion rearing up near the back. He was trying to protect his herd in captivity. Whoever picked his number was sure in for the ride of his life, Logan commented to herself.

"Ed sure has a fine stock in this year." She turned to see that the man was gone. "That's odd. He was just here, right behind me." Logan shrugged it off and decided to go look for Riley.

"I was wonderin' when you'd get here." Riley stated as she came up to the corral seeing her friend.

"I had to check out the challenge today. Wild Mustangs, I envy you." Logan commented.

"All you have to do is sign up." Riley knew her friend was an excellent rider. But she wasn't too keen on riding a horse that wasn't broke in first.

"I have children to think of." Logan begged off. Dale spotted the two women near the chute walking up to them while he put on his gloves. He was working the chute this afternoon. He let them know the horses weren't waiting any longer and for Riley to be ready.

The barrel racing event was near the end. Katie and Brooke Moore, Beau's younger sister were tied for first place. One last ride for each girl would decide the winner. Riley strolled over to the fence with Logan to watch. Brooke was an excellent barrel racer but she was a bit wide on the turns, which cost her a few seconds. Katie on the other hand knew her competitors weakness and held tight in the turns making up those few seconds. The crowd was on its feet when the announcer declared two first place winners. Katie lacked in style what she made up in speed. Brook was the opposite.

The announcer raised the excitement by announcing the start of the saddle ride. Riley tightened her gloves on each hand knowing this was the only real protection she had against these horses. The first horse was finally loaded into the chute and Dan Morgan was lowered into the saddle. As soon as the gate was open the horse shot out into the ring to the applause of the grandstand. Huck climbed onto the rails waiting for his mount that was being pushed and pulled into the confined area.

Dan's ride was clean with the horse bucking enough to give a show but Dan clearly made the eight second horn blast. He was riding around the ring to the cheers and applause of the audience.

Huck was in the saddle and ready when Dan rode out of the arena to the barn.

The gate swung back hard this time slamming against the rail fence. The loud sound made Tess jump. She turned in her seat just in time to see the next rider climb up the rails of the chute and being lowered onto the saddle. The crowd roared as Huck stood tall in the saddle. The mount was trying it's best to throw the strange weight off it's back. Huck was a disciplined rider and would stay on until the horse gave up out of sheer exhaustion. Riley was up on the fence rails getting ready to lower herself down. The horse suddenly jerked sideways almost pinning her legs against the rail. She jumped back on the fence quickly to avoid the blow.

"Be careful Riley." She nodded in response as she pulled her cowboy hat down firmer on her head. Riley tried again to lower herself onto the saddle and succeeded this time. When she lifted her head to signal she was ready Riley looked into the stands. A moment passed as the woman with dark hair and sun glasses turned around.

The gate swung wide and the wild Mustang took off rearing high into the air barely clearing the fence near the front row of the bleachers. Riley fought hard to stay in the saddle before the horse came down hard on it's front feet pitching her forward. The crowd was on it's feet. This ride was by far more exciting than the first two. Maybe it was because it was Riley's ride. The stands cheered her on.

Tess stood in complete shock watching Riley ride by in a whirl of dust. "Damn, she's good." Tess hadn't realized she spoken out loud until the lady next to her looked over at her.

"Honey, Riley Jones can out ride any man in this county and she's done it plenty of times." The woman remarked in a friendly way.

"I can see why." Tess replied never once taking her eyes off of Riley.

Riley tried getting the Mustang's head down but the horse had other ideas. They flew past the bleachers in a blur and she could hear the cheers. The second turn Riley pushed down hard on the stirrups to regain her balance. The horse took off when Riley heard the sharp snap of leather right before the saddle started to slide from the horse's back. Riley hit the ground hard with the saddle falling on top of her before she even realized she was falling. Riley could hear the screams from the stands when she tried to get up. She saw the hoof come out of the cloud of dust striking her in the right hip knocking her back down on the ground realizing she hadn't cleared the horse. The men were on their feet running towards the center of the arena. Riley felt the pain searing down her right leg but she knew she had to get up. She managed to raise up on her left knee when out of nowhere she heard someone scream her name. Riley never saw the second hoof coming from behind.

Tess was on her feet and over the fence running to where Riley lay. An ambulance was on its way into the arena. Medics jumped out from the back with a stretcher. A group of men had the frightened horse under control leading it back towards the barn out of the way. Riley could hear everyone around her but couldn't focus. The pain was so intense. The medics placed her on the stretcher and started to close the doors to the ambulance. Riley opened her eyes looking into those crystal clear blue pools of water. "Tess." Riley called out before losing consciousness

Chapter Five

The rain had let up by mid morning turning into a slight drizzle. Barges were being loaded along the Columbia River to transport goods to the Mississippi River then on to the final destination. A sedan was parked between two warehouses back in the shadows. The detectives shut the doors cautiously looking around. There were a group of men loading boxes onto pallets then stacked on the dock with a forklift waiting to be loaded onto the a cargo ship.

"Right over there Wes." Detective Reed pointed towards the huge building towering above the smaller one in front. It was almost half hidden in the shadows directly in front of them. The windows were painted black making it impossible not to go and investigate. It was locked up tight and the detectives were one search warrant shy of breaking in. Det. Carson looked closely at the ground around the structure. The area was clean □□not even a cigarette butt laying around. "Your hunches were right. This has to be the lab. The other buildings are too large to be secured as tight as this one." Det. Reed commented.

"This part of the docks have been abandoned for years." Wes stated. He walked behind the building looking around at the others. "Right over there at that warehouse would be a perfect place for

67

surveillance." The building had several floors, which offered an overlook view of the building in question. A few patrol cars for backup hiding under the interstate over there." He pointed up a large hill where the on ramp. "And we could get a bust."

"Let's do it." Reed agreed looking at the name on the old building, Wilburn Brothers. Must have been quite an operation during it's time. He thought to himself as they headed back to the car.

Mrs. Kelly waved at Jesse from the porch when the Jeep drove into the driveway. Jesse went over to say hello. "I haven't seen you for a few days." Mrs. Kelly stated once Jesse stepped on the porch step.

"You know, I used to dream of the day when my dues were paid and I'd get my first recording contract." Jesse sat down on the porch swing. "That's what has kept me going all these years. But now that day has come and it isn't a damn thing like I expected it to be."

"It never is." Mrs. Kelly looked at Jesse as though she was reflecting on her own memories. "I wish Toni had the sense and determination that you have. Both you girls have the talent. I'm a light sleeper." She smiled and winked referring to those nights Jesse and Toni would be up all hours of the night playing their songs.

Jesse had to laugh. She had no idea they had been so loud that the Kelly's had heard them practicing. That's was not going to happen any longer. Those days are gone forever with her partner. "You sound as though you had similar experiences." Jesse had to change the subject to keep her emotions in tact.

Mrs. Kelly's eyes held a sparkle when she answered. "I was a back up singer for Miss Patsy Cline and those were one of the best few years of my life." She waited for Jesse's reaction and wasn't surprised from her look.

"You're kidding?" Jesse was surprised.

"I sort of landed the job by accident when Miss Patsy heard me singing backup duet with Mr.Hank Williams. The Rebel himself." Mrs. Kelly leaned her head back on the old rocker letting the memories surface. "Back then everyone wanted to be on the Grand Ol' Opry. I made it several times with Hank But the night Patsy's back up singer had the flu I stood in for her on Pasty's performance. Her accident sort of ended all my ambition. That's when I met Frank and then we got married and the kids came soon after. I had my fifteen minutes of fame and then some." She leaned up looking directly at Jesse. "I wouldn't trade what I have now for the life of fame. I can see that you're gonna take your talents to unbelievable heights. Don't lose any part of yourself along the way."

Jesse had a hard time believing after all these years she had lived above Mrs. Kelly had never let on she had any part of the music business. "I never would of guessed." She said a bit shocked.

"No one has yet. Those are my memories and now you will be making your own." She smiled.

"I will always remember that. Thank you." Jesse was going to miss this woman more than she even realized. Mrs. Kelly was as sweet as southern ladies were known to be. "I best get upstairs and let you about your business." Jesse got up then instinctively she went over to the older woman and bent down to give her a hug surprising Mrs. Kelly. Their relationship had always been friendly but this was the first time Jesse had shown affection and Mrs. Kelly had shared any of herself with her. She bid goodnight and took her mandolin off the swing before walking towards the back stairs. Once upstairs she checked her messages and Toni's mother had called to make arrangements to come to Tennessee to pick up her daughter's things. Jesse had already boxed up everything in Toni's bedroom expecting that someday soon her family would want to come for them. Toni's room was bare except for the bed. She kept the bed covers on it thinking it wouldn't make the room so empty.

Jesse sat down on Toni's bed and laid back against the pillows and closed her eyes. The band was the opening act at the state fairgrounds tonight for Nadine. She wanted them to have exposure and Hop Harris, Nadine's manager and record producer would be there to check out the band that his star had been raving about. If there was anyone in this industry that could make or break a carreer it was Hop. Jesse still had a few hours before she had to get ready. She closed her eyes letting her mind relax. Back home this time of year would be the annual county rodeo. This was the time of year she got homesick. If she was home now she would be like everyone else in Stanford getting ready for the festivities. She had been to one several years ago when she went home for a brief visit. The last few years her parents had kept her informed. They had mentioned Riley had shocked the whole town by riding in the last few years. But that was

69

Riley and from the sound of it she hadn't changed much. Jesse found herself drifting back in time.

The day couldn't have been better for summer. The sun reflected off the water. The girls had climbed to the top rock being supported by the stack of limestone slab. The rock was flat and large enough to spread out a couple towels and room for the portable radio between them. The first thing this morning both Riley and Jesse had rushed through their chores just so they could lie out in the sun all day. The summer was almost half over and this would be their last year of high school. One more homecoming game, one more Christmas break and one more last day of school before their lives took on different directions. Jesse had been trying to convince her friend to go with her to Tennessee for a year and then decide if the Air Force was what she really wanted. The idea of moving to a huge city like Nashville scared Jesse more than she let on. Riley didn't seem to be in much of a hurry deciding on her future anyway. College had not been a option for Jesse but Riley on the other hand was toiling with it. The one thing both girls did agree on was to get as far away from Stanford as they could.

Jesse's dream was to go to Music City and play her mandolin for a living. Every teenager's dream at one point was to be a star but she was willing to just be part of a band. A successful band would be nice and maybe one day play on the Grand Ol' Opry. Jesse had the talent and everyone who heard her play knew it. There wasn't a Saturday night that went by where she was playing somewhere between the summer festivals and just get together with Dale's uncles who had started their own Bluegrass band. Riley on the other hand wanted to go further beyond Tennessee. There was a whole world out there and she didn't just want to sit in Stanford and read about it anymore. Riley wanted to go out and experience those stories. Live in places only others can read about. The military would provide her those opportunities since she wasn't a millionare it would be her only option.

"Are you playing anywhere this weekend?" Riley asked trying to shade the sun from her eyes.

"No. Want to do something?" Jesse had been waiting for her friend to ask.

"Like what?" She asked, suddenly realizing how quickly Jess reacted to her question. Riley knew her too well to know that Jesse already had their weekend planned.

"I thought maybe we could go into Springdale." She sat up to look out over the quarry.

"And look at the old city women going in and out of craft stores? I think I'll pass." Riley would rather stay at home.

"No stupid. I have an idea." She leaned closer to Riley as if there could be anyone around to hear. "Dale told me his uncle is playing at the Shucker's Inn. We could go and see what it's like in a real bar."

"What if we get carded?" Riley could feel the pangs of trouble brewing.

'We're in the band, get it? I'll bring my mandolin just in case." The mischievous grin spreading across Jesse's face. "It's not like it will be a lie. They'd let me sit in on a number or two. What do you say?"

"Hell, like I would have a choice either way. What time will you be picking me up?" Riley knew it would be useless to argue. This was supposed to be their time for adventure and going into a tavern at seventeen years old would promise adventure or just plain trouble.

"Think you can get away at seven?" Jesse asked.

"Not a problem." Riley's parents were liberal about her going out on the weekends especially in the summer.

"You know if you want you could bring Harlan McCoy with you." Jesse teased and just managed to duck as Riley's T-shirt just missed her head by inches and going over the edge of the flat rock they were on. "Nice move, now your shirt is in the water butt head." She laughed.

"Maybe you need to go in after it." Riley jumped up suddenly as Jesse let out a scream backing up off her towel.

"Maybe you need to kiss my ass." She yelled as she jumped from the rock going feet first into the water with Riley following. They had swam in these quarries ever since they were allowed to make the trip by themselves. They explored every slab of rock around and underneath the water to check the depth of the water. Some quarries had rock not one or two feet down and if a person not knowing jumped into the water at that point they would risk sever injury or a broken neck. It had happened many times before. They knew where

71

every piece of slab was lain and on this particular spot none were in the deep end where they swam.

Saturday night arrived and both girls went to Shucker's Tavern on the pretense Jesse was a member of the band, which meant Riley had to sit just off stage and not go near any liquor. When the bartender wasn't looking she would sneak over by the pool table and watch a game. It was there Riley saw Mr. Simms from the mercantile coming out of the men's room. He didn't notice her she thought, but he also wasn't looking to either. Riley took this as a sign in getting the hell out of Dodge. If their parents find out where they really were tonight there would be some serious hell to pay. Riley quickly made her way back to the table and wasted no time in getting Jesse's attention. She pointed over near the pool table and Jesse's eyes bugged out. Jesse took the hint and told the guys she had to leave early and now was a good time. Once outside the music faded in the background as they ran towards Jesse's truck.

"That was close." Jesse replied breathing hard in excitement and from sprinting halfway down the parking lot. She didn't want to park her truck too close to the bar in case someone recognized it.

"We don't know that for sure. It wasn't like you was hidin' up on stage under all those lights." Riley had a good point. "I wonder if his wife knows he comes here."

"She's probably why he comes here." Jesse started the engine and pulled out of the parking lot. "You know something? Tonight was cool." She looked over to see Riley looking at her. "I mean when I was up on the stage. The crowd was different than the festivals we've played. I was in a bar. That's like a huge step."

"From the look on your face it looked as though you belonged." Riley stared out her window. It was true. Soon her friend would find that out for herself.

Jesse slowed down and looked over at Riley. "Sometimes I get this eerie feeling that you feel exactly what I feel. How do you do that?" She grinned and Riley laughed.

"Hell, I've known you since kindergarten. There isn't much we don't know about each other growing up together like we have." Riley didn't even want to think about what it was going to be like next summer without Jesse.

Jess nodded in agreement. She wandered if Riley was thinking the same thing as she was at this moment. "So what do you want to do now before we spend the rest of our summer in our rooms?" She gunned the engine. "We could go see Harlan."

"When are you goin' to give that a rest? I went out with the boy twice. That's it. What's the big deal?" Riley started laughing unbelievingly. "What about Dale? Or Thad Greene for that matter? You wench." Those were the guys Jesse had dated and still went out occassionally with Dale. If Huck was around all four went out to even out the boy girl ratio.

Jesse was laughing hard by now and could hardly speak. "Did you know the veins on your neck pop out when you get mad?"

Riley couldn't look at her as she was trying to control her laughter. She hated it when Jesse brought up Harlan McCoy. She only went out with him because he had an extra ticket to the Grand National Rodeo at the state fairgrounds in Albany. "God I can't wait to get out of this town. No more guys with a wad of chew in their mouth and spitting it into a beer can they keep on the dashboard. Then they expect you to kiss 'em. Like, the wad of tobacco really turns me on." Both busted up laughing knowing how true it was. That was all they were used to in Stanford where the pick of boys was slim.

"So what does turn you on?" Jesse asked surprised at the look coming over her friends face.

Riley had never given it much thought. "I don't think I know yet. What about you?"

"I can tell you it's nothin' around here." She grunted as they turned into her driveway. Riley was spending the night. At least they could be truthful about this part of the night.

The next few days went by as usual until towards the end of the week. The girls met Jesse's mother coming back from the quarries on their horses. Jesse rode Nelly and Riley rode her horse Lily. They were hanging up their towels on the clothesline when her mother came out with a load of wash. "Make sure you take off your suits before sittin' on the furniture. That quarry water stinks." Mrs. Monroe instructed noticing how Jesse rolled her eyes.

"It's not like we have a city pool with chlorine we could go to." She said it with more sarcasm than she intended and her mother picked up on it.

"Well, I'm sure you both would find something else to do. Maybe go to a bar?" Mrs. Monroe turned to see the expressions on both girl's face. This was one of the benefits of being a mother. When the kid gets caught and watching the reaction. "Is there something you want to tell me?" She asked sternly. Riley decided this would probably be a good time to leave before she got the idea to call her parents. Sometimes Mrs. Monroe was pretty cool and let her slide on things that her own mother would bean her for. Hopefully this would be one of those times. She prayed to herself. But she was only dreaming. "Riley maybe you could explain to me how two seventeen year old girls can get into a tavern?"

Riley slowly turned around willing her mind to work fast. It was confirmed. Mr. Simms had spotted them and ratted them out. "We weren't there long, Mrs. Monroe. Honest. Just long enough for Jesse to get back her picks she lent to Dale's uncle." That sounded too simple. And from the look on Mrs. Monroe's face she wasn't buying it either.

"You girls will be the death of me yet." She tried hard in keeping the humor from her voice. There's no backing down when a teenager is involved and never let them see you faulter in punishing.

"Oh, Mama it wasn't a big deal. I need the practice." Jesse interrupted.

"Practice for what? Playing in bars? Is that what you want to do with the rest of your life Jess?" Mrs. Monroe had to get serious. She knew all about the love for music her daughter had. But there came a time when morals had to intercede. This morning she stopped in at the mercantile to pick up a few things when Mrs. Simms began to enlighten her by telling on the girls. Both girls had the reputation of finding trouble but they took their little adventure too far by going into a place that served liquor. She had always encouraged her daughter's dream but she was growing too independent to soon. "I think spending some extra time here at home will keep you from finding trouble young lady. For starters there's weeding the garden. That will give you time to think about how you want to live your life. Maybe then you'll think twice."

"Oh Mama." Jesse whined.

"Hey, no one forced you to go in that place and now I have to hear it from the grocery store. No 'Oh Mamma's'. I can't believe you would do that." The thing is she wasn't all that surprised when she heard it. "You can start with the garden. And if you give me any lip there's always the stalls that need cleaning."

"Fine." Jesse sighed defeat. Riley followed her towards the barn and she was heading home. "I'm going to head over to Grandpa's since you're grounded." Riley replied. She untied Lily from the fence and followed Jesse towards the garden.

"Wait til you get home. I'm sure your mom knows by now." Jesse took the hoe off the wall. She really didn't mind the extra chore. It would give her time to daydream. That was the only way she managed to get through most of her punishments. Retreat to her fantasy world. "Picks? You could of come up with something better than I lent out my picks." She shook her head.

"She had me with that look. It was the best I could do under that kind of pressure." Riley defended.

"Mom has got to understand that playing in bars will be my life for awhile. How many musicians do you know that just walked into a studio one day and made a hit record?" Jesse was venting.

"In a year you won't have anyone to answer to but yourself. Just bear with it for now." She bent down and pulled a few weeds out between the tomatoes.

"That's easy for you to say." Jesse made quick swipes of the blade around a dandelion unsuccessfully. "This sucks."

"Sure does. It's our last summer and I don't want to be spending it pullin' weeds out of your mother's garden." Riley stated.

"How are we going to do that? If we ain't lookin' for trouble it will always find us." Jesse retorted.

"I guess I'll go home and face my sentence. I'll call you later if I can." She put her barefoot in the stirrup and swung her right leg over the saddle.

"Good luck." Jesse bid a farewell. She watched them ride down the drive until they reached the road. A sudden loss came over her. Their time was running out. It was going to hurt real bad when the time came to say goodbye to Riley. Jesse didn't want to think about that so soon. It was still the better part of a year away. She beat at the ground in frustration getting most of the weeds in one or two swipes.

Chapter Six

The excitement from the grandstand was at a climax by the time Jesse, Jackson, Bobby Jim, and Joey known now as the Wayward Weeds made it to the side of the stage. Nadine was still in her dressing room waiting for the show to start. The atmosphere back stage was rushed. Someone was yelling for the announcer to return to the stage. A Deejay from one of the local radio stations had the honor of being tonight's master of ceremony. "Are you ready?" Jackson asked leaning over close to Jesse's ear. She nodded and looked up at Bobby Jim. He had never shown any emotion so no one knew if he was excited, nervous, or near hysterics. He looked as calm as he did four days ago. Jesse wished she could feel the same way. Her plans in breaking into the business never included center stage. She would of just been content on staying in the background. Nadine Nash had other plans for her. As long as Jesse had they boys and the band she could manage.

Suddenly the stage lights came on to the huge roar of applause and shouts from the audience. The stamping of impatient feet on the bleachers created its own rhythm. The announcer had been found and was at the microphone. "What a show we have in store for you tonight!" He yelled with his voice booming above all the excitement.

77

The Dee Jay was working the crowd. That was the honor of being master of ceremony. "Let's get this show on the road. WCHT welcomes to the stage a band who has been riding up the charts and now you can see why. Put your hands together for Jesse Monroe and the Wayward Weeds!" He screamed above the noise.

The band took the cue and headed for their instruments as Jesse waited behind a big speaker at the side of the stage for the first chord to start. Then she walked out to the cheers, whistles and clapping of hands. Her mandolin poised high, her mouth close to the microphone, she closed her eyes and felt the music run through her. The husky whispering of her voice cut through the night air as smooth as silk blowing in a gentle breeze. She told the story of a woman who loses her man in the mines of old Kentucky. The heartache and pain poured out through her voice and caught the attention of every single person beyond the bright lights of the stage. Her mandolin wailed in the loneliness and sorrow that she too felt the tears at the corner of her eyes. Jesse had blocked out everything around her but the music. A silence filled the arena at the last chord of the song before a burst of applause brought them all back to reality. The band immediately went into a fast tempo mountain tale that had everyone remotely around the stage foot stomping, hootin' and hollerin'. The set only ran five songs and an encore followed to everyone's surprise. The band had gotten more than just the attention from the fans. The buzz backstage was proof Jesse and the boys had made an impression.

Nadine was waiting behind the curtain when they came off the stage. "Do you hear that honey? That's for you." She shouted near Jesse's ear to be heard above the applause. Jesse couldn't believe it and the smile on her face was answered any doubts they had at what heights the band would climb. It was a good feeling Jesse thought to have earned this kind of recognition and the years it took to achieve it. Her parents would be so proud if they could see all of this going on.

"Don't get too excited I need you on the duet. Third song and I will introduce you again. Oh and bring that stick of wood with you." Nadine teased. She was so happy for this young woman. It had been a long time since she had witness a dream come true for someone as deserving in talent as this young woman had.

"Thank you so much Nadine. If nothing else comes of this I will always remember tonight." Jesse replied right when the announcer was introducing Nadine and her band. But Nadine wasn't in any hurry.

"Honey, you best take a good long look at that crowd. There's goin' to be a lot more nights like these for you." She patted her arm. The grandstand began a slow chant of the star's name, "I guess it's my turn." She winked at Jesse before strolling out onto the stage in her sequin jacket that sparkle under the lights

The clouds kept the moon from shining through to the city below making the night even more dark than it already was. The two detectives wouldn't have any trouble keeping a low profile safely hidden on the lower level of the Wilburn Building. Another detective was placed on the third floor with a sound receiver pointing directly at the structure below. A few patrol cars were hidden under the overpass with a view of both directions. The radio cracked and a uniform officer let them know an El Camino had just made a turn towards their station without its headlights on. Both men glanced out towards the road. The car was coming very slowly and parked right in front of the building in question. Two men came out the door each carrying a couple of stacked boxes towards the car. Det. Carson stood back and radioed to stand by. The same men went back into the building. The door opened and closed soundlessly. This would be the right moment to nail them when they came back out. Take them by surprise. Wes checked his pocket where he had put the search warrant before backing away from the window.

The detectives cautiously made their way towards the shack and positioned themselves at both ends. They didn't wait long before the door opened again and three men filed out carrying more boxes. Two were arguing and not paying much attention when all of a sudden flashing red lights came from out of no where and shouts for them to stop right where they were and drop to the ground. Det. Carson came from behind the door with his 357 magnum pointed right at the first man. Det. Reed coming around from the front. A shot was fired from inside as Reed stormed in through the door firing a few shots for cover. Two men were stood before a table covered with plastic bags and several sets of scales. They were too shocked to react. Both men dropped their guns knowing they were surrounded by cops. There wasn't an easy way to escape since there wasn't a back door. It wasn't worth getting killed for. The detective ordered them down onto the ground and proceeded to handcuff them both.

"I'll be damned. Look what we have in here boys." Det. Carson replied as he stood in the doorway. "Paddy wagon is on it's way boys."

"What do you think Wes? Make it, bag it and send it on down the river. Can't get any easier than that." Reed watched as Wes walked around the room looking closely at the set up. He came to a back room used for storage and had no clue what he was looking for until he just missed hitting his head on the shelf above a stack of boxes. Wes took a closer look at the boxes contained plastic baggies. On the shelf turned over on its side was a rusted can her could hardly read the label. Wesley looked closely and noticed the powder contents had spilled out and was covering the top layer of bags.

From the doorway Reed stood watching. "What did you find?"

"I don't know but it looks odd. I think this is rat poisoning." Wes pointed to the can. "It looks like it tipped over spilling onto these open boxes. If I'm right and this is rat poison then we have our men."

"You got to be kidding. You're telling me that can caused all those people to die?" Reed shook his head in disbelief. What are the chances of that happening?

"That's the chance an addict takes. One might get a hold of some bad stuff and it doesn't matter how it gets into the drugs. In this case I have a gut feeling that's exactly what happened." Wes walked out of the small room just as the last of the men were being loaded into the police van. A small crowd of curious on lookers had gathered at a distance. They wanted to find out what happened but not willing to get involved.

A uniform cop walked over. "You guys doin' the report on this?" he asked.

Reed nodded. Wesley looked around the rest of the lab. The equipment that was used was highly sophisticated with the capabilities of producing mass amounts bigger than this operation. Something wasn't right. "Frank, you've been on this beat for a long time. What's you're opinion?" He had worked with this officer many times on the drug enforcement task force and there wasn't anyone more knowledgeable about this part of town than Frank.

"You're instincts are right. For this size of an operation with only six men running it? No way." Frank commented. "I've been around long enough to know we just caught the middle men."

"You're right. If anything, whomever is the head honcho of this is going to pull back til the heat is off. We won't see anymore action for awhile." Wes replied wearily as the adrenaline reduced in his body.

"I was surprised Hank Moleson wasn't in this group. This fits his profile." Frank checked his gun to make sure the safety strap was over the hammer.

"I don't think it's over yet." Wes watched the crowd of people slowly disperse as the last of the men were hauled away. He had a strong feeling the Mole wasn't too far away.

The concert was over and the audience was leaving the fairgrounds. A group of fans made their way towards the back of the stage to get a glimpse of the entertainers. All they really wanted was too meet Nadine Nash for an autograph. Just to see the Queen of Country Music up close even if it was only a glimpse as she got into her limousine. Bobby Jim had made his way over to the crowd and shook hands with the people. He told them Nadine would be heading to her car shortly. If they stuck around they might get a wave out of her. Jesse took the opportunity to go back out on the stage now that it was almost empty of the equipment. She could see now without the bright lights how huge the arena was. Every seat had been filled. Nadine had told her the concert was sold out. A thought Jesse just couldn't comprehand. So the response she got from tonight performance was true. Their style of Bluegrass music was accepted and loved. Man, she knew this day would come if she would just hang in there a little longer. And boy did she. Tonight Jesse Monroe from Stanford, Indiana had played for a sell out concert. Granted it wasn't she who they came to hear but someday it would be.

"Looks a bit scarier when you can see out there." The stoutly man in a western cut suit and cowboy hat with boots to match walked up to her. Hop Harris, Nadine's manager. The King of Music Row. He alone is responsible for more successful careers than any one talent agency. Just to have Hop say your name in this town was a privilege. "Very nice show tonight lil' lady."

Jesse could feel the color rise in her cheeks. "Thank you." That was all she could manage to reply.

"We have some talkin' to do. Call my office next week. Then we're gonna put you and those boys of yours in a recordin' studio." Hop grinned and put his cigar back into his mouth and walked on past Jesse like she wasn't even there.

"Yes sir." Jesse replied to his retreating back. There it was right in front of her. Jesse's dream served on a gold platter. The duet had brought the house down as Nadine and her sang the life of two women vowing for the love of the same man. Nadine had taught her one good lesson and that was to act out the songs for the audience. They come to be entertained not just for someone to stand at the microphone and sing. This was the entertainment business and that was exactly what the two singers did. Jesse followed Nadine's lead just as they rehearsed. When Nadine got up into Jesse's face swearing she would fight for her man the audience cheered her on. Jesse was the other woman and she loved every minute of the confrontation they displayed for thousands of people.

"Hey, was that Hop Harris talkin' to you?" Jackson asked. Jesse was so into her thoughts she hadn't seen him approach.

"He wants us his office. How about that?" She watched as his expression changed to excitement.

"You're kiddin'? Oh my God." Jackson couldn't believe it. "We have to get together before Monday. We have to have a proposal of some sort." His mind was working.

"Right now all I want is sleep." She picked up her mandolin case.

"Want some company?" Jackson teased.

"Don't flatter yourself. Toni has a big mouth." She walked off the stage with him following at her heels. Jesse still couldn't use her friend's name in the past tense. She was still with her and Jesse she knew it. At times Jesse could feel Toni around her. Tonight Toni's presence was felt during the songs she and Jesse had written together.

"I thought I explained all that." Jackson retorted.

"Call me tomorrow and we'll get the boys and put something together for the meeting." She walked up to her Jeep and got in. "But don't call too early. I don't think I'll be sleeping much after tonight."

"I know the feeling. Be careful." He stepped back when Jesse started up the engine.

The police station was a busy place tonight. The six men that were brought in were in a holding cell waiting for questioning. Det. Reed sat down at his desk sighing wearily. "The evidence is in forensics. When the report is done they'll send it up."

Wes was sorting through the stack of files on his desk. "Do you know where I put that woman's number?"

"Why in the hell would I keep track of your women? You need to find someone and settle down like the rest of us and you won't have that problem." Reed remarked. This had been a long shift and he was ready to get the hell out of there.

Wes glared at his partner with the, I'm with stupid expression. "Tag number four's roommate, asshole." He shifted through a more files before finding Toni Griffin's folder.

"Are you sure that woman is on the up and up? How many musicians do you know in the business that aren't into drugs or any other illegal activity?" Reed asked. One thing he didn't want to see was his friend hook up with any trouble. "Ever thought to check her out?"

Wes admitted Reed had a point. But he wasn't going to deal with that tonight. He had put in enough overtime on this case and he was beat. All he wanted was to go home and go to bed. "I might give it some thought." He wrote down the number on a piece of paper before standing up. "Let's get this questioning over with."

"I'm right behind you." Reed followed.

The sun crept through the open window creating lines of shadows across the room. The quiet of the morning right before the alarm clock went off. The figure laying on her back with the sheet pulled back exposing a long shapely leg. Her body jerked from the unconscious. Jesse's eyes flew open and she gasped for air. She sat up trying to calm her breathing. Strands of damp hair falling into her eyes. The same reoccurring dream of the light, the very bright light and the train whistle blowing right before she fell. Hearing someone cry out her name and then she would wake up never knowing who's voice it was. It was if this person was trying to save her or warn her. Jesse pulled back the sheet and flung her legs over the side. Her t-shirt was wet with sweat and she took it off. Jesse got up and went to the window and pushed back the curtain. The day looked promising. Only six-thirty in the morning and the heat had settled in the air. This would be a day to take off to regroup. Last night had a huge impact on her. The apartment seemed stifling. A drive through the country might be what she needed to clear her head and let destiny lead her way.

Two hours later Nashville was in her rearview mirror. Jesse turned on the radio to WCHT and let the wind blow through her hair, heading northeast. A few small towns passed by but she wasn't out quite far enough. She was in search of quiet. So many things have been happening lately with the record, Toni's death and now a recording contract. Things had to level out at some point and run smoother. She just had to keep her senses about everything and just flow with it. Trying to do everything at once will only drain any energy she had lately. The more Jesse could let go of her mind the better she began to feel. The road took her further away. Before long she was feeling hungry.

The jeep pulled into the first place to eat that she had seen in a few miles. Bulls Gap Diner was painted on the front window. Jesse quickly ran a brush through her hair and pulled it back into a ponytail to get her baseball cap on. Glancing around she noticed the view of the mountains lining the trees behind the buildings. How far had she driven? She wondered. Jesse looked up the street that was lined with old buildings. The town was surviving but barely. The bell above the door went off announcing her presence. A few people at the counter looked over then went back to their meal when they didn't recognize her. Jesse smiled and took a seat at a booth near the window. It would give her some diversion. A glass of water was placed in front of her by an aging Tammy Wynette look alike.

"What can I git for ya?" The waitress asked in her deep southern drawl.

"I'll have a cup of coffee and a turkey sandwich." Jesse answered.

"Have it out fer ya quick." She turned to leave when Jesse noticed the woman' name tag. Her name was Tammy. The place shone from the spotless chrome around the counter and stools to the linoleum floor. The tables were wiped clean and the menus didn't stick to the table. Jesse got up from the tableto get the local paper from the rack next to the booth. She turned to the classifieds and noticed only three listings under real-estate section. One was a brick home in town asking price twenty thousand. She scanned the next but found interest in the last ad. A farmhouse with a barn and an out building on fifty acres just outside of town off Mountain Point Rd. Miss Tammy brought her lunch and sat the plate down in front of her.

"That paper is about two weeks old honey. We ain't current around here." She smiled revealing a huge set of teeth.

"Where would I find out information about this ad?" Jesse showed her the ad in the paper.

"Oh hell. Ed is the Williamson's place still up for sale?" Tammy turned around towards the man sitting at the counter.

"Yea, you interested?" Ed asked nonchalantly.

"If I was wouldn't I have asked you about it before now?" She replied sarcastically and winked at Jesse. "This here young lady is asking about it."

"That's who I was askin' not you." He got up and came over to the table.

"I might be. I'd like to take a look at the place and see how much it is." Jesse took a bite of her sandwich.

"I might save you the trip. The house is over one hundred and thirty years old and in need of major repairs. The barn is in better shape but not by much. The people that have owned it in the past never took proper care of it. Let it get run down and it's been vacant for over three years. There is alot of acreage with a pond the size of a small lake. If you're looking for a some land to build a house then you might want to see it." He replied.

Jesse wondered how many times he had given that sales pitch. Ed didn't seem to eager about selling it. Maybe she was the first person to inquire about the property. "It doesn't sound too appealing but I would like to take a look at it anyway..." She replied.

"Really? Well, I can drive you out after you finish your lunch." He smiled.

"We can go now." Jesse laid down some money and finished her coffee.

"It's not far so you can follow me. Can't really get lost." Ed remarked as they headed out the diner. He got into his Ford Taurus. Jesse had no idea what she was doing but it felt right. With a

85

recording contract in the works she would be bringing in royalties and a lot more money. It was time to for some stability in her life. This town had character. The people seemed friendly and Bulls Gap was small against the huge back drop of the mountains. This place reminded of home.

Jesse followed the car in front of her as it turned down a country road and then slow down to turn right into a lane. There was but little gravel left that the weeds hadn't taken over. The two-story house was to the left of the barn. She understood now what Ed had meant about rebuilding. The barn was made out of stone that Jesse later found out came from the creek that ran just south of the property. A dirt ramp went up to the second level leading to the double doors of which only one was intack the other no where to be seen. They parked the vehicles and got out.

"This is it." Ed opened his arms. "The house is just like I said. In need of major repair."

Jesse kept her eyes on the barn. "Mind if we go in?" She asked.

"Can't promise we'd be the only ones in there." Ed referred to the wild animals that probably made their home in the abandonded structure. He saw the smile spread across this woman's. He opened the huge door making as much noise as he could to scare anything off. There were a few stalls to the right, a tack room of sorts on the far back wall with a staircase leading up to the hayloft. Jesse looked up at the beams of solid oak. The loft only went part way along the wall. Her heart began to beat faster. There was an energy about this place. She could sense it. Ed seemed a bit bored. Real estate wasn't his chosen career.

"I like it. There are alot of possibilities here." Jesse commented while the plans of renovation swam in her mind turning this place into a beautiful home. "Can we look around outside?" She noticed the look of complete shock on Ed's face. He never thought in a million years anyone would be interested in this old place. Wait until he told the guys back at the bank.

"Look at that view." Jesse could see the mountains from the side. A huge picture window along the north wall and she could have the view of a lifetime. "What's the elevation?"

How the hell would he know that? Ed thought to himself. "That would be on record at the courthouse." He looked at her hard. "Are you really serious about buying this? I mean I've shown it to a few people but once they saw the property and the work involved they shied away."

"Yes Mr., I don't think I got your last name." Jesse couldn't keep her eyes off of the barn. So many possibilities brewing in her mind.

"Hawsey. Ed Hawsey." He looked embarrassed. "I was just checking. I honestly thought you would take one look and decide it would be a waste of your time."

"Mr. Hawsey I have to go back to Nashville and get my finances together but I would very much like to put an offer on this place." Jesse replied being quite the business woman.

"You are serious. Well hot damn." Ed shook his head in disbelief. "Here's my card. I'm at the City Bank. I can go ahead and put your offer in. It's safe to say there aren't any more interests but can I ask why this place?"

Jesse sighed. "I don't know yet. I just have a feeling about this." She continued to look around.

One thing his daddy taught Ed was to stay as far away from a woman when she gets a feelin' about something. Wise words he took to heart.

The neon signs lit up Music Row in the night. The tourist settling themselves in their motel rooms until the action started in the clubs that lined the streets. The Grand Ol' Opry would be airing it's broadcast in a few minutes. Bogg's Tavern was having a good night. Jesse met Jackson at their booth back against the far wall. Bobby Jim and Joey were at the pool table and Jesse was telling Jackson all about the place she saw earlier that day. Who in the hell had ever heard of Bull's Gap? The place sounded painful to Jackson. Their first decision for the band was to go ahead and release the demos they had made after hours at Blue Ridge Studio. That would give them enough tracks for an album. Their sound was bluegrass with a rockabilly beat. The ballads were strong and mournful. They wrote their music from their own experiences and the perception of life around them trying hard to stay as far away from the honky tonk cheating songs as they could. This band had a story to tell and it was up to them to get it across the only way they knew how from the heart. As long as they didn't stray from their style and kept their heads on straight then they would gain respect. These musicians were a band together and together they would stay.

"So when are you going to move out of Nashville?" Jackson asked.

"Not for awhile. The barn needs total renovations but the broker Ed Hawsey has a cousin who does this sort of work. I can't wait for you to see it. Maybe it would be best once the renovations have started and you can see just how perfect this place is. You wouldn't believe the view I have of the mountains." Jesse answered.

Jackson shook his head in disbelief but for the first time he saw how excited she was about having a place of her own. "How on earth did you find it?"

"I just went for a drive to get away and clear my head. The further away from Nashville I got the more peace I found and the rest just fell into my lap." She smiled.

Frieda came in through the back via the kitchen and was in the process of tying on her apron when she noticed the Jackson and Jesse sitting at the back table. She went over with a huge grin on her face. "I have been hearing you all on the radio." Jesse started to laugh. "I'm serious my sister-inlaw went to Nadine's concert last night and there you all were. I'd figure you'd be wantin' to hang in a much nicer place than this dump."

"Well honey, we just might do that." Jackson winked at her.

"Carl said you were in awhile ago looking for Toni. Then I saw the article in the paper. It's an awful shame." Frieda remarked sadly. She had known Toni just as she knew Jesse, Jackson and the rest of Bogg's customers.

"Yea, well the police are investigating it." Jesse stated.

"You think so?" Frieda asked coyly. She had been a bar waitress long enough to know about the Nashville Police Department. The cops would make their appearance on this side of town but only when they were looking for information.

"What do you mean?" Jesse asked trying to figure Frieda out wasn't easy.

"Check out the pool table when you get the chance." She loaded up the empty bottles and walked back to the bar. Jesse looked at Jackson for a meaning and he only shrugged.

"I'll be back." She got up going towards the back to see what Frieda meant.

"Jesse, now don't get into something you can't get out of." Jackson started to follow her but she was too persistent. Jesse didn't walk far before she recognized the man at the back pooltable wearing a sleeveless denim shirt and a dingy white cowboy hat perched slightly back from his forehead. She recognized him as the man whom that old man described that afternoon she was in the bar looking for Toni. This man was the Mole and Frieda had remembered him also. He fit the description down to the look in his eye when glanced her way.

Jesse took her beer bottle and wandered over to the tables. Joey was playing a game with thise man of eight ball. She stood next to Bobby Jim and watched. "Who's winnin'?"

"So far Joey's got his ass parked up to the swing. Depends on this guy's next shot." He watched closely as the stick hit the cue ball sending it into a solid ball then into the right pocket. Joey laid out his money on the table and put his stick up.

"Too much for me." He replied.

"You up?" Moleson leaned against the table. Jesse looked up into the darkest eyes she had ever seen.

She had seen his type before in Bogg's but knew enough to stay clear. She wished Toni had too. "Yea, why not." She stated sitting her bottle on the table. "It's been awhile since I've played."

"That's what they all say. How much you layin' out?" His voice was deep and almost at a whisper.

"I ain't layin' nothin' out mister. I just lost interest." Jesse put the pool stick back in its place and turned to walk away.

"You got some sass." She heard him reply up close to her back. "I like that." He was too close for her comfort. She noticed the boys walking up out of the corner of her eye. She might have gone a little too far.

Jesse turned around looking at him straight in the eye never faltering. "Whatever." And walked past him towards the ladies room. What he couldn't see was the fear that went through her when she looked into those cold dark eyes. There was nothing but evil about him. To think this is the man responsible for her friend's death made her shudder. Once inside the bathroom she looked at her reflection in the mirror. Jesse was on the curt tail of her dream. This place was no longer a part of her being. Freida was right. There were other places and a different social scene to explore. Bogg's just became to dangerous of a place for her. Jesse smiled in the mirror and opened the door. Out of nowhere a hand grabbed her arm and twisted it around her back, pushing her up against the wall. The violence knocked the breath out of her.

"No one ever talks to me like that. Especially not a two-bit whore like you." Moleson threatened through gritted teeth with his hot skunky breath against her ear. Jesse tried to free herself from his grip which made him push her arm further up her back tightening his grip. She knew he could just as easily break her arm than to struggle with her. "Now we are gonna go out this door and have us a little fun. Are you as fun as your friend was?" His laugh penatrated deep.

Jesse's eyes grew wide with fear. This son of a bitch was trying to kidnap her. She opened her mouth as if to scream but Moleson was too quick in anticipating the move as his hand came down crushing her lips against her teeth. She gave him a fight as he pushed her through the door into the alley. She tried to break lose but his grip on her was vice like. He maneuvered her towards a beat up truck trying to get the keys out of his pocket and not let her go at the same time. When he eased up on his hold she took advantage of it by throwing her whole body weight back against him enabling her to get her feet up on the door of the truck and pushed hard with all of her might. Moleson lost his balance and fell backwards with the weight of the woman landing on top of him. Instantly Jesse was up and running as hard as she could towards the street. He was quick getting to his feet running after her. She ran past the front entrance of the tavern looking back she saw the Mole was gaining ground. She heard the shouts but kept on running. No one was out on the street this time of night. No one to help. She ran faster turning the corner on 16th Street she saw a stairwell near a brick building and ran under it to hide in the shadows. Jesse held her breath when the pair of cowboy boots go by. A second later two more appeared and one stayed. She heard voices. "He got away. Took the fence near the construction sight and booked. Where's the woman?"

"I don't know. I saw her turn the corner." Wes stopped when he heard a noise coming from around the steps. Both detectives walked over and saw Jesse on her knees breathing hard. "Ms. Monroe?" She looked up recognizing the detective from the police department. Fear and relief coming over her face. She was safe now as Wesley offered his hand in helping her up. "He's gone. It's all right."

"That was him. The one old man told me about. That son of a bitch killed her. He almost admitted it." Jess ran her hands through her hair trying to control the fear and anger rising in her. With anger came tears. Out of instinct Wes drew her into his arms for comfort. Reed had went back towards the car to call in an all points bulletin on Hank 'the Mole' Moleson. If they were lucky they just might get him yet.

"I know but proving it is the hard part without evidence." Wes knew without physical proof nothing holds up in a court of law without evidence. "Are you going to be all right?"

Jesse clung to him not realizing how fiercely. She took a step back leaving this man's arms wiping at her tears. "Normally I'm not like this. I guess everything is hitting me all at once." She tried to apologize. Jesse heard her name from down the street and thought of Jackson and the boys. "I best get back to my friends."

"Would you mind telling me first what happened in there?" He asked as the policeman in him took charge of the situation. Jesse filled him in about the events leading up to the abduction and the comment he made about Toni. In her mind it happened so quick she was surprised she reacted in knowing how to get away from him. A hidden strength deep within herself that she didn't even realize she had. Wes had just by chance seen a ruckus in the back and thought a domestic dispute was in progress. When he went to investigate he had seen Jesse running out of the alley and Moleson in hot pursuit from the back door. He had signaled Reed and went after them.

Once the guys were convinced Jesse was all right they offered her a ride back to her apartment but Jesse didn't want to leave her jeep overnight at Bogg's. The detective had more questions for her and she took him up on his offer to follow her home. "I'll be fine. I'll call you in the morning if it'll make you feel better."

"I could spend the night. It's not like I have anywhere to go or do." Joey offered. With Jesse being the only girl in the band the guys felt protective of her.

91

"I'm tougher than you all give me credit. Go. Do what you came here to do. I'll be okay." She pulled her hair back in frustration. But they relented. She went over to the police car. Wes turned around as she approached.

"He got away. We'll have a uniform police officer watching his truck. If he comes back for it we'll get him then. Are you sure you're all right?" He could tell she was shook up and had every right to be from what just happened.

"I just don't know everyone Toni was involved with. I think the best decision the guys made was to release her from the band. If this is evidence of how low an addict gets then I don't want any part of it. I told her that. I really tried everything. Even the tough love bit. I don't know." Jesse pulled her keys from her pocket.

"You have to live your own life Miss. Everyone does. It's when you start living it for others that pulls a person down. Sounds to me like Toni had more than just a drug problem." Wes commented.

He was right and Jesse knew it. "I'm parked over there." She pointed down the street.

"I'll follow." He got into the front seat of his truck and pulled up next to her jeep.

The short distance it took to reach her place Jesse rode in silence. The events of the evening kept going through her mind. She glanced a few times in the rearview mirror to see if the detective was behind her and he was. She pulled into her drive and he parked his truck next the Jeep and got out.

"I know this is kind of frank but you've been so nice. Would you like to come up for some coffee?" Jesse asked. The man had saved her life tonight. Coffee seemed mineute compared to his actions.

"Yes, I would. Thanks." Wes walked with her to the stairs. She stopped at the top step noticing the door was ajar. Jess knew she had locked it when she left earlier. She remembered losing her balance and leaning into the door. It would of opened if it wasn't closed tight. Wes noticed her expression and instictivily told her to stand aside. He took out his gun and slowly pushed the door open further. At the end of the short hall the apartment door was standing wide open as he approached with caution. Jesse couldn't stand it and followed him in. He glanced back at her before going into the rest of the apartment. Checking rooms, closets and under the beds. Nothing. The first bedroom was trashed. Boxes overturned and clothes laying all over the bed and floor. Whoever had broken in was looking for something in particular and from the look of it he didn't find it. Jesse looked around. It was as though someone came in here in a rage and just knocked everything over onto the floor.

"No one is here, ma'm but don't touch anything." Wes instructed as he found the phone on the floor and called the station. He had a hunch about who would do this and if he was right Moleson was not playing games. He wanted Jesse Monroe and this was his way of letting her know he wasn't finished with her yet. Wes asked the desk sergeant to run a profile on Hank Moleson and give it to Det. Reed to bring with him. He watched as Jesse sat down on the sofa and put her head in her hands.

This was too much. She thought to herself. What in the hell did Toni think she was doing when she got involved with this man? She was at her limit and she had enough. "This was Hank Moleson's doin' wasn't it?" Jesse waited for the reply but from the expression on the detective's face she already knew the answer. He must of came straight here when they lost the chase. But why? For the life of her she wished she knew the answer.

"That would be my guess. From the busted door frame he wasted no time. Any idea what he was looking for?" The cop in him needed answers.

"If I knew I would save him the trouble and just give it to him." She responded strictly out of emotion. Just the idea of knowing this Hank Moleson knew exactly where she lived and had been in her home made her feel violated. The way that man leered at her made chills run through her body. He could still come back and get what he wanted. Maybe she should of took Joey up on his offer. The sirens could be heard coming from down the block. Wes sent the uniforms down to the landlords to see if they had heard or noticed anyone on the premises. A report was filed and Reed as promised gave him Hank Moleson's file. He would study it later. Finger prints were taken and sent off to the lab.

Mr. Kelly had heard what he thought was Jesse moving things around. With everything that has happened to her they just thought Jesse was grieving. They hadn't seen anyone physically. The fact that Jesse kept odd hours so niether thought about anything being amiss until the policeman came to their door. Hank worked quickly and stayed one step ahead of the police. He was known for his evassiveness.

"Miss Monroe," Wes started to speak before Jesse interrupted him.

"Jesse. When someone comes to my rescue not once but twice in one night then you have the right to call me Jesse." She tried a timid smile.

"Okay, then it's Wes. Not detective anymore." He offered his hand and noticed a sign of relief when she grasped it. For the first time since Jesse went to the police station she looked at this man other than just a police officer. He wore his dark curly hair short and sported a well groomed beard. She remembered his sensitivity when Wes took her into his arms finding her hiding behind the stairs. How long had it been since a man had held her like that? The last relationship she was in was over a year ago. His name was Johnny Banks a free lance songwriter who had several songs recorded and was making a comfortable living at the time. They met at Blue Ridge during a recording session for one of his demo tapes. His long brown hair pulled back in a ponytail. Johnny looked as though he had stepped out of the seventies. An authority fighter who strived in being different. That was the attraction to him. The whole relationship was weak from the start but Jesse was looking for more than Johnny could give. A mutual agreement to try to remain friends. She never heard from him again. Right then she made a vow to never get involved with anyone in the music business again.

"You know, I just got off work about half an hour ago." Wes looked at his watch. "I could stick around and help you clean some of this up." He waited for her to accept the offer.

Jesse looked around at the mess. "That would be appreciated but solely up to you." She felt her cheeks flush hoping he didn't notice.

"That's final then. So how about that coffee?" He smiled breaking the tension. Jesse welcomed the smile that came across her face as she went into the kitchen stepping over things as she went. Wes bent down and picked up some of the pictures that were strewn everywhere. He couldn't help but look at them. Pictures told more about the person. There were a few of Jesse with her parents and a horse. He wondered if the animal was hers. From the look of the other photos it probably was. There were several of her and another girl about her age.

"I don't understand why this man wanted to scare me bad enough to do this?" Jesse came back into the room.

"Hard telling with the type of man the Mole is. Let me show you." Wes went over to the coffee table where he had lain the file. Jesse sat next to him on the sofa as he leafed through the pages. "Two theft convictions, a possession and he served three years for it. Plus with the intent to deal. My guess is he is on probation and will stop at nothing to stay out of prison. Connecting him to Toni's death could get him twenty years to life with all these priors." He looked at her face as she focused on the mug shot.

It was his eyes. She could not get the evil of this man's eyes out of her mind. The way they bore into her when he pinned her against the wall. To think this was the last person Toni saw before she died. Jesse couldn't help but chill at the thought. "Do you think he will be back?" Jesse asked straight out and expected the answer just as straight. She never was one to beat around the bush or walk on egg shells around a subject. She wanted answers and didn't want to be spared. This man knew exactly where she lived. How many times had Toni brought him here? Or did he follow her home? In a few days she would have the closing on her property and would move out there if she needed a place to feel safe again.

"That's what worries me in this situation. If he wasn't looking for something then this was a scare tactic. He is a psychopath." He pointed to the file. "You rejected him. In his mind maybe every woman in his life rejected him. Who knows." Wes knew this information was not comforting and but he felt she had the right to know who she was up against. "I can tell by these photos you grew up in the country?" He decided to changed the subject. She had been through enough tonight.

"Stanford, Indiana. And you're right it was a farm. This picture here is me and my horse Nelly. I really miss her." Jesse comment showing the side of the girl of about seventeen up in the saddle gleaming for the camera. She was still holding on to her youth.

Wes could see it in her face and her movements. What was gone was the innocence. For some reason this city and it's business was known for taking that away from the people.

95

"Where are you from? I mean you don't seem city born and bred." She picked up the frames and laid them down on the table so they wouldn't fall. She really had no desire to clean this all up except to put it all away in boxes.

"Bowser, Tennessee. It's near a small town at the base of the mountains called Bulls Gap. No one has ever heard of it." He noticed the surprised look come across her face. He hit a nerve.

"You're kidding?" Jesse laughed. "I'm in the process of buying some property in Bulls Gap. You knew that didn't you?" She could feel her mood lighten.

"No, really? I didn't think anyone knew where that town was. What property are you buying?" Wes was intrigued now.

"The Williamson's place." She answered.

"You're kidding. I know the place. I thought the house was falling down and unrepairable." He remembered the property well. Every kid in the area did.

"It is. I'm going to renovate the barn. It's the most stable structure there is on the property." Jesse couldn't believe it. That was too ironic.

"Let me guess, Ed Hawsey the loan officer at the bank sold you the property and you probably shock him silly." He chuckled at the look she gave him in total disbelief. "He's been trying to sell that place for years."

"I had the impression he didn't think I was serious." Jesse shared.

"He's got a brother in-law who does construction and remodeling. Earl is a good man. Ed will recommend him and he'll treat you fair." This woman was now becoming a part of his past.

"The town reminds me a lot of the town I grew up in. We have a town north of Stanford called Springdale. That place is a major tourist attraction. Always has been because they kept the buildings just as they were in the 1800's and added a lot of craft shops. It's pretty cool." The coffee was done and before either even realized they had talked well into the early morning. Each telling the other stories and pieces of their past. Wes was inspired by the courage it took the first few years after Jesse arrived in Nashville to pursue. His own move was a lot easier due to the fact he just transferred from a deputy position in Madison. This woman left home at eighteen and moved to an unknown city with all the fears going through her mind.

He never understood the passion a person has when they first arrive in Music City only to lose to the wild side of the business and that's usually when he met them. When they broke the law. He couldn't ever remember ever having that strong of a desire that it completely took over your life.

At some point in the early hours both had nodded off to sleep while talking. The sun was trying hard to peek through the curtains casting a bright ray across Jesse's face. The warmth felt so good she thought as she tried to turn over. She wasn't in her bed. Jesse opened her eyes and saw the detective at the other end of the sofa fast asleep. His leg was placed on top of hers making it difficult to move. She watched him as he slept. He was very handsome she thought to herself. She let her gaze go lower to his neck down to his chest, which was rising from his breathing. Jesse noticed the hairs coming from under the collar of his shirt. His body was lean and muscular. She couldn't suppress the arousal creeping down deep in her stomach. Her foot started tingling from lack of circulation and she tried to move it without stirring him. No success. As soon as Jesse moved his eyes flew open and looking straight at her.

She smiled. "Sorry, my foot is going to sleep."

Wes looked like he was trying to remember where he was. He regained his senses and lifted his leg. "I don't remember falling asleep." He grunted as he sat up.

"That's what I call police protection." Jesse managed to joke. Normally she wasn't a morning person but for some reason this morning she felt good. "It was late." Jesse stretched trying to get the stiffness out of her muscles.

Wes sat watching her. She was even more beautiful in the morning he thought to himself. He wasn't quite ready for her next move when she placed her hand on his arm. He felt so comfortable just being around her that it seemed natural. He wondered if she felt it also. "Thank you." She whispered to him. Wes reacted without considering the act and leaned closer to her and placed a soft kiss on her lips. Jesse was not surprised at her reaction. She felt all resistance fall when he pulled her closer to him. He didn't press any further and released the kiss and placed his forehead against hers.

"I've never met anyone quite like you before." Wes was honest. After last night he felt he knew this woman more than anyone else.

He too had shared with her things he had never told anyone including his ex-wife. Anything he did seemed like the natural thing to do. By offering no resistance Wes knew Jesse had simular feelings.

"Honey, no one has or so I'm told." She gently tugged on the hairs of his beard. A spark came from her past. He laughed producing one from her also.

"I want to see you again." Wes attempted to be serious. Jesse sat up and looked at him. It was as if he could read her mind and emotions.

"I would be disappointed if you didn't." She looked deep into the brown of his eyes. There was sincerity in them. A detective's job might require toughness from him but the eyes never lied. And right now they weren't so tough.

"How about tonight? Do you have any plans or appointments?" He didn't want her staying in the apartment by herself especially at night. Not until they knew where Hank Moleson disappeared to.

"None that I know of." And if she did she would cancel all of them to be with him tonight.

"Is seven all right?" He mentally checked his schedule.

"I will be ready." Jesse got up with him when he went by the door she had offered more coffee but Wes had to get into work. They stood together by the fireplace when he put his arms around her pulling her close against his body. He kissed her one more time. Jesse placed her arms around his neck and let herself lean into him. Last night must have been special for him as well. She knew now that the feelings were planted the first time she had met Wes at the police station. Circumstances had thrown them together. A force she doubted either one could control.

Chapter Seven

The saddle sat on the Sheriff's desk. The scene playing over and over on everyone's mind. Who was behind the gate in charge of saddling the horses? How many people were there and why in the hell would anyone want to do this to Riley Jones? Plain and simple the cinch strap on her saddle had been cut almost to the edge. The right amount of pressure and it snapped. Who in their right mind would do that? Huck stood by the window looking out lost in his thoughts. Dale and the Sheriff tried talking it out. "What did Riley do in the military?" The Sheriff asked.

"I don't know. She never talks much about it." Dale replied. He was tired from going over and over every possible angle.

"Intelligence." Huck offered. He knew a lot more about Riley Jones than anyone but maybe Logan. He had already been over that possibility. "I doubt some Middle Easterner is terrorizing Riley. Her job wasn't that important."

"It's hard to tell from the tourist in this county who is a stranger and who is just visiting." The sheriff took his handkerchief out of his back pocket and wiped at his forehead. The day was just too hot. "Have you heard how she's doin'?"

"Logan is supposed to call. That girl sure took a hell of a beating." Dale remarked. "When I saw that hoof come down on her shoulder I thought for sure…" He sat shaking his head at the memory. Everyone who saw the horse kick Riley thought at that moment she was a gonner. The force of a wild horse's kick in the back of the head would kill anyone. The damage to the saddle was a clear act of attempted murder.

"I need to get some air. Maybe go feed her stock." Dale go up and turned to Huck. "You want to come?"

"Naw, I'll stay til I hear word." He answered.

"Let me know when you hear word from the hospital." Dale headed for the door.

The rest of the time was spent going over whom Huck remembered in the barn or around the area. Someone they might not of seen before. Most of the volunteers were from the Horse and Pony Club and everyone knew each other. Someone had to have seen someone they didn't recognize around those horses.

"Maybe this wasn't directly aimed at Riley." Wilbur got up from his chair and went to the map of the county on the wall. Whoever was responsible was probably long gone by now. His guess would be escaping up in the holler.

"What do you mean?" Huck was interested in where he was heading with this.

"Maybe it was a scare tactic of sorts." He rubbed his head. "I don't know. I guess I'm grasping at straws. People are always interested in the land in this county. I don't know why. It's just full of sandstone and clay in most areas. But deep down I think he is after Riley."

Huck had no answers. All he knew was his friend was laying in the hospital because someone wanted to see her hurt or dead. How bad of an enemy could someone make that would so carefully plan this type of accident?

Machines were placed near the bedside with tubes going in to Riley's right arm. Logan stood near the window. Riley was in and out of consciousness due to the medication given for the pain. She had sustained a concussion caused by the second blow that knocked her into the ground. If the horse had been any closer to Riley the force from the hoof would have been much worse and may even of

100

fractured her skull. The doctors had declared fate was definitely on her side. The bruising on her upper right thigh near the hip was what was causing the worst of the pain. The concussion alone would keep her overnight in the hospital for observation.

Riley was slowly coming out of the shock opening her eyes trying to focus on where she was. The last she remembered was the door closing in the ambulance. Logan saw her stirring and put her hand on Riley's arm.

"Doesn't look like you'll be doin' much of anything for awhile." She grinned. A huge scratch led down from Riley's eyebrow to her cheekbone. It must of happened when the kick knocked her face first into the ground.

"You think so?" Riley tried to move but it hurt too much.

"Yea, I think so." She hoped more than she believed. "I need to be getting home. I wanted to stay til you woke up. You gave us all quite a scare for awhile." Logan was being comforting. She couldn't begin to image losing her friend. "Besides you have another visitor who's been waitin' to see you."

"Thanks. You know for being here." Riley's throat was dry and whispery. She found the button for the bed and raised it until she was in a sitting position. The move of the bed made her wince but she didn't like being flat on her back.

"Yea, well don't let it happen again." Logan stated teasingly. "I'll stop by tomorrow." Riley nodded.

She heard the door close before looking over. Riley watched as Tess materialized at the side of the bed. She hadn't been seeing things. Tess had been there. "I thought that was you." Letting down any resistance Riley reached for Tess' hand. "You were sitting in the stands. I saw you when I got into the saddle. Then you were by the door of the ambulance." Riley had thought she was delirious from the pain when she saw those eyes.

"I didn't think you saw me." Tess couldn't hide the relief in her eyes. She cleared her throat, which was tightening with the threat of tears. "I was afraid you got the wrong impression when you came to Albany and I wanted to set things straight. I stopped in town to get directions and was told I would find you at the fairgrounds at this rodeo. Tess started to rub her thumb across the back of Riley's hand as she told of why she was there. "I had no idea you were a cowboy now."

Riley started to laugh at the reference. "I'm not a very good one obviously."

Tess leaned over and tenderly touched the scratch on Riley's cheek with her fingers. "When I saw you fall from the saddle it felt like I was going to lose you all over again. I felt the pain each time that horse kicked you and I don't care what you think I couldn't stand it..." She broke. The tears fell and she tried to look away when Riley placed a hand on Tess' cheek turning her head back to look into her eyes.

Riley had never seen Tess like this before. They had their ups and downs in their relationship but anger was always behind those moments. This situation was different. They both were different people. "I'm not going anywhere." She stated not knowing what made her say that. But it felt right. Tess managed a smile and squeezed Riley's hand in response. "So what did you come down here to talk to me about?" Riley couldn't resist. She may feel like a truck hit her but she had her sense of humor probably brought on by the pain medicine.

"Ah, I think that is irrelevant now. Don't you think?" Tess sat down on the side of the bed.

"No, I'd really like to hear it." Riley laid her hand on Tess' thigh. The intimate contact did not go unnoticed.

"We can talk about it tomorrow." Tess side stepped the issue. This was not the time nor the place.

"Do you need a place to stay the night? My house isn't too far." Riley offered.

Tess hadn't thought about where she would stay but took Riley up on her offer. After writing down the directions and Riley's insistence her farm wasn't hard to locate she handed the paper to Tess. "I don't think the house is locked but if Huck or Dale fed my animals then they might of locked it knowing I wouldn't be home. The key is in the first pole of the clothesline. The cap comes off. You'll see it."

"Get some rest I'll be fine. You look like you're about ready to fall asleep. Are you in any pain?" Tess asked.

"Not really. But the medicine is making me fade." She slurred.

"I'll see you tomorrow morning. Do you need anything?" She asked.

Riley shook her head and closed her eyes. What she needed Tess wouldn't be able to give her. How would be able to convince her of that. She didn't even hear the door close before sleep claimed her.

The evening was getting dark making it harder to see the road signs as Tess followed the directions. A left turn then a right turn just past the old church. She stopped her car when she came up to the bridge in the drive. Tess looked at it and wondered if the Jag would make it over or would it just collapse with her on it? She slowly drove over the wood planks hearing the creaking until she was on the other side. Just around the bend Tess saw the house standing tall on a slight hill. Every picture of a farmhouse was molded into this one. The barn stood several feet down the hill. A few horses were out in the pasture eating bits of grass and turned their attention towards her. She went up the walk and around the back where the clothesline was. Just in case the door was locked. She had no trouble finding the key and went around to the front. The view from the porch was astonishing. How many artist she'd known who had put these scenes on canvas. Once inside she took a deep breath. The house was beautiful. Hardwood floors, a stone fireplace, the furniture overstuffed and inviting. The kitchen was also the dining area. A solid wood table placed in the middle with benches on both sides. The sink and appliances lined the far wall. A few steps up behind the fireplace wall was a landing with a bathroom just behind the stairs. A door across the hall was probably Riley's bedroom. She thought to herself. Tess opened the door and stepped in. Two steps down a four poster bed of dark mahogany wood stood in the middle. A rocking chair sat near the window by a small table with an oil lamp on it. Another fireplace was against the side wall near the bed. She sat her bag down. This whole house was filled with antiques. Even the stove and refrigerator looked to be made in he late 1950's. It was amazing. She sat down on the bed with the knitted bedspread. It all seemed to belong. So this was the escape for Riley. Tess was beginning to understand a part of Riley she never knew about. She lay back on the pillow and found herself falling quickly into the first restful sleep she had in a long time.

The next morning Tess heard the strangest noise that broke through her dreams. It kept screeching until she sat up in bed. The sun was barely up but she went to the open window and looked down. She located the noise from the rooster sitting on top of the fence pole near the chicken coop. It was true. Roosters do crow at sun up. She went back to bed but found it hard to go back to sleep. She decided to shower and change her clothes. The thought occurred to her that maybe those animals needed to be fed. Abandoning the shower put on her shoes and headed outside towards the barn. She had been around a few horses in her time to know what they ate. The chickens were another story. She had no idea what to feed them but surely the food would be labeled.

Riley was up at the crack of dawn staring at the light starting to come through the window. Her thoughts were on the accident yesterday. Late last night in her sleep she had remembered the sound before she fell. The snap of leather and the only piece of leather that held the saddle on the horses back was the cinch strap. The problem she couldn't figure out was the saddle was in perfect shape with hardly any wear. The strap had to have been cut making her accident deliberate. But for the life of her she couldn't figure out who would want to do that to her. She remembered the screams when she hit the ground and the pain. She knew she had been kicked twice but she hadn't seen either blow coming. Why? Anyone who would go to the lengths to cut a cinch strap knowing she could of been trampled to death had wanted her out of commission. The door to the room opened causing Riley to jump. The night nurse came in to see if the patient was awake.

Riley recognized her. "Hey, Charmaine."

"How you doin' this mornin'?" Charmaine came to the side of the bed and checked the machines behind Riley's head. "You didn't use hardly any medicine last night. That's a good sign. Are you in any pain?"

"Not a whole lot. I have a high tolerance." She answered.

"Good chance of getting out of here then." The nurse leaned over and proceeded in taking her blood pressure writing down in the chart the vital signs. "I think if we can get a doctor in here to look at you he might release you. Your vitals are good. You're not medicating yourself. Good chance."

"Good. Something to look forward to." Riley raised the bed so she could sit up.

"Any idea what happened yesterday?" Charmaine asked.

"You mean do I remember the accident? Then yes. Why it happened? No." She tried to smile.

"Kind of scary. But you're a lot tougher than you give yourself credit. I'm sure Wilbur is on it." Charmaine assured. "You know we've known each other for a lot of years. Hell, everyone grew up with everyone in this place. I can't imagine you having any enemies. I can't figure it out."

"I can't either. When I lived in Albany I had met some odd characters but no one I can think of who hated me. Who ever it was is a coward." Riley tensed up. One good thing was Stanford was so small a town a stranger would be noticed. And after yesterday he or she wouldn't go unnoticed.

"I'm goin' off duty in a few minutes. If you're not here tonight then I'll stop by your place later in the week to see how you're doin'. I'll bring the girls. They'll get a kick out of your horses." Charmaine offered. "I should warn you that Hannah Murphy is on at seven." She chuckled. Hannah was a dear person but she spoke her mind and didn't care much about anyone else's opinion. Riley grimaced and turned on the television to kill the time until a doctor came to see her.

A little after eight the door opened and Tess walked in with a surprised look on her face. Riley was standing at the window and turned when she heard the door. "You're up!" She exclaimed as she put a bag down on the bed. She thought to get Riley some fresh clothes to wear home but she didn't think it would be today.

"I get to go home. As soon as I sign some release papers I'm outta here." Riley noticed the bag. "Are those clothes?"

"Yes. By the way your wardrobe needs some enlightenment. All you have are jeans and T-shirts."

"There's a few shirts and blouses. Just not a lot besides have you ever known me to wear anything else?" Riley asked.

"Oh yea, the flannel." Tess smiled.

"It gets cold in the country." Riley tried to rationalize her clothing choices. She new Tess was only joking. Just like they always used to do banter back and forth about her wardrobe. Always playful. "Could you give me a hand?" Riley turned her back for Tess to untie the strings of the gown. Tess pulled back the material and looked down to Riley's seeing the bruise for the first time. The area looked hideous with the dark skin and the red patches where the blood vessels had broke. Riley could feel her gaze. "Looks worse than it feels."

"What are you doin'?" Riley and Tess both turned at the sound of the authoritative voice at the door. Hannah stood with Riley's chart in her hand looking annoyed.

"Just seeing how bad it looks." For some reason Hannah made Riley feel like she was doing something wrong. Tess just looked at her humorously. Hannah ws not known for her comforting bedside manners.

"How are you feeling otherwise?" She asked looking at Tess then back to Riley.

"I feel fine. Just let me go home and I will feel ever better." Riley sat down on the end of the bed.

"How do expect it to look? You got kicked by an angry horse." Hannah chided. She really didn't mean to come off to people as rough as she did but that was just her. "Here's the papers for you to sign. They're going to send you home."

"Great." Riley took the pen and read over the forms before signing them.

"Are there any instructions for her." Tess asked.

"Any that she would follow?" Hannah chuckled. "Bed rest for the next couple of days. She's not going to feel like doing much anyway.

"If it will get me out of her any quicker then I'll do anything you tell me." Riley handed the papers back.

"Most do honey. I'll go find you a wheel chair and get you on your way." Hannah looked over the forms before leaving.

"There are only five wheelchairs in this place so she'll be gone all day. Let's see if I can get dressed." Riley commented.

Tess opened the bag and pulled out a T-shirt and a pair of jeans. "I couldn't find any shorts or loose fitting pants." Tess remarked.

"I don't have any." Riley sat down on the bed.

"Let me help." Tess got the jeans over and up her legs. "Let me know if it hurts."

Having Tess so close to Riley began to stir old feelings as she watched her ex-lover carefully help her on with her clothes. Tess had only become more beautiful over the years. There was a certain air about her that was different and it totally confused Riley. Maybe it was Riley's vulnerability. For the first time in her life she was going to have to rely on others. Tess pulled the shirt down over her head and Riley slowly got her arms through the sleeves. Other than the dull headache she really didn't have a lot of pain.

Tess was fighting all the urges that overcame her at seeing Riley in this state. She wanted to wrap her arms around her and hold her. Hold Riley forever. Tess kept her eyes adverted so Riley wouldn't see the desire on her face. "Where's your shoes?"

"In that locker with the clothes I wore yesterday." Riley answered softly.

Tess opened the door and saw the clothes folded neatly and a pair of brown cowboy boots on a separate shelf. "You know something? The cowboy look is good for you." She bent down working on getting the boot on her foot.

"Think so?" Riley smiled.

"Yea, now push your foot down." The boot slid on as with the other.

"Let's get out of here." Riley stood up and headed for the door.

"I don't think it works that way. Aren't there rules you have to leave the hospital in a wheel chair? A liability thing?" Tess asked.

"When have you known me to follow the rules?" Riley asked as she opened the door looking both ways down the hall. She didn't see Hannah nor anyone near the door. The nurse's station was down the hall and almost hidden by a wall. Tess relented and followed Riley out going along the hallway. They made it to the elevator when both women heard a shout from behind which stopped them in their tracks.

"Ms. Jones, get your bruised ass back here now." Hannah said sternly standing near door to Riley's room with the wheelchair.

Tess turned to Riley. "You just got busted."

"Me? You're aiding and abetting." She turned around facing the nurse. "We were just coming to see where you were."

"That's what I thought." Hannah helped Riley into the wheelchair and wheeled her out to the front door. "Before you go I was serious about taking it easy. That's the only way you're gonna heal faster."

"I know and I'm going to listen to you Hannah. Honest." Riley replied. Tess pulled up to the curve in her car. She got out to help Riley into the front seat.

"Be careful." Hannah looked at the Jaguar with raised eyebrows. Someone made a good living, she thought to herself.

"Thanks." Riley winced in pain when she bent her leg to get into the seat.

Tess shut the door then turned to the nurse. "I'll make sure she follows your instructions to a T."

Hannah looked at her with a smile in her eyes. If this woman thought she could keep Riley down for a few days then all the power to her. "Make sure she locks her door at night. A lot of those homesteaders out in the country don't think of security. You all be careful." She took the brake off the wheelchair and turned to go on back to work. Tess was taken back by the sincerity these people shared for others. It wasn't something she was used to seeing.

The ride out to the ranch was silent except for an occasional direction. Riley leaned her head back against the headrest letting a stream of air from the open window blow through her hair. Her eyes were half closed thinking this would have been the last place she expected to be sitting beside Tess. "Tell me the reason why you came down here." She stated out of the blue.

Tess just stared at the road before her. She really didn't know the answer. All she knew was she was following her heart and not her head for the first time in her life. "I was hoping you could help me find out. Of course I had no idea this was going to happen." She glanced over to find Riley looking at her intently.

"There is something different about you, Tess. I haven't quite figured it out. Maybe the years have changed you." Riley reasoned.

"I think the years have changed us both." Tess pulled into the drive almost stopping when she got to the bridge. The Sheriff's car was parked in the drive with Wilbur leaning against the hood waiting until the Jaguar was parked.

"You know I should write you a ticket for the shape of that bridge." Wilbur opened the door for Riley as he helped her out.

"Like I can do anything about it now." She retorted. "Wilbur this my friend Tess McGuire. Tess this is our Sheriff." They nodded in acknowledgment before going up the walk into the house. "So tell me what you know." Riley got right down to the point.

"The cinch strap was cut to the edge. The pressure you applied to the stirrup was just enough to cause it to snap." He took off his hat. "We have no clue who'd do that to you. How many enemies you got girl?"

This was the first Tess had heard Riley's fall was not an accident and the authorities felt that someone was deliberate in sabotaging Riley's saddle. The shock showing on her face she glanced first at the sheriff then at Riley.

"I don't know maybe three." She replied sarcastically. "How does anyone know that?"

"Now don't be a smart ass when I'm tryin' to help you. No one saw a damn thing yesterday out of the ordinary and I find that next to impossible to believe." Wilbur stated. "I've had to contact the state boys on this. So they might come a callin' on you asking their own set of questions. Thought I would give you the heads up."

"I'm as baffled by this as you are. I have been racking my brain trying to come up with some kind of reason." Riley sat down on the sofa. Her head was throbbing as the pain medicine Charmaine gave her early this morning was beginning to wear off. She was tired from not sleeping last night as she tried to trace her steps from the time she arrived at the fairgrounds until the accident.

"I'll let you rest. Do you know when Doc Garvey is due back?" Wilbur inquired still standing by the door.

Riley had to think what day this was. Lucas had told her he wasn't able to make the rodeo since he had to make an emergency trip to Lexington. "He said he would stop by late Sunday or early Monday morning."

"I'll check his office in the morning then. If anything pops up call me, okay?" Wilbur stated.

"It was nice meeting you Sheriff." Tess spoke up. He nodded back at her as the screen door shut behind him. She then turned to Riley who was looking up at her. "That settles it. I'm staying. You didn't tell me this was not an accident and that someone had deliberately done this to hurt you."

"You don't know what you're getting involved in." Riley tried to reason with her.

"And you don't either. It'll be a lot safer with two of us here than just one and being injured at that. You're going to need some help at least for a few days. I don't want to hear another word about it." As far as she was concerned the matter was settled.

Riley was too exhausted to argue. "All right. You're a grown woman and you can make your own decisions." She smiled. That was what worried her. "I could really use a hot bath."

"See that's the first thing I can do for you." Tess stood up and went up the steps to the bathroom. A few minutes later she came back out seeing Riley in the kitchen taking a pill. The pain must be really bad for her to succumb to taking medicine. Riley never even took an aspirin for a headache the whole time they were together. "Are you in a lot of pain?" Tess asked out of concern.

"Just my head. I'll feel fine after a good soak." Riley followed Tess into the bathroom. Tess took over and helped Riley get her T-shirt off and pulled at her jeans as Riley placed her hand on Tess' shoulder to steady herself. Riley had no qualms about Tess seeing her naked. Tess managed to get Riley's left leg into the water. The hot liquid immediately took effect.

"This feels so good." Riley closed her eyes. The pain seemed to subside slightly or it could be the painkiller she just took. Tess knelt down by the side of the tub and began soaping up a washcloth. She wouldn't have been human if she didn't notice the beauty of Riley's body. The hard lean cut muscles of her arms and legs. Riley had never been fat but she never had the muscle tone like she did now. Her body was tanned and showed the tan lines of her swimming suit. Tess looked up and noticed Riley was staring at her smiling. Riley knew exactly why she was staring catching Tess off guard and feeling the heat on her cheeks.

"Let's start with your legs." Tess gently lifted Riley's right leg and began rubbing the cloth over the skin from her foot up to the bruise. She stopped when she noticed a long scar down the side of her thigh away from the discoloration. She touched the pink welt. "What happened here?"

"Quarter horses like to ride out the fences. Something spooked the one I was on and ran us into the fence. I got a splinter." Riley answered in matter of factly. She rested her head against the inflateable bath pillow feeling so relaxed but fully aware of the woman washing her body.

Tess just shook her head in response. The scar looked like there was more to the injury than just a splinter. She leaned over reaching for Riley's left arm their faces so close Tess could feel Riley's breath on her cheek. Tess turned her head just as Riley's lips found hers taking her totally by surprise. Tess parted her lips and their tongues touched as if for the first time. Tess braced her arms against the tub once the desire weakened her body. Tess thought of the times she had lain in bed yearning for the feel of those lips against her own one more time. She regretted what she was about to do next because now was not the time. Tess lifted her head to look down into Riley's green eyes. She saw the the first glimmer of hope. Tess took the wash cloth and threw it gently in Riley's face.

"Hey!!!" Riley exclaimed playfully.

"You need to cool off." Tess teased and continued to was the rest of Riley's body gathering all the composer she had to finish. She couldn't' let things get too out of hand. Tess was there to help and get to know the woman she so desperately fell in love with years ago. "Can you scoot up so I can wash your hair?" Tess took the plastic cup that was placed on the edge of the tub and supported Riley's head while she ran water through the long strands of hair. This idea might be harder than she planned.

Once out of the bath Riley decided to lay down in her room. Tess helped her onto the bed and combed out her long hair. "When did you decide to grow your hair so long?"

"Hmmm, I haven't cut my hair since I left the city. I've had it trimmed but I decided change was what I needed. It's the longest I've ever had it." Riley leaned back against Tess. "I'm sorry."

"For what?" Tess put her arms around her.

"Over stepping my boundaries in the bathtub." Riley answered attempting to stifle a yawn.

Tess breathed in the floral scent of Riley's wet hair. "I didn't realize there were any boundaries between us. I want to get to know you. We never took the time before and I think that was our demise. We went into our relationship pretty fast back then."

"Yea, the first night we met we were hitting the sheets." She remembered that night of Fernando's party... "So you think by sharing a few memories will make everything right and bring us back together?" Riley thought about it. How would it work? Stanford wasn't Albany and the people here all think the same. Her whole business was based on the reputation she had earned by years of hard work. Being known as the town lesbian just might hinder her business. Times have changed but not so quickly in Bradford County.

"I think that's something we both are going to have to find out." Tess kissed the back of Riley's head. "Here lay down. I'll check on you later." She got up propping up a couple of pillows. Riley laid back and as soon as she closed her eyes she was asleep.

Tess stayed for a few minutes and watched as she slept. The memory of their kiss still burning in her mind. She knew deep in her heart Riley still loved her. But she was also afraid. Tess could sense it. That was one of the issues they could work through together if given the chance. She decided to go downstairs and call Lynn to fill her in on what happened and she may have to stay down here longer than planned.

Riley slept for most of the afternoon and was up around four-thirty. Tess was in the kitchen fixing something for them to eat later when she appeared on the landing. The sight of Tess busy was intriguing. She had an organized way of doing several tasks at once. She must of made a sound cause she suddenly looked up.

"I was wondering if I was going to have to go wake you up for dinner." She smiled then continued slicing at some vegetables.

"What are we having?" She asked as she sat down at the table.

"Just some steamed veggies over rice. Would you like something else?" Tess asked.

"No. That's fine. I don't feel much like eating a heavy meal." Riley watched as she continued cutting up some vegetables. She noticed the wisps of black hair that fell around Tess' face escaping the pony tail she wore. The way Tess was standing with half her back towards the table Riley let her eyes roam down the curve of her waist then to the tan shapely legs. She remembered how those legs felt when Tess would wrap them around Riley's waist when they made love. The memory caused her to shiver slightly.

Both women heard the footsteps on the back porch before the knock. Tess went to the door to unlock the hatch. "Is Riley here, ma'me?"

Riley snapped back into reality when she recognized the voice. "Lucas, come on in." Riley greeted him as he walked into the kitchen.

"I just got back from Lexington and heard about your accident." Lucas walked in the kitchen. Riley introduced Lucas to Tess and both shook hands. "I had a message from Wilbur and he filled me in on the details." Lucas took the chair Riley offered. He reached out to touch her hand when Riley suddenly leaned on the table ignoring the gesture. "Do you think you're safe out here by yourself?" He asked concerned. Until this person was caught no one was really safe.

"I'm not going to let some creep run me off my property. Besides, Tess is staying with me a few days so I'm not alone." Riley retorted with more sarcasm than she intended. She was just tired of everyone worrying about her. She was fully capable of taking care of herself or she would have failed a long time before now. She didn't want to take it out on Lucas. That wasn't fair. "How was your trip?"

"Okay, I get the hint." Lucas knew when to quit. She did have a point and it wasn't up to him to decide what was best for this woman. " Jethro Howell has some mighty fine horses. I love the chance to work with thoroughbreds. Amazing athletes." Lucas replied.

"Are you talking about the Howell horse ranch outside of Lexington?" Tess interrupted.

"Have you been there?" He wouldn't have pictured a woman like her interested in thoroughbreds. She just seemed to have a class about her. Not to mention her beauty.

"Years ago. Elizabeth Howell, the daughter is a sculptor with a talent beyond the imagination. I showed some of her work at my gallery. Sold quickly too. Have you seen her work?" Tess asked. What she didn't say was at what level Liz took her imagination. Liz could be very persistent but Tess was not interested. Liz took rejection as a challenge.

"Her Daddy has a lot of her pieces in his office." He remembered also how at odds Lizbeth was with her father. Jethro had been a friend of Lucas' since he graduated from veterinary school. He had enough confidence in Lucas' ability he gave him his first job as the ranch's Vet. Lucas wanted more out of a practice and after a couple of years he headed north. He was visiting his cousin when he heard about the county vet in Stanford was trying to find a replacement so he could retire. This job was exactly what Lucas was looking for. He wasted no time in accepting the position.

Riley was beginning to feel uncomfortable. There was her ex-lover and the man whom was interested in her more than just talking about horses. Both in the same room. Things could really get complicated. She couldn't just ignore Lucas nor the feelings he had for her because Tess was whom she really wanted. Riley knew she never lied nor let on to Lucas that she wanted more than friendship from him. The night of the dance when he kissed her gave Lucas the interpretation there could be more.

Lucas didn't stay long since he had things to get caught up on from being away for a couple days. He promised to stop by again and see how she was doing. Dinner was finished and Riley suggested they eat out on the front porch. A slight breeze was blowing cooling down the evening.

"Do you like it?" Tess asked.

"Good as always." She chewed slowly allowing for the taste. One of Tess' talents had been her cooking skills. "It's a nice evening out tonight."

Tess agreed as she looked out at the view. The sun was lowering in the sky just barely above the tree tops. Riley looked over at Tess deciding now was a good time as any to have their talk. "What took you so long to get in touch with me?" She noticed the cloudy expression come over Tess' face.

"Mostly, anger. When I came home from Chicago and saw you had packed your things and moved out. I was so angry with you before the realization that you were actually gone hit me. How could you just up and leave?" She paused as the memories of those times came back to her. "A year or so ago I did meet this woman. She was everything I thought I wanted. She was a graduate from Brown University and had this indescribable love for art." Tess swallowed hard. She had wanted to love Rae as deeply as she did for the woman sitting next to her.

Riley felt the twinge of jealousy hit the pit of her stomach. Tess had been involved with someone else. All these years Riley had no one. But that was her choice and she had no right to expect the same from Tess.

"Rae saw right through everything. She knew I was someplace other than with her. She made me realize I had not come to terms that you were out of my life. It took guts for Rae to not only realize this but for her to help me see it." Just then a brown truck came speeding around the bend and stopped just short of hitting the gate near the barn. Katie got out and waved before going into the barn.

"That's Katie Wilson. She helps me around the ranch." Riley informed.

Tess nodded. "Should I go help her?"

"Naw, she's just going to feed the horses." Riley remarked. She wanted to hear more about this Rae.

"Just the same I'm going to be here for awhile I may as well earn my keep." Tess smiled as she stood up and headed down the steps towards the barn. Riley stared after her. What the hell was going on? Was this a ploy of Tess's to make Riley fall back in love with her? The fact being she had never fallen out of love with Tess. Riley didn't need another woman nor man to realize her feelings. Riley put her plate down on top of Tess' on the table between the two rockers.

A few minutes later she saw Katie rounding the horses up from the pasture. She heard a yell and looked up in the barn loft. There was Tess throwing down a couple of bales of hay. There would be no way in hell that E.G. would believe that Tess McGuire owner and operator of the most exclusive art gallery in the state was doing farm work. She grinned to herself.

Riley looked out over the landscape and up into the trees of the holler. There was something very dark within those trees. She could feel it in the air. Martha Cowen taught her to always listen to what her instincts told her. He was out there. Riley knew it would be the only safe place for anyone to hide especially if the law was after him. The holler had places hidden that no one knew about even those that have lived in the area all their lives. There were caves all through the hills that this man was probably hiding out in. Riley knew it would only be a matter of time before he was found. If she had anything to do with it then it wouldn't be long.

Katie came out of the barn looking up at her on the porch and waved. A few minutes later both her and Tess made the way up to the house. Katie took the porch steps two at a time. "How are you feelin'?"

"Stiff and sore. How about yourself?" Riley asked.

"I didn't get kicked by a horse." Katie was used to Riley's sense of humor by now. She walked behind the rocker and lifted the back of her shirt as Riley leaned forward. "Man, he hit you hard. Look at that bruise." She exclaimed. "You know when he kicked you so close to your head it sent the church ladies into a faint. You should of heard them scream." She made Riley laugh.

"How does it feel to the rodeo barrel racing champion of Bradford County?" Riley asked.

Katie's smile stretched across her face with pride that Riley remembered after all she had been through. "Pretty good. I don't even mind sharing the title."

"You worked hard for the honor Katie. You deserved it." Riley praised before turning her attention to Tess who plopped down in the rocker next to her. "And you sure know your way around a barn."

"I'm definately out of shape." Tess commented.

"You get used to it." Riley remembered the first few months after she started training horses. There were mornings where she could barely get out of bed. After months of constant training the work became easier.

"She's a pretty interesting lady." Katie remarked. " Never met anyone who's been to all those foreign countries like you have."

"You can just as easily go to those places as well as anyone. Riley has been to a few." Tess said. She really understood Katie's excitement to explore new places. She had the desire to go beyond Stanford but wasn't quite so sure about leaving the security of home. Everyone had those same feelings the first time.

"No way. What ones?" This was the first she heard.

Riley leaned back in the rocker. "There was a year in France and Italy. Two years in Iran. The longest two years of my life." Riley rarely talked about why she was in the Middle East other than admitting she had lived there.

"You're not going to elaborate any further are you?" Katie knew more about her boss than Riley even realized until that moment.

"It's not as exciting as you think living in Iran would be. Let's leave it at that." Riley explained. She had to give the girl credit though for trying.

"In that case I'll go home. At least Tess can talk about the places she's been." Katie complained getting up from the porch swing. Tess was was trying her best to keep from laughing at the comical way adult and teenager carried on. Katie turned around on the last step. "Oh, Mom wanted me tell you if you needed anything to let her know. I'll let her know you have a babysitter." The comment set Tess into a fit of laughter.

Riley was doing a better job at hiding the humor even though she was cracking up inside. "What's so funny?" She turned to glance at Tess. "Tell your mother thank you for the offer. And if I was you I'd keep in mind I'm on medication and can't be responsible for my actions." Riley started to get up from the rocker when Katie threw up her hands.

"You need to keep in mind that in your condition I can out run you." Katie took off down the sidewalk running to her truck.

"Oh my gosh, I haven't laughed that hard in a long time." Tess calmed herself down.

"Really? And what was so funny?" Riley teased.

"She's got some sass." Tess saw a different side to the life Riley had built in this community. How good it was to see the world through the eyes of a teenager. Katie waved once she got into her truck and sped off down the drive.

"She does at that. I love to get her riled. I have to admit she was in rare form this evening." Riley looked over at Tess who was looking worn out. "I am quite impressed with you Miss McGuire. I had no idea your talents extended to the barnyard. I've been sitting here watching you sling those bales down from the hayloft then I remembered last week when I saw you in a Claiborne original. Quite a difference." Riley leaned over her knees to stretch out her back while she looked up at Tess.

"There's a lot about me you don't know." Tess took a drink of her ice tea. "I've been on a few horse ranches in my time." She caught herself too late at what she implied. Earlier at the mention of knowing Liz Howell she had seen the look come over Riley's face. "My parents sent my sister and I to summer camp when we were teenagers. Every summer for four years."

Riley got up going over to the railing finding it more comfortable to lean against. Why after all these years were her and Tess sharing

117

parts of their past when they should of been doing it the first few month of their relationship? "I know I can never change who I am and I'm comfortable with that. I also know that this lifestyle is not acceptable in this community. I don't know if I'm not comfortable with knowing that."

"I don't think you give these people much credit. Are you willing to give up your happiness for them? I doubt they would expect that much gallantry from you." Tess could tell her words hit home. She stood up and took the dishes into the house not waiting for any response.

Riley thought about that word gallantry. Was that the impression she was giving? Tess didn't realize she lived in a different world than Riley's. She was so deep in thought she didn't even here the truck coming until it was parked and Huck got out yelling a hello.

"Glad to see you're up and about. Let me see the damage." Huck came up the steps as Riley turned so he could see the back of her head. Huck grimaced at the bruise at the base of her neck knowing full well the pain that went with it.

"It looks worse than it feels. Hey, did you bring my saddle?" Riley asked changing the subject. Talking about her injuries was growing tiresome. They all needed to concentrate on it never happening again.

"Wilbur still has it. It's evidence." He heard a noise from inside and looked through the screen door. "Who you got stayin' with you?"

"A friend of mine from Albany. It's Tess." She noticed his eyebrow raise in surprise. Huck knew a little of the situation.

"Is that wise? I mean you've been through so much and from what you told me about her." He implied.

"That's the weird part. I can't say Tess has changed completely but I can say there is something more serene about her. We never took the time to get to know each other before and I think all that is about to change." Riley could see Tess at the sink washing up their dishes through the screen…

"That's your business Riley. It doesn't change our friendship one bit." Huck did the unexpected and wrapped his strong arms around her taking her totally by surprise. Huck had never been one for showing any emotion. Her accident must of really shook him up. She put her arms around his waist and hugged him back. They will always have a bond between them. She would never do anything to hurt this man who had been there for her more than she could remember.

"How would you like a beer?" Riley asked as they let go of each other.

"Now that's an offer I can't refuse. Besides I think it's best I meet this woman. I want to know what kind of person she is to be getting herself involved with you." He gently rubbed her arm. They walked into the light and Tess turned around as they came into the kitchen.

"Tess I want you to meet the best friend anyone could ever have. Huck Hopkins this is the Tess McGuire." She stated with a smile in her eyes.

"Nice to meet you." Tess offered her hand and Huck took it in his own. It didn't take long for Riley to see that look come across Huck's face. Everyone was infatuated when they met Tess. It was as if no one had ever met anyone with beauty and grace. Wait until Dale met her she commented to herself. He would be tripping all over himself.

"Nice to meet you." Tess turned on her charm. Riley had told her about this cowboy. And he looked the part from the callused hands to his checked shirt down to his Wranglers over his pointed boots. She also felt the warmth in the smile across his face and felt in some way she had been accepted.

"So you're the one who gets to babysit Riley. You got a job ahead of you." His smile was sincere.

"Here's your beer and stop drooling." Riley took two more out of the refrigerator and handed one to Tess who took it willingly. It had been over six hours since she had any medicine and felt a beer wouldn't do her harm.

"Thanks. I wanted to let you know Doc Garvey, Dale and I are going up into the holler in the mornin'. Can we use a few of your horses?" He asked taking a huge gulp from the bottle. The cold hit the back of his throat.

"Sure. Leave the brown mare. The Hartley's are supposed to be out sometime this week to ride." Riley replied. "What are you looking for?"

"Tracks. There are a couple of detectives coming with us from the State Police Post in Greendale. They think whoever did this is still loose out there and the holler would be the only place he could live

119

undetected. That is unless we find something solid." Huck wanted to be straight up with his friend. The more she knew of the situation the more precautions Riley would take.

"Be careful." Tess interjected. "This person doesn't seem to playing with a full deck."

Huck liked this woman. He figured Riley was running from something and he saw exactly who it was now.

"There's no one who knows those woods better than Huck and Dale, unless it's Martha Cowan. She's this old woman who has lived up in the holler for more than what fifty years?" She looked over at Huck.

"At least. She married and they moved up there and raised a litter of children who have all moved into the city or around the county. Martha lives strictly off the land and always has." He tilted his bottle and drained the remaining contents.

"You're kidding? I never would of thought there were people still out there living in total seclusion." Tess commented. These people were interesting beyond those she knew in the city. They definitely cared about themselves, others and their heritage. Those qualities have been long forgotten where Tess was from.

"I need to get going. I just wanted to see how you were doing. We'll be leaving early before sun up and we'll be sure not to wake you. Doc has appointments in the afternoon but wanted to make the trip with us." Huck threw the bottle away in the trash can by the back door.

"That's fine. Thanks for stopping by." Riley reached out for his hand when he walked past her.

"It was a pleasure to meet you Tess. I'm sure we'll be seein' more of you." Huck winked at her as he went out the back door whistling while he walked down the hill to his truck.

Huck decided to head to Miss Mayme's for a sandwich and see if Logan was still around. When he parked next to the curb he saw her car out front. He also noticed Sara Bensons standing behind the counter when he went in. She didn't even try to hide the smile on her face when she saw him. "Hello there stranger." Sara replied.

"How are you doin' tonight." Huck was never comfortable at flirting and wondered if she could tell. "Is Logan around?"

"In the office. Want me to go get her?" She no sooner said it than Logan came through the swinging door from the kitchen.

"Hey Huck. How's it going?" She asked.

"Just came from Riley's place. She's up and moving around like nothin' happened. Except a bit slower than usual." He ordered his sandwich and kept and eye on Sara as she prepared it.

"I was going to give her a day before I went out to see her." That was one of her reasons and the fact she knew who was staying with her. Logan wanted to give them some time alone.

"She'll be out working in the barn by tomorrow. I bet you." He took a sip of his iced tea.

"How's the investigation going?" Logan hadn't seen Wilbur when he had been in at the cafe.

"We're going up in the holler in the morning to see if we can locate any tracks. Everyone seems to think whoever did this is hiding up there." Huck remarked. Riley's accident was big news in Stanford. The whole town was trying to solve the mystery.

"And what do you think?" Logan had also heard the rumors.

"They're probably right. Where else could he go?" Huck had a point. "We just can't figure out how no one saw a thing out there yesterday. You'd think a stranger would be noticed if he was back by the horses." He took a bite out of his turkey sandwich.

Huck's last remark clicked in Logan's memory. When she went over to look at the horses she remembered that man she saw whom she didn't recognized. He was there one minute and gone the next. "Maybe not." She stated. "I had been back by the corral to look at the stock. There was a man at the fence. I asked him a question and when I looked back he was gone."

Huck stopped chewing. "What did he look like?" He swallowed hard.

"Like everyone else around there. He had on a dirty straw cowboy hat and his shirt was just as filthy. Reminded me of those carnival guys you see at the fair." Logan remembered making that comment to herself.

"Now that is something. You never saw him before?" He had to make sure.

"Not unless he worked for Harlan or Ed Bancroft. I just thought it was strange for one second he was there and the next he wasn't. I

121

didn't see him near any of the saddles but that doesn't mean anything." She looked concerned. "You think this was the man?"

"It's something to go on. I don't think we'll know til we find him. I best inform Wilbur." Huck finished his meal.

"Let me know what happens." Logan replied after him. Huck nodded and paid for his supper leaving a generous tip for Sara.

Once outside Huck looked across the street and didn't see the patrol car. He decided to wait until tomorrow and maybe they would have more information on this guy from their trip. There wouldn't be anything done tonight.

Riley was at her desk going over the accounts for the month and paying a few bills. The boarding checks had arrived the first of the month and she needed to go into town to the bank sometime tomorrow. She put the pen down and turned off the lamp. Time to head for bed. Riley went up the steps without much pain from her hip and saw a light coming from the partially closed door to her bedroom. She opened it quietly and saw Tess toweling off from her bath. Her dark hair was combed back from her face. A sudden burning sensation went throughout Riley's body as her stare followed the towel as it went over every inch of Tess' body. She must of sensed Riley's presence and looked up towards the door to see her standing in the doorway. The towel came up to cover herself making Tess feel a bit embarrassed by the look on Riley's face.

Riley couldn't help it. Tess' body was so beautiful. Her breast were jsut the right size to in porportion to her body. Riley shook her head to dispose of those thoughts but she couldn't break the eye contact. Those light blue eyes were enough to get totally lost forever. Riley remembered the first time they made love in her old apartment. That was the night she lost her way. Riley stepped down walking slowly until she was within inches of those eyes. Riley saw Tess' hesitation before her lips touched Tess's. Her arms went around Tess' waist drawing her into a deep kiss. Riley let all her inhibitions down. Nothing in this world felt better to her than the taste of this woman. Tess put her arms carefully around Riley's shoulder's her hands into her hair. Their tongues found the familiar warmth and sensations. Riley ran her hands up the curve of Tess' waist feeling the softness of the side of her breast. Tess's lips found the side of her neck near her ear and she leaving little wet kisses. The arousal becoming intense.

It wasn't time yet, a voice inside Tess' head interrupted the passion. She fought to ignore it but it was no use. Tess had to listen and gently pulled away breathing hard into Riley's shoulder. "I can't resist you when I should." She whispered. "This isn't going to work Riley unless we give each other time. It would be so easy to just pick up where we left off. But you know it can't be done." She hid her face in Riley's shoulder. God how she wanted her.

"I know." Riley tightened her arms around her. She never wanted to let her go again. But Tess was right. They stood there holding on to each other until Riley thought it best Tess got dressed.

"I forgot I didn't have any clothes on." Tess chuckled lightly. She went to the dresser and pulled out one of Riley's T-shirts. "Do you mind?" She took the grin coming across Riley's face as yes.

Riley unzipped her jeans stepping out of them as she sat down on the bed. She checked the alarm clock to make sure it was set for five thirty. Tess had went to the other side of the bed and got in. Riley's body felt weak with desire and she knew this was going to be the hardest part. Sleeping next to Tess and not being able to touch her.

Riley propped herself up on the pillows and tried to relax. Her shoulder was aching as well as her hip. She turned off the lamp and tried to settle on her left side. Riley's eyes adjusted to the darkness and looked at Tess laying on her back. She let her gaze fall on her breast which were taunt against the shirt. She felt the wetness between her legs grow. There was no way on earth either one would be able to keep a distance between them. The desire and passion were too great. She could tell Tess was struggling with it now. Riley reached over finding Tess' hand and held it tight. Tess moved slightly to look at her with the saddest expression touching her deeply. At that moment Riley knew she had never stopped loving Tess.

Chapter Eight

The sun was just barely peeking up over the trees as the horses followed the trail leading to the old homesteader's place. Long ago the cabin had burned to the ground leaving the stone chimney and fireplace. Every hunter and at times a camper would use the sight as their campsite. No one knew who actually owned the property but most took care of it leaving the sight as they found it. On past the site was a not so known trail that led up to the ridge taking the scenic route. Dale reined in his horse next to the fallen structure. Huck, Lucas and the State Police detective Jenkins followed. "It's a lot cooler in the thicket." Huck remarked.

The fireplace was empty except for a few leaves blown around. They dismounted to have a better look around. Dale went to check the weight on the packhorse. Him and Huck always brought supplies to Martha Cowan when they made trips up into the holler. Other than a few times a year she lived primarily off the land and woods around her place. Dale adjusted the straps around the kerosene jugs. "This mount is tiring out. I'm going to head up to the old lady's place and let you guys go on."

"Fine. We'll meet you there." Lucas replied as he took in the ground around them looking for any signs of tracks. Huck was around the other side of the fireplace. Nothing seemed unusual and no evidence of anyone being there but maybe a few animals. Dale rode off going north while the rest would head due east before turning north. Martha Cowan's cabin sat up on the northeast ridge.

"Hey check this out." Lucas shouted to alert the others. He pulled back a few branches from the briar bush to reveal a few pieces of charred wood. Huck let out a long whistle. The wood was still warm.

"How old do you think it is?" Det. Jenkins asked.

"A few hours maybe." Huck looked further back into the bush. Nothing else hidden. This guy was familiar with the outdoors. Might even be a survivalist, which would be harder to pick up on his tracks. He could be anywhere out there and watching them now. "Let's go."

They got back on the horses and headed due east and kept at a slower pace. Huck had the gut feeling they weren't the only ones around.

Dale made it to Martha Cowan's place just before mid morning. She was outside at the fire pit stoking up the fire. He called out to her but he knew she heard him coming long before he got there. "Have I made it for lunch?" He asked.

"Of course. Why do think I'm out here cookin'? You younguns have got to be more sensitive. You'll live longer knowin' that." She straightened up when she saw the horse packed with supplies. "Where's Huck?"

"He'll be a long shortly. I wanted to get these supplies up here before the horse tuckered out on me. Borrowed some of Riley's horses and they're not use to a long trip up hill." Dale started to unpack the horse.

"Just put the kerosene on the porch. I can get it down to the root cellar. Andy Tucker was up here yesterday fishin' in Eagle's Lake and brought me a mess of trout. Hope you're hungry for it." Martha stated.

"Sure am. It's been awhile since I had any fresh fish. Been too busy." Dale put the kerosene kegs on the porch as instructed.

"Cause you all are so damn used to that fast food stuff. That'll kill you quicker than a bullet. I had never tasted one of those damn things and I'm eighty-six year old." She professed.

125

"You don't look a day over sixty." Dale didn't think it sounded the way he intended but it brought a toothless smile from the old woman.

"Bless yo' ever lovin' heart. How's Riley?" She asked as she turned over the fish in the skillet.

"That's part of the reason we came up here." He glanced over at the trees where he expected Huck and the Doc and detective to come through. "Last Saturday at the rodeo Riley took a bad fall. She got a concusion and got some bad bruising on her hip." Dale wasn't surprised that the old woman reacted as though she already knew the whole story. "The thing is someone cut the cinch strap on her saddle. We think maybe the person responsible has headed up this way."

Martha sat on the tree stump and stared into the fire. "I understand now why the trees have been howling. There is evil amongst them." She glanced over at Dale. He understood the meaning. The woods and all that lies in it were her family. She knew them better than anyone. "How is Jesse?" She asked suddenly.

Dale was taken back. "I haven't heard from Jess in a long time." He answered.

"I think you need to find out. Riley needs to know so she can heal." Martha turned her head just before they heard the boys coming in from the ridge. Dale didn't have a chance to ask what she meant by her comment. He took everything this woman said or did to heart. She was the Wise Woman to those who had the privilege of knowing her. She smiled over at Dale and added more fish to the skillet.

"We could smell that fish a mile down the bluff." Huck's stomach growled. "Martha Cowen do you remember Doc Garvey. The county Veterinarian?"

"All of you sit down. Yes, I remember Lucas. Who else you got?" She referred to the detective standing near his horse in wonder. He had no idea people still lived up in these woods.

"I'm Detective Jenkins from the Indiana State Police. We're working on an attempted murder case and think maybe the suspect might be in the area." He replied taking a seat next to the others near the fire. "We didn't pick up any tracks. Have you noticed anything amiss going on around here?"

Martha shrugged her shoulders as she turned the fish. "If yo' askin' if I have seen anyone around the answer is no. But I have noticed a lot."

Huck looked over at Dale who nodded slightly towards him. He would explain later. They stayed for awhile then headed back down the holler. Huck left his rifle with the reluctant woman who chose her own twelve-gage shotgun. He felt better knowing she had something new and quicker if need be.

The wind blew within the tree tops casting shadows through the night. She kept running trying to keep up with her friend. The railroad tressle was just up ahead. They could make it. But without warning the tip of her boot hit a rock sending her face down into the hard ground. The whistle blew louder than her shouts before the blinding bright light coming down upon her from the tracks. She looked up to see Jesse standing right in the middle mesmerized by the light. The train was coming fast. She had to get to her friend. Her legs wouldn't move. The whistle was getting louder and louder as it grew near. She squeezed her eyes shut and tried to scream. The train whizzed by creating a gust of wind that lifted her up throwing her hard against the ground.

Riley's eyes shot open as her body jerked sending a wave of pain down her leg. Had she hit the tree? She tried to clear her mind. It was a dream. Tess turned over and leaned above Riley pushing the wet strands of hair from her face.

"A bad dream?" Tess asked softly.

Riley nodded and lowered herself back down on the pillows. It had been a long time since she had a nightmare. She closed her eyes trying to remember everything that happened. The night was so familiar which was why it was so haunting. "May as well get up." She turned towards Tess who was resting on her elbow. "How did you sleep?"

"Better than I have in a long time. Must be the fresh air." She grinned sleepily. "What was your dream about?"

"Like everything else goin' on around here I can't make sense of it. I bet that's why I'm dreamin' crazy." She got out of bed and tried to stretch. The pain was dull but throbbing.

Tess laid back on the bed and thought about last night. Was this what she really wanted? She glanced over at Riley who had successfully put on her jeans. "Do you need some help?" She asked.

"Nope. The only way it's gonna get better is to keep moving. I noticed Huck and Lucas's trucks outside along with a State Trooper car. I didn't even hear 'em pull up." She sat down to pull her boots on. This was the most difficult part of dressing and undressing was dealing with her boots.

"Are you upset about last night?" Tess crawled over to lay next to where Riley sat.

"No." Riley thought about her next words. "When I left Albany I also left that lifestyle. There has been no one since you. I fought myself day and night trying to get your memory out of my mind. My life had taken on new direction and I threw myself into this ranch. But it didn't help at night when I would lay here in this bed thinking and wishing you were lying here next to me. I could almost reach out and touch you. I knew deep down what I did was right but I also know how cowardly it was to just leave while you were away. It was a lot easier. But it haunted me for the longest time. When I came to see you I knew then it was a mistake." Riley took a deep breath. "The feelings came flooding back and it scared me. I didn't want to spend the next three years going through that loss again. But I have no control where you're involved Tess. I just don't. It's been so long since I've been intimate with anyone. I honestly think you saved me from making a grave mistake." Riley touched her cheek lovingly.

"How's that?" Tess reached up and took hold of her hand.

"Saturday before my visit Lucas Garvey had taken me to the festival dance at the Inn. When he brought me home he kissed me." Riley waited for a response, which she didn't get. "It felt so good to have someone hold me and touch me in that way that I did lose sight for a moment. He stirred feelings within myself I had thought were buried. All of that in just one kiss. I knew it was wrong and I could never love a man like I have loved women. If you didn't come back into my life when you did I really don't know what would of happened. I don't feel anything but friendship with Lucas but I know he has strong feelings toward me. I have to take this careful and not hurt him."

"It doesn't sound like any damage has been done. I mean it was just a kiss right?" She would have never of guessed.

"No just that one kiss. I'm going to have to tell him the truth. Huck knows that I'm a lesbian. He has since I moved down here. He's been my friend since high school. Dale too. That was why he wanted to meet you the other night. I guess he had to approve of you or something." She laughed.

"Did I pass?" Tess perked up.

"Yea, you passed girlfriend." Riley stood up and gave her a gentle noogie.

Chapter Nine

The squad room was hot and unbearable. Wes pushed himself back from his desk. The radio was sitting on the window ledge near the desk. Something Reed had brought in to listen to at work. The case of the poisoned heroin was closing and Wes felt the decision was harsh and too soon. The lab results confirmed the can they found in the warehouse did in fact contain strychnine or rat poisoning. Those bodies that now lay in graves were just a result of bad luck. Being in the wrong place at the wrong time. The fact is the operation probably moved on down the river to a new location. These guys were small time. It's the big time boys who are too smooth to get caught. No one gave a crap about the little guy that takes the fall every time. It was useless to try taking on the whole drug cartel. Right now his main concern was locating Hank Moleson who hasn't turned up anywhere nor has anyone seen him around. His truck had been impounded but that wouldn't have stopped him. Moleson was the type that would of just stole another vehicle to get himself out of town. But where? He'd turn up just as trouble was reported. Evidentially they all get caught. It would be some other police department's worry now. But why would he want Jesse so bad? Enough to break into her apartment and destroy everything. He had it out for her and in his psychotic mind he would stop at nothing. At least if Moleson was out of town she would be safer. But until when? With her career taking off, Jesse will be out of town more and in different cities. There would be no way of protecting her. There was always security at these concerts and backstage. Still he would feel better knowing Moleson's whereabouts. Wes turned his head towards the radio when he recognized the voice. A ballad of hard times and heartache. This was the first time he had heard Jesse sing. He wondered if she experienced those words she sang. What kind of life did this woman have? Wes remembered holding her in his arms the other night when he took her out for dinner. She felt so comfortable in his arms. When he kissed her she tasted sweet. This was the first woman who has ever touched him in the ways that Jesse Monroe has. The confines of the office were getting to him. He suddenly needed fresh air.

"Where you goin'?" Reed asked looking up from the paperwork as Wes walked by.

"Out for the day. Call my cell if an emergency comes up." He stopped at the door and looked back to make his point. "Only if an emergency."

Once outside the sun felt good even though the humidity was high. Wes wandered over to the park benches down the street. Tourist season was at its peak. All different kinds of people from everywhere in the world came to this city in the summer months. They just didn't see the dark side that Nashville had. He walked over to the 16th Street Diner. The place was near empty except for a few people at the counter. He took a booth near the window.

"Kind of early in the day for you to be in. What's up?" Thelma sat a glass of water down.

"Too damn hot to be cooped up in an office all day. I'll take a piece of apple pie and a coke." Wes ordered without looking at the menu he had long ago memorized. He had eaten more meals at the diner than he did at his own apartment.

"Be right back." She wrote out a ticket and placed it on the table. Wes was staring out the window and didn't notice the woman walking towards his booth.

"I thought you guys liked the donut shops." He looked up at the sound of her voice. "Or are you tailing me?"

131

"It would seem that way." He couldn't help the grin spreading across his face and motioned for her to take a seat. "Let me guess you found the best kept secret of Nashville too."

"Oh good Lord, don't tell me you know this guy, Jesse." Thelma sat his pie and glass of coke down in front of him. Jesse just smiled as she thought she spotted some color in his cheeks beneath the beard.

"It looks that way." Jesse teased.

"Shit." Thelma replied and walked off with her order.

"She's quite a character." Jesse sipped her coffee. This is my favorite place in Nashville. I love diners. As a matter of fact I was at the diner in Bulls Gap when I found my place."

"Sounds like they're good luck for you." Wes suddenly didn't feel so hungry any more.

"You might be right." She looked him square in the eye holding his gaze.

"Ah, I've been hearing you on the radio quite a bit." He tried changing the subject. Wes was amazed at how he could be thinking about this woman all day and then to have her show up unexpectedly. Some force was behind this and trying to put them together. And he was not about to fight it.

"Yea, things are moving right along." Jesse commented. "Tomorrow morning we're meeting with Hop Harris."

"You're kidding?" Wes had heard of the man though he never met him personally.

"He manages Nadine Nash's career, which as you know is how all this started." Jesse fiddled with her spoon as a distraction.

"You don't seem as excited as one would think." Wes did notice whenever the conversation turned to her music she tended to tense up a bit. "Are you afraid it's too good to be true?"

"Partly. I just don't know if I'm cut out for all of the attention. I love the music. When I'm upon the stage I feel so totally free. It's hard to explain. But with it comes the understanding of the business aspect. It just doesn't seem real yet. Does that make any sense?" Jesse asked a bit embarrassed to be telling him her thoughts and feelings. But she knew he cared. "So enough about me. Any word on Hank Moleson?"

"No, I think he's left town until the heats off. Which is good news for you." Wes took a drink of his soda.

Jesse checked the clock above the door and saw it was time to be getting on the road. She had an appointment at the bank in Bulls Gap. A sudden thought came over her. "So are you off duty today?"

"Sort of." Was knew what she was going to ask.

"How would you like to drive out to Bulls Gap with me? I have the closing on the place today. Actually I need to be leaving now." She started to reach for her check when Wes quickly took it from her.

"I would love to." He put the money and the tip down for Thelma and they headed out the door.

"Let's take my jeep since it's a pretty day. I have the top off." Jesse walked over to the curb.

It was a good thing she offered since he had walked from the police station.

Ed Hawsey sat across from Jesse explaining the forms that needed her signature. The financing had gone through and she was set to start remodeling. Deciding to stay local she gave Ed's brother in-law the job. Hopefully with luck and his skill Jesse could move in soon.

"Everything seems to be in order." Ed glanced over each page she signed. Then he stood up offered his hand and welcomed her to Bulls Gap. "I think Norman is already out at your place. He's got quite the job ahead of him."

"I got complete confidence he can do the job." Jesse stated. It was a good feeling owning your own home. Now to get it livable.

"Norm's good. The best around these parts." Ed replied. "Anything else we can help you with just let me know." He walked her to the door of the office.

Wes rose from his chair in the waiting area when he saw the door open. "Nice seeing you again Wes." Ed offered his hand.

"You too." Wes took it. "Let's go check this place out." He looked at Jesse.

Jesse clocked the distance at three and a quarter miles from town to the driveway. The area was secluded by the trees and weed growth. She would need a bushhog to cut a lot of it down before she could get a mower to it. No one would ever known there was a house back in the thicket if it wasn't for the drive. Wes was quickly falling in love again with the peacefulness the country brought. He had been cooped up in the city too long. This was exactly what he needed.

"There it is." Jesse drove up to the barn next to the tan Suburban. That must be Norman's truck.

Norm spotted the Jeep when he came around the corner from looking at the foundation which seemed the only stable part of the structure.

"Are you Miss Monroe?' He asked.

"Yes. Are you Norman Jones?" Jesse shot back friendly.

"Afraid so." Norm answered.

"This is my friend Wesley Carson." Both men nodded. Norman wore a pair of faded blue jeans and a gray pocket T-shirt with top of a pack of Camels sticking out. His company logo was printed on the cap, Jones' Remodeling and Construction Inc. The sign on both sides of his truck said the same but offered a toll free number.

"Well, I've been lookin' around. I found some minor crackin' in the foundation but considerin' the age that ain't bad. How is it you want the inside?" He went over to his truck to get a note pad and to write down some measurements for a blue print plan on paper to work from.

"My ideas may not be totally possible so tell me if they're not." Jesse noticed the nod. "I want the two trees just behind where the house stood cut down and used in the remodeling. I would like a huge picture window where the barn door is now." She walked over to the door. "Have you ever seen the movie with Jane Wyman and Rock Hudson, 'All that Heaven Allows'?" She asked.

"Naw, unless it's sports I don't watch it. Ask my wife. She watches all the old movies." Norm chuckled.

"You're going to have to see it to know my ideas. I want a stone fireplace and a bedroom downstairs and I want to salvage the loft. The rest like the bathrooms and kitchen and everything else that makes a house. What do you think?" Jesse stood back trying to vision the barn once it was finished.

"If I have to watch that movie then I'll let you know then. But there's the heating and air unit, the plumbing and electricity. First I want to get it all cleaned up and see exactly what we have to work with." He made a few notes on paper. "I'll have a crew out here tomorrow."

"Do I need to be here?" She remembered her appointment with Hop Harris in the morning and the outcome of that meeting will determine how much of an expense she can afford for the house.

"Naw. I'll get the blueprints made and go over them with you. Then we cans start puttin' up the walls." He grinned at her.

Jesse liked him. He was so laid back but yet also very knowledgeable. Ed was right. The whole town seemed just as nice. It reminded her of Stanford. Here she spent her whole adult life trying to get out of the small town environment to only go back. She was more than ready this time. Like the saying went, you can take the girl out of the small town but you can't take the small town out of the girl. Wes walked up to them after he checked out the old farmhouse.

"Looks to me like you have your work cut out for you Norman." He replied.

"Yea, but it's not impossible. Might be pricey but we'll try to keep the expenses down. I can see what you all see in it. Hell, every kid within ten miles of this place has explored every inch of the land." Norman remarked.

"I know I was one of them." Wes said.

"I thought you looked kind of familiar. You from Bulls Gap?" Norman tried to place the name.

"No. Corbin. Just up the road." He answered.

"Yea, you played football. Wes Carson. We used to go up and watch you all play back in '82." He face lit up at the memory.

"You're pretty sharp." Wes commented.

"What're you doin' now?" Norm wondered.

"I'm a detective with the police department in Nashville." He down played his job quite a bit.

"You don't say. Do you remember Dottie Wilson? She was a cheerleader for your school. Probably a few years ahead of you." He asked.

"Blond gal?" Wes faintly remembered a girl by that name.

"I married her. Hey, I played for Bulls Gap but I got about five years on ya. Yea, me and Dottie got married right after she graduated and been together ever since. Got three girls just like her." Norm was proud of his family.

"Well I'll be." Wes was genuinally surprised.

135

Jesse stood back and the admiration she had at that moment was beyond words. Wes wasn't the tough city cop but a country boy who knew his roots and didn't forget the people there. Jesse had come all the way to Nashville to meet someone with the same values as she was taught.

"You didn't get any football players?." Wes chuckled.

"You haven't seen my youngest. For a girl she can hold her own." He replied. "Well, tomorrow we'll get started. I don't know who is more excited about this project. I never had the opportunity to turn a barn into house before. Don't worry I know what I'm doin'."

"I have an appointment in the morning. I'll give you my number and you can give me a call when you come up with the expenses." Jesse took his pen and wrote it down on his note pad.

"If you don't mind me askin' what do you do for a livin'? If it's personal just ignore the question." Norm asked out of the blue.

"I'm a musician. Ever hear of Jesse Monroe and the Wayward Weeds?" She smiled when recognition hit his face.

"That's you I hear on the radio? I'll be damned. You're not kidding are you?" He lifted his hat and scratched his head. "Wait til I tell the Mrs."

"I'm not that big yet." Jesse stated a bit self-concisously.

"We ain't never had a celebrity in Bulls Gap before. How about that." Jesse couldn't help but grin. She really liked this man.

"I wouldn't go as far as saying I was a celebrity." She remarked.

"Modest aren't you. Okay then, I'll give you a call in a few days. Once everything is cleaned up we'll know what we have to deal with. Here's my card. If you have any questions or ideas give a holler." He turned to Wes. "It was nice seein' ya again buddy."

Wesley nodded. Norman went back to his truck and left. Jesse turned to look at Wes. "You know just about everyone now don't you?"

"Just about. You're going to have a nice place here when ol' Norm gets through. What made you decide to buy this?" Wes was curious. If her career was taking off she definitely could afford a house that was already built and ready to move in.

"I really don't know. It grabbed me. Do you have any idea who the Williamson's were?" She asked wanting to get a feel of what this place was about.

"No. I'm sure county record's or even the library could give you that information. It has just always been here." He looked over at what still remained of the house.

The homestead had been turned over to the county for taxes over thirty years ago. No known relative was ever located. The place had a mystery to it and maybe someday Jesse would spend the time to figure it out. A few things were strewn about like an old screen door, pieces of glass from the windows and a lot of dead branches. At one time this was someone's home. Maybe even children were raised here. Why would anyone let it get in this condition of abandonment? No use trying to analyze people she never even met. Now it was all hers.

"How about having dinner with me tonight?" Wes interrupted her thoughts.

Jesse walked over towards him and put her hand on his arm. "I would love to."

Wes looked down into her blue eyes and saw a sparkle. This woman was so unbelievable beautiful and so down to earth.

They drove back into Nashville and stopped at a restaurant to eat dinner. The whole time sharing bits and pieces of their lives and dreams they had while sharing a bottle of wine. Several times Jesse caught Wes looking at her and she smiled back. The feelings were there and they both knew it. After dinner Wes asked her to take a walk down the street. He held Jesse's hand and never wanted to let go of it. The evening seemed to have gone by so quickly and they ended up back at Jesse's apartment. The gentleman he had been all evening, Wes walked her up to the door. She unlocked it and opened it slowly turning to face him. Half expecting and fully wanting he took her into his arms and kissed her softly. Jesse showed no resistance when Wes took a step into the apartment still holding her. She leaned back in his arms breaking the kiss long enough to look up into his brown eyes. What she saw was sensitivity mixed with desire. This was one of those times where instinct took over. Jesse ran her hands through his wavy hair drawing his mouth back to hers. Wes rubbed his hands down her back feeling aroused touching the curve of her waist to her hips.

"Normally I don't act this way on a date." Jesse breathed against his ear when his lips touched her neck. Their want and desire exceeded beyond any sanity. Jesse led him to her bedroom before their clothes started falling to the floor. Wes laid her back against the pillows and took into memory every single inch of Jesse's body. From her long muscled legs up to her flat stomach and the rise of her breast. He ran his fingers across her lips ever so lightly. His touch passed over the boundaries she had long ago placed and now she was accepting him. Jesse was falling in love. Wes took her to the heights of desire and caught her in his arms when she fell. Jesse's head hit the pillow as she grasp for air after waves of orgasms spread through her body. Wes, released his passion and rolled off of her to lay by her side. Both were still breathing hard. It was as though they had been waiting their whole lives for this one moment and for each other. She turned over to face him and ran her hand across the mass of curly hairs on his chest.

"I don't know what to say." Wes drew her close.

Jesse caught the gleam in his eye as he looked at her. He as falling just as hard for her as she was for him. She smiled back at him and replied. "You don't say anything. You just hold me and kiss me 'til we fall asleep in each others arms."

Wes did as he was told. It wasn't long before they were kissing and touching, which brought them together once again.

Early the next morning Jesse was up at the crack of dawn. She wanted to be at Hop's office early. She got out of bed slowly so she wouldn't wake up Wesl who was sleeping soundly. Once the coffee was brewing she took her shower and thought about last night. How long has it been since she felt this way about a man. Or even allowed herself too. The few men in her life had come and gone. Wes was different. Maybe it was because she was different. She didn't quite know. Going back into the bedroom to get dressed Jesse looked at him. He was lying on his back. She let her eyes roam over his face and down his chest to the trail of dark hair disappearing beneath the sheet. Bending over she placed a kiss gently on his lips before she left reluctantly. What she would give to stay in the comfort of his arms all day. The day would come she thought as she hurriedly grabbed her keys off the counter and headed out the door.

Traffic wasn't too bad on the main thoroughfare as she made her way over to Music Row. Parking was more difficult. The tourists were up early and took a lot of the spaces along the street. Jesse found a space on the back row of the office building parking lot. Jackson and Joey were standing nervously in the lobby waiting for her and Bobby Jim who came in behind her out of breath from jogging across the street.

"Hey, guys." Jesse greeted.

"I've been givin' this some thought last night. We can't make any decisions today or he is goin' to think we're anxious and give us a screwed deal." Joey replied.

"Let's just hear his offer. This is one time beggars can't be choosy." Bobby Jim pushed the elevator button going up. Once on the fourth floor the doors opened to the plush carpet, mahogany woodwork and desks. The office reeked of money and power. The receptionist was expecting them and directed them towards the office where Hop's secretary showed them to his door. The room was huge. Records of gold and platinum lined the walls with the photos of each artist he represented. The decor was American Western with a few modern conveniences such as the computer and the stereo system along one wall. The window showed the view of Nashville's skyline and all along Music Row below. Mr. Harris stood when the group walked in and shook everyone's hand offering coffee. They accepted Then he sat down behind his huge desk and got down to business.

"I'm not one to sit and jaw about all that I can do for you. Take you all so far up the ladder of success you'll get a nosebleed. You all know that already. Here is my offer." Hop leaned back in his chair and ran over the terms of what he could offer professionally. And in return he would have their full cooperation. There was some legality, which could be worked out between the lawyers.

"What are the percentages and will that be per person in the band or as a whole?" Jesse asked. Nadine had went over everything they should ask for and expect from this man.

"Nadine got to you first." Hop recognized a rehearsal when he saw one. Nadine was famous for her coaching abilities in backing a new group. He had seen her in action before and fully expected a performance today. He was prepared. "She looks out for her interests. That's what I love the most about that woman. You are a band. Miss Monroe just happens to be the lead singer. It wouldn't hurt for you all to hire an attorney to look over these contracts. I

139

don't screw people. If I did I wouldn't be where I'm at today. You give me good honest work and I will do all I can to see you get rewarded for it." Hop took on a serious tone. "I'm trying to bring a new sound to the business and I see it in you guys and hear it in your music. It's been tried before to bring bluegrass back on the charts. Skaggs and Krause has tried. Neither with much luck in my opinion. This town is ready for a change and you all are it." He lit a cigar.

Jackson looked over at Jesse who sat surprisingly calm. Her reaction depended on the trust Hop was willing to give. "And the percentages?" She asked never blinking an eye.

Hop Harris looked at Jesse wondering if she heard a word he said or was she that tough a businesswoman. He wasn't willing to take the chance. He placed his elbows on the desk slowly exhaling smoke. "Standard. I'm having the contracts drawn up as we speak. Lawyers can go over the details. Hell, they're going to anyway. We'll go from there. For right now I'm working on a deal with RCA Records for you. I want you in a studio recording as soon as possible. Your song 'Whispering Way' is slowly climbing the charts but still it's climbing. You need to be represented and quickly. The royalties are coming in and we've set up an account in the band's name. There's so much to get set up that I can guarantee within a month your heads will be spinnin'."

Jesse and the boys looked at each other in disbelief. Hop e was serious. This man had more faith in their music than they probably had in themselves. "Let's do it." Jesse replied. Hop stood up to end the meeting.

"Get the attorney and call me." He offered his hand to each one and they left his office. So this was it. All the years of struggling and going through disappointments. In a few short minutes they had one of the biggest talent agencies representing them. A few months ago they were studio musicians and now according to Hop Harris they were about to be the latest sensation in country music. They made it the elevator before letting out a sigh almost at the same time.

"Oh my God. I don't believe this!" Jackson exclaimed. "We are really goin' all the way!"

"Let's go find a good entertainment attorney and quickly." Jesse's mind was working fast. "We can't lose this. We've come this far and from what that man said he can take us further. Are we ready for this?" Everyone looked at each other and there was no doubt in their minds and in unison they all exclaimed. "Yea! Let's do it."

By that evening Jesse Monroe and the Wayward Weeds had an attorney and an accountant. The attorney was led to them by fate. Jesse had heard about a law firm that specialized in entertainment law. Hollingsworth and Roberts. Their offices reminded her of a depression era private investigator's office. Any moment she had expected to see Dick Tracey come walking around the corner. It was the feeling she got when they walked in and announced their intent. Dean Roberts had the reputation of one of the best negotiators in the business. He was young but his reputation was starting to thrive. They paid the retainer fee and gave him Hop's number and that he was expecting his call sometime today. Dean Roberts was very familiar with the Hop Harris Agency and knew this could advance his career even further. Everyone wanted a piece of the pie and this band was going to put a lot of sugar in his. It was on his advice they get an accountant to handle their income and expenses. Dean gave them a reputable firm not far from his office.

Together lay out their plans and along with the determination to go as far as they could with their music. The songs were to stay in the band's control and retain the rights to their work. It would be up to the lawyers to battle it out. But fame wasn't worth much to them without that control. Nadine had a serious talk with her about the rights a songwriter has over their material. Jesse followed her advice to the last spoken word. If the record label wants you bad enough knowing you're going to make their company alot of money then they will try compromise before giving into the terms. All Jesse and the boys wanted was to keep control over their songs. Plain and simple.

It was late in the evening when Jesse arrived home. Wes wouldn't be waiting for her in bed as she left him this morning and didn't even realize she left his truck was at the police station when they took her Jeep to Bulls Gap. She checked her messages as she went into the kitchen to fix something to eat. Wes had left two messages. Last night was so special even to him. That was a rare find in a man. Or at least the one's she was used to.

The streets were quiet for this time of night. Wesl sat parked near the Ryman Auditorium. There was a peace about this old building that once was used as a church. Maybe that had something to do with it. The dreams of many people started and ended right through those doors. Now it was just used for tourism and anniversary shows. He remembered as a boy his parents took both himself and his sister to a Grand Ol' Opry show. Wes had sat mesmerized by the talent on stage as well as far as he could see backstage from his seat. When they moved the show out by the theme park the old building never seemed to lose its identity. The only thing a person could count on was change. Always. He sat and watched the people walk by and every one of them would stop and look at the big doors up the steps. Then they would continue on down the street.

It was here the last he saw of Hank Moleson and that had been quite some time. It was as though he just disappeared. He could just be hiding out somewhere or left town completely. Wes couldn't shake the feeling they haven't heard the last of the Mole. That wasn't his style to just leave no matter how hot it was to stay. Moleson sought out revenge and for some reason he was bent on making Jesse suffer. Suddenly his cell phone rang bringing him back to reality. "Detective Carson." He answered. His heart skipped a beat when he recognized the voice on the other end.

Chapter Ten

The sun sat high in the sky over the hills of Bradford County. The air was so thick with humidity a person could almost cut it with a knife. The horses were grazing in the pasture near the pond. Riley walked out to see if the water was drinkable. Other than a limp, and a sore head she felt better than she did all week. The fresh air and sun had more to do with the healing process than just the medication, which made her tired. Huck and Dale filled her in on their visit with the old woman up in the hills. They were more than convinced the perpetrator was hiding out near the ridge. The only decent view that over looked the valley where most farms can be seen was up on the ridge. Especially Riley's ranch which bordered the base of the holler. The back pasture led right up the center.

That afternoon when the expedition came in Lucas had appeared to be distant towards Riley when she offered to rub down the horses after their trip. He asked how she felt but not in his usual tone. She wondered if he had a notion about Tess but quickly thought different. What would give him that inclination? Once Riley reached the edge of the water near the cattails she looked up towards the hill. The wind was blowing the very top of the trees not making its way lower to cool the sweat running down her back. The water looked fine but she'd fill the trough anyway. She knew day was coming when she would have to answer a few questions and wondered if she would have the answers. Lucas was not an ignorant man and she owed him that much. Other than the kiss she had never led him to think a relationship was a consideration. Now she was realizing she had done the same in her relationship with Tess. Having Tess staying with her these last few days has taught her how she treated people who tried getting close to her. Riley was afraid of giving all of herself to just one person. There always has been a wall of protection built around her heart. When times became difficult she booked and she could admit it now.

Tess and Riley had spent the evenings asking questions about pieces of their lives. They shared their dreams, their childhood and what each wanted from life. Riley was beginning to trust again.

"How long are going to stand there looking at those trees?" Riley heard her voice and turned around as Tess came towards her. "Should we fill the trough?" Tess asked suddenly noticing the grin on Riley's face. She wondered what caused it.

"I got an idea. The crick is just down that hill. How would you like to go swimmin'?" Riley had that mischievous expression on her face.

"I don't know I have never swam in a crick before. Is it anything like a creek?" Tess teased at the way Riley pronounced the word. This was Southern Indiana and everyone south of Albany seemed to butcher the English language. But it was cute coming from Riley.

"Honey, if you're goin' to hang with us country folk you really have to work on your pronunciation or no one is goin' know what the hell you're talkin' about." Riley put the dialect on thick for her benefit. She led the way down to the swimming hole.

Tess saw the clearing and the creek that ran deep with the clearest green-blue water she had ever seen. She was a bit hesitant of the fish or any other creature that might be waiting to take a nibble out of her. A long rope hung from the branch of the tree that stood at the edge of the water. Riley was quickly taking off her clothes not conspicuous at all and Tess decided to do did the same. Riley half ran and limped taking hold of the rope and swinging high out into the water. She let go at the highest point splashing as she hit the water feet first.

"Use the rope." Riley shouted back when she came up for air. Tess took a running start grabbed the rope and swung far out releasing her hold and landing within inches from Riley splashing water at her when she hit the surface. The water felt cool over her hot skin and goose bumps rose on her arms but it felt good. Riley swam over and playfully splashed her in the face to which Tess returned vigorously.

"All right! I give!" Riley shouted above the noise of the water hitting her square in the face. She reached out and grabbed Tess' head trying to dunk her. Tess gave a convincing fight until the end. She came up gasping for air as Riley came up from behind her and put her arms around Tess' waist pretending like she was going to pick her up and throw her. Tess turned in Riley's arms instead placing her hands on each of her shoulders. They both started laughing and Riley leaned in fighting the urge to kiss her. Tess placed her hands on top of Riley's head before jumping out of the water in attempt to push Riley under the surface. Riley was stronger and she stood lifting Tess higher into the air.

"Okay! Okay! I give in." Tess laughed. "Put me down Riley Jones!"

Riley gently let her slide down the length of her body still keeping a firm grip on her. She watched as Tess' breast slowly passed her eyes and fought every urge not to reach out with her tongue and lick the water from her taunt nipples. A slow fire began to build in her stomach. Damn she wanted this woman in the worst way. The passion would soon win out and it was stupid to think other wise. Their eyes met and held for an instant before they kissed. Riley remembered the other night and what Tess had said and pushed herself off Tess floating back into the water.

"I have never seen you laugh so hard." Riley commented. She still felt the impression of the kiss on her lips.

"It' been a long time since I've acted like a kid." Tess tipped her head back into the water cooling off her scalp. There were large rocks at the bottom covering the mud and she stepped carefully. "I have to tell you this has been the best vacation I've had in a long time."

"When was the last vacation you took?" Riley asked out of curiosity. She saw a darkness come over Tess' face while she thought about it.

"About two years ago Rae and I went to St. Croix. It was nice but it wasn't fun." Tess remarked. "We mostly laid out on the beach and drank fruit drinks, dinner in the evenings and walks on the beach at night."

"That sounds like fun." Riley wondered just what kind of person this Rae was. She seemed like the intellect type just from what Tess had mentioned here and there about her.

Tess looked at her. "I think it has to do with the person you're with. Rae would never try to dunk me and would be appalled if I had tried to dunk her. I never gave Indiana the chance. You have a resort right in your backyard. Horseback riding, swimming, and weight lifting if you count how many times you lift a bale of hay or pitch a pile of manure."

"I never thought of it like that." Riley swam up next to her. "You're right tho'. It all depends on who you're with." She placed herself right in front of Tess. "Hop on and I'll take you down with the current."

"What about you're shoulder?" She was hesitant of hurting her.

"It's good therapy and if it hurts I'll just dump you off." Riley stated. Tess hopped on her back. In the water she was weightless. She wrapped her arms around Riley's neck avoiding the bruised area on her back feeling good against her bare skin. Never before had she felt so right with someone. Already in the short time she had been there Riley had opened up more to her than the year they were together. By the end of the workday Tess was so tired it was hard to stay awake. For the first time in her life she found herself fast asleep by nine thirty and up before six the next morning. The best part of the day was the wee hours between dawn and sunrise.

Back in town Wilbur and Lucas sat in the corner table at Miss Mayme's. The lunch crowd was starting to thin out and they had the time to talk. Huck had already informed the sheriff about the information they found up in the holler and what Logan had told him the night before they went. The State Police investigators had a meeting with him yesterday to discuss getting a posse of sorts together and scanning the hillside. It was the only lead they had so far even though it wasn't solid. The next step was getting enough men to scour the area.

"My main concern right now is for Riley and the asshole that tried to kill her. I know that guy Logan saw out by the horses that day is the man we're looking for but what is his connection with Riley? She never talks about those years away from Stanford and that's a lot of growin' years for a young girl." Wilbur was at his wits end trying to piece together this case.

"I don't understand what she has to be so secretive about?" Lucas took a sip of the hot coffee. He couldn't quite figure it out himself. This was a very attractive woman living on a farm all by herself. She had never been married nor has any children. And from the looks of it she didn't appear to want any. Her horses were her life. And it really didn't make any sense to him either.

"Her family was well respected in these parts." Wilbur remembered. "Her grandpa lived his whole life here in Stanford. His wife Irma died of pneumonia in the early seventies. I don't even know if she remembered her or not. I do know she was close to her grandpa. Her parents Randall and Carol moved south about a year after Riley left for the military. Her father was in finance and the opportunities were a lot better south. Once Riley came home four years later she spent a lot of time with her grandpa. I wasn't a bit surprised that she bought the farm when he passed. That's about the time you moved into town." Wilbur commented.

"I guess a person needs their space." Lucas remarked.

"You got it bad for her don't you?" Wilbur asked bluntly. He was never one to beat around the bush. That's what made him a good sheriff. If a person has something to say then just say it.

Lucas about choked on his coffee. He didn't realize it was that obvious. He had been giving a lot of thought lately to the possibility of something going further on a personal level with Riley. He just had the gut feeling it wasn't possible. She was a very complicated woman and very independent. At times he felt he should just keep it as a friendship. "Can you imagine Riley settling down with anyone?" He asked to save face.

"Doesn't mean it's not possible." Wilbur winked at him.

"I think you'd have a better chance on finding the guy up in the holler." Lucas remarked. He knew the odds were not in his favor. Lately Lucas had been sensing that Riley had been purposefully keeping him at a distance.

147

"Hey, have you've been listening to the radio lately?" Wilbur decided to forgo the lovelorn situation. "I don't think you ever met Jesse Monroe. Roy and Laura's daughter? She and Riley were the best of friends growing up. Kept us all on our feet. After graduation Jess went to Nashville, Tennessee to pursue a music career. That girl could play the mandolin like nobody's heard. It just sang it's own song when she plucked the strings."

"I've heard her name a few times here and there but never had the pleasure." Lucas looked at his watch realizing he had appointments at the office. "I need to get going. I have appointments lined up all afternoon."

"Right behind you." Wilbur had to get back to the office and see if the state boys have come up with any news.

Towards evening the stock was fed for the night and lounging in the pasture. The chickens cackled and searched the ground for a few specs of seed. Up at the house both women decided to go out tonight. Riley was feeling itchy and Tess wanted to see little of Stanford. The first place she'd take her would be Cooter's. It wasn't the weekend so it shouldn't be too crowded. They could eat dinner and drink a few beers. Riley waited patiently as Tess came out from the bedroom. Since she had no idea she would be staying as long as she has she didn't have anything to wear but Riley's clothes. She looked really good in gauze tank top of Riley's and the pair of shorts she wore her first day in the country. She putting her hair up in a braid when Riley walked in the bedroom and swallowed hard at the sight before her. Tess saw her in the mirror and turned around.

"I see you're ready." Riley commented, as she looked her over. She was so beautiful it was becoming more and more difficult not to show Tess how she felt. A few kisses here and there had sent her into a frenzy but she wouldn't show it. Not yet.

"Let's go." Tess headed for the door fully aware of the look on her ex-lovers face.

Cooter's Tavern was busier than expected. The parking lot was almost half full and it was not even seven o'clock and on a Wednesday evening. They walked through the swinging saloon doors and the jukebox was wailing a song of heartache. Logan saw them first and waved as they headed her way. "I was beginning to think I'd lose these chairs." Logan replied as they sat down. "The whole town was hopping today. I see Riley hasn't been working you to death." She smiled warmly at Tess making her feel welcomed.

"Not yet but I have acquired a few blisters." Tess showed her hands.

"You have to wear gloves." Logan offered. "She don't cause her hands are as rough as leather."

"No they're not. They may be a little callused. Riley rubbed them on her thigh as if to soften them up. She was right they were pretty rough. She never really gave it much thought. Never cared to until now. "Let's get some brew started here." Tess was studying the bar. Everything about this town was old and historical.

"I doubt they serve a house wine so I'll just go for the beer." Tess remarked. Riley got the waitress' attention and she came over.

"Hey, Riley. How you feelin'?" Betty asked.

"Pretty good. And very lucky. Bring us a round of Miller Lites and keep 'em coming." Riley was in the mood tonight. She had been cooped up in the house too long.

"All righty." She put the order in. And brought them back their drinks.

"This is a pretty cool place." Tess observed.

"It gets happening in here every now and then. How do you like Stanford so far?" Logan was doing a bit of fishing and wondered when Riley was going to open her eyes to what she had right in front of her.

"I really like it. Everyone has been so friendly. I was beginning to give up on humanity up in Albany. Here's to my restored faith in people again." Tess toasted and they lifted their bottles in a toast. Betty came back to the table.

"So have they caught the guy yet that did this to you?" She asked.

"They're working on it." Riley didn't know much more than anyone else did.

"You about scared the shit out of all of us. When I saw that hoof come down and knock you right into the dirt. Thought for sure you were a goner." Betty shook her head and noticed the next table trying to get her attention.

"You saw more than I did. It happened so fast I didn't have time to react." Riley commented.

149

"Man, don't these people let up." She held up her hand to let them know she saw them. "If you need anything let me know. I'm glad you're feelin' better."

"Thanks Betty. Means a lot to me." Riley smiled as she walked over to the next table.

"She is a character but a damn good waitress." Logan had tried on many occasions to get Betty to work for her but the tips weren't as good as they were at Cooter's. People were more generous drinking beer than coffee and she had to make a living. "Riley there's an estate auction in Seymour next weekend do you want to go check it out?"

"What are they auctioning off?" She asked.

"Who cares. Do you want to go?" Logan retorted jokingly before turning to Tess. "You wouldn't believe the crap she would get me into when we go auctioning." Logan ignored Riley's protest. "We're out looking for wood planks from old barns that have either fallen down or was near collapse. That's how I remodeled the coffee shop. We pull up to this old lady's house with the perfect wood that I needed. Riley goes up to talk with the woman and the next thing I know we're picking green beans for her in exchange for all the wood we could haul. Seven rows and three rows of tomatoes plus we had to tear down the wood and load it in the truck." She laughed.

"It was a good deal not too mention good exercise." Riley interjected. It had saved her friend a bundle. Logan just ignored her and continued to talk to Tess.

"I understand how Riley is so if you want to kick her ass or something just go right ahead." Logan commented and Tess busted out laughing.

"I don't think she's that bad yet but I will keep that in mind." She looked at Riley lovingly.

"So what's your opinion about the accident?" Logan wanted to know Tess's view of all this.

"I think it's a scare tactic or revenge of some sort. Whoever it is has the capabilities of homicide. He probably has a long history of crimes and probably a prison record. If he really wanted to Riley I think he would of done the job. I doubt he just got unlucky. She has something he wants and he needs you alive or that saddle would have done the job." This was something Tess knew Riley already thought of but she needed to get it out in the open and run it by to figure out the details.

"You may be right. Someone is trying to put a scare into you, Riley." Logan had to agree. This was actually the first time she had the chance to know this woman who had vexed her friend not once but twice. Tess wasn't at all what Riley had described the few times they talked about her. Logan couldn't quite describe it just as being she had a certain air about her. At the hospital when everyone was in the waiting room she knew right off who the dark haired woman was. They chatted briefly when Logan realized she was there for Riley and not any other patient.

"I haven't a clue to who this man could be. That thought will sure make me sleep good tonight." Riley was actually too distracted to think of anyone but the woman that was laying next to her. She gestured for Betty to bring another round when she felt Tess' hand on her thigh. A reassuring touch nothing more. "It's a good theory but there's no sense to it. Why would anyone plot revenge against me? And why now?"

"I don't know. I just hope at some point you can figure it out cause who ever this is he won't stop until he gets what he is after." Logan replied.

"What did this guy look like?" Tess asked.

"Like everyone who was around that day. He had dark hair and a filthy straw cowboy hat, kind of long dark hair but it was his eyes. They were dark. I only saw his face for an instant and it didn't take much mind to him. I thought he was one of the hands Bancroft hired to work the horses. It never occurred to me he what he was really doing. But all of the rider's saddles were right there. They would saddle the mounts before they put them in the chute. They were tagged with each name which is why they were lined up according to the order of the rider." Logan informed. Every night since the accident she would close her eyes and try to remember this man's face. He was there one minute then gone the next.

"I don't have a clue and I'm not going to let any son-of-bitch try to put a scare into me." Riley stated. "I'll be cautious but I'll be damned if he thinks he can scare me that easily." Tess looked over at her and saw the anger in Riley's eyes.

"Don't try to be a martyr. It very well could get you killed." Logan knew this was frustrating her but she was still a woman. She may have a muscular build but when it came down to it anyone with a psychotic trying to kill them had to be scared. Riley would not only show it but would never admit it. She would go down fighting. The rest of the evening went by quickly as it was almost ten o'clock when they decided to call it a night. They walked outside and breathed the fresh air. Riley felt a good buzz going and from the looks of Tess, she wasn't feeling much pain herself.

"Be careful going home." Riley replied as Logan go into her car.

"Country roads all the way." Logan backed out and waved as she turned onto the road. Riley started the engine as Tess tuned in a music station on the radio. "We don't get very many stations down here unless you like country music. The hills block out any reception."

"Why not? Country music isn't all bad and I'm doing a lot of things now that I would have never thought of before." Tess smiled as she scooted closer to Riley. The song attracted Riley's attention. The soft bluegrass sound as the woman's voice was low and husky. Most bluegrass songs go with the high pitch tenor such as Bill Monroe or Ricky Skaggs. This song drew you into it. When Riley heard the soft whine of the mandolin she caught her breath. The style was unmistakable.

"What's wrong?" She heard Tess ask.

"I think that's Jesse." Riley leaned over to turn up the volume. They made it home just as the song came to a finish. She turned off the engine but left the battery on so they could finish listening. Jesse sang of the loss of someone she loved. The song never identified whether it was a man or woman or just a friend. Jesse had done it. She finally conquered her dream. Riley placed her arm across the back of the seat and turned to Tess. "She could always make that mandolin of hers sing."

"That's your high school friend?" Tess remembered some of the stories Riley told her the previous nights. A sudden chill ran down Tess' spine as the song ended.

"Damn. She did it. She actually did it." It had been so long since they had said their tearful goodbye the day after graduation. It had taken Jesse a long time but she was there. Riley wondered what all she had gone through to get there. The disappointments but the determination had to keep her going. Jesse would never give up until she had what she wanted no matter how long it took. A sense of pride swelled up inside of her. Riley dropped her arm around Tess' shoulders and when the deejay came on he announced the new Nashville sensation from Stanford, Jesse Monroe and the Wayward Weeds. It was true.

Tess leaned into Riley and looked up into her eyes. "This is nice. Having your arms around me as we sit in an old truck listening to the radio."

The dashboard light made it easier to see Tess' face. There was no hesitation when Riley leaned down and gently kissed her lips. Tess responded by parting hers until their tongues touched. This was different than the kisses they had shared earlier. This was intimate and slow. As though each were savoring the sensation their tongues made to their bodies. The fire of passion was lit and neither wanted to put it out. Not tonight. No more denying the feelings they both shared of their wants and desires. Riley broke the kiss and looked at the woman who flatly refused to give up on them both. Tess' lips were red and slightly swollen. Her eyelids drooped and Riley knew from this moment on there was no turning back. Everyday from now on was a positive step forward. She suddenly opened the door and half-pulled Tess across the seat. The steering wheel bumped against her hip. They both started to laugh. Once inside they barely made it to the steps on the landing without tripping over each other.

Riley gently backed Tess up against the bricks back wall of the fireplace completely lost in their passion for each other. She held Tess' arms up over her head and began kissing her neck as her thigh parted her legs. Tess grinded her hips against Riley's leg until neither could take much more. A few more steps and they were in the bedroom. When Tess went into her arms going at a slower pace as their clothes fell to the floor. The sight of Tess' naked body made Riley ache between her legs which she knew was wet with desire. She laid Tess gently back against the pillows and placed herself on top of her looking into her ice blue eyes seeing the love Tess' neck down to her breast. Her body was so beautiful. Riley took her breast into her mouth letting her tongue flick against the taunt nipple. Tess moaned in response. Riley ran her hand down letting her fingers roam over soft skin pf Tess' stomach gradually making the way between hre legs.

Tess parted her thighs allowing for Riley's touch. She ran her fingers through the silky wet dark curls stroking the places Riley could never forget. She lowered herself between Tess' legs and let her tongue replacing her fingers. Her taste drove Riley wild as she increased the pressure of her tongue making Tess wither in desire. "Oh my God, Riley!" Tess breathed hard between her moans. Riley continued the rhythm never letting up. Tess raised her hips and grasped the back of Riley's head to steady herself. Not yet she didn't want to reach climax just yet. She gently pulled back. Riley looked up at her and moving slowly towards her mouth to which she kissed deeply. Tess could taste herself on Riley's lips and gently rolled her over onto her back.

She took Riley's breast into her mouth hungrily sucking each nipple as though this would be the last time. Tess remembered the places and certain touches that drove her lover wild. In turn she gently let her tongue leave a wet trail going down between Riley's legs. Riley gasped when she parted her legs and let Tess' tongue do its magic. Both women were on the verge of orgasm when Tess sat up and stradled Riley's face while continuing with the pressure of her mouth. Riley grabbed Tess's hips and started the climatic rhythm. Their bodies moving together as sweat glistened on their skin. Riley arched her back right at the moment both women gave in to the sensation as they climaxed into a breath taking orgasm.

"Oh my God." Riley breathed heavily as spasm after spasm flowed through her body uncontrollably leaving both gasping for breath. Tess slowly rolled off Riley and turned herself around until she lay in her arms. They were spent from the pent up desire and the final release. Their bodies throbbing still excited.

Tess placed her leg across Riley's her arm resting on her stomach. "I don't know if you're ready to hear this Riley." A slight hesitation. "I'm still so much in love with you." She lifted her head as Riley placed her mouth on Tess'. The tastes of each other still fresh on their lips. The desire was building again.

"I've never stopped loving you Tess McGuire. For three years I have ached for you." Riley whispered against her mouth.

"Why did you stay away for so long?" Tess asked. A tear developing at the corner of her eyes.

"I don't know." Riley wrapped her arms around her. The wall was crumbling down around her heart that she had so painstakingly built up over the years. There was no control where Tess was concerned.

Tess kissed her back. There would be no sleep tonight. There was only lost time to make up for and all night to do it in. The sky was beginning to lighten when they finally lay entwined completely exhausted. Sometime before morning Tess got up to go to the bathroom. When she came back to bed she looked at Riley sleeping soundly. This was woman who found her way into Tess' heart and wouldn't leave. What kind of person had she been three years ago? Tess knew things between them back then were not the same as they were now. She had taken the time to get to know Riley as the person she has always been. Riley would never leave this place to go back to Albany and Tess didn't know if she could live so far out in the county away from the happenings of a big city. She never had to make this choice. It would have to be worked out cause after last night Tess wasn't going to let her out of her life again. She had been right that Riley couldn't deny her feelings for her.

Tess walked over to the window and looked out over the yard and to the fields spreading out as far as the eye could see. She noticed a glow coming from behind the line of trees to the west. The sun wasn't due to come up for a couple of hours yet. Then she noticed the smell in the breeze that blew through the window. It was smoke. She looked again and was convinced it was a fire. Quickly she ran to the side of the bed and shook Riley awake.

"Riley, wake up!" Tess exclaimed. Riley slowly opened her eyes questioningly. "I think there might be a fire." Riley sprung up out of bed. "Look beyond those trees. See the glow at the top?"

"Oh my God. Do you think…" She couldn't finish. Something was definitely wrong. She noticed Tess was almost dressed before she could get her jeans and boots on.

"Riley, I don't understand this." Tess stated as she hurried. They were dressed, down at the truck and on their way towards the glow.

"I think it might be at the Monroe farm." She drove in that direction and soon found she was right when they pulled into the

155

drive. Fire trucks, police cars and an ambulance was parked up near the barn. "Oh shit!" Riley exclaimed as she parked as close to action as she could get. The barn was completely engulfed in flames. The firemen had given up on trying to extinguish the blaze it was too late. They concentrated on keeping the house watered down so no sparks would ignite it. Riley saw the Monroe's standing near one of the firemen. She and Tess hurried over as Mrs. Monroe turned around as they approached. "What happened?"

"We don't know. Roy woke up hearing a scream and saw the barn going up in flames. He got the stock out but I'm afraid Nelly took the worst of it. Doc Garvey is over by the fence tending to her. Jesse's heart will break if that horse dies." She quickly looked away. Laura Monroe had been like a second mother to Riley ever since she and Jesse had became friends. Riley quickly ran to the fence not prepared to see the sight before her. There on the ground lay the horse with a blanket over it's head and Lucas leaning over her heaving sides.

"Nooo!" Riley cried out. She fell to her knees taking Nelly's head onto her lap. She saw the burns covering most of the animal's body. She looked up at Lucas with tears streaming down her face. "She's dying isn't she?" She asked knowing full well even if Nelly survived the horse would be scared for life. Lucas couldn't look Riley in the eye as he prepared a shot of medicine to help ease the pain.

"She wouldn't leave the barn Riley until all the other animals were out. Roy couldn't even coax her out." He stuck the needle in her neck. Maybe if Nelly was younger he could save her but she would be ruined. Riley continued to stroke her neck and softly nuzzled her nose. Tess stood back and watched trying her best to control her own emotions. She had only been back in Riley's life a week and she had seen so much damage brought on by someone hell bent on revenge for reasons no one could understand. She watched as Riley bent over the horse's head to whisper in its ear. A few minutes later the horse exhaled a long sigh. Nelly was gone. Riley continued to stroke her face not wanting to give up this part of her life. She wasn't able to keep holding on to her childhood nor her past. Someone was trying to take that away from her. And Riley vowed the bastard was going to pay. Even if she died trying.

Tess walked up behind Riley placing her hand on her shoulder. Riley stood up going into Tess' arms for comfort. She couldn't control the sobs that racked her body. Everything that has happened the past couple weeks seemed to take its toll on her tonight.

Lucas replaced the blanket over Nelly's head and stood back glancing over where Tess was holding Riley as she cried. He saw the tender way Tess held Riley stroking her back and then the thought hit him hard. There was more than just friendship going on between these two women. Lucas shook his head and walked away feeling the fool.

The moon gave off just enough light to show the path through the trees. The figure running looked back at the glow in the night. It wouldn't be long before a posse of lawmen would come looking for him. He expected them and but he was also beginning to lose his edge trying to out smart the law. The other day was proof enough when those men showed up in the woods. He decided now was the time to make his final move. Living all those weeks in the woods wasn't so bad but he missed a soft mattress. A cowboy has to spend his time out on the range or in the woods to keep himself toughen to the elements. But tonight he had to get out. Setting fire to the barn would cost him his freedom. No way in hell was he going back to prison. He had one more thing left to do and he was gone. Riley Jones was still alive. He ran faster cutting across the pastures but always keeping to the edge where the trees gave him some coverage. The sun would be up soon and he had to make it to her barn to finish off his revenge. All in one night he would destroy Jesse Monroe's dreams.

This holler would be filled with the law and he needed a horse to travel faster. He couldn't believe his luck when he ran past a bend of trees and saw her barn up ahead. This had to be her place if he calculated the distance correctly. The last few weeks all he had done was stare at the backside of her property memorizing every detail. What he didn't expect was the girl inside the barn doing chores when he silently slipped through the door. He needed one of those horses badly.

Katie went into the tack room and started filling the buckets with feed. The sun wasn't quite up but she wanted to get an early start since she and Milly were thinking of going down to the reservoir later

157

this morning and spend the day on the beach beside the lake. The college students who stayed in Greendale through the summer usually hung out there. Of course no one else knew that was their reason for going. She hoisted up the buckets and stepped back. Her boot stepped on something hard and when she tried to turn around a huge hand come down on her face over her mouth. She wouldn't have been able to scream even if she could. He had a vice like grip she was afraid he would snap her neck in two.

He placed his mouth close to her ear. "You make one fuckin' sound and I will break your neck. Do you understand?" He hissed. Katie knew right off that this was the man everyone has been looking for. She nodded her head in agreement. She felt her legs grow weak. What would he do to her? "Now you go saddle up two of those horses. We're going to take a trip." He shoved her up against the boards of the stall. She wasted no time in doing what he asked. He stood and watched until she had both mounts ready. "Get up there." He pushed her towards one of the horses. Once in the saddle he took both of Katie's hands and tied them to the saddle horn. He mounted his horse and led her out of the barn and towards the house. Now was the time. He wouldn't burn the barn but he would leave his mark. He jumped down and ran up the steps so fast taking one of the rocking chairs on the porch and throwing it through the front window. Stepping back Hank Moleson took a piece of paper out of his pocket and flung it in the broken glass and wood pieces. Katie felt the terror seize her. What the hell was this man doing? She asked herself not daring to speak. She kept looking down the drive expecting Riley or someone to come up the lane. Where were her and Tess? Why wasn't Riley home? She never prayed so hard as at that moment. But no one came. Before she knew it he was back on the horse and pulling her along at a trot until they reached the trail at the base of the holler. No one around for miles to hear her scream Katie realized. For the first time in her young life she was scared to death.

The house was really taking on a shape. Norman and his crew had done wonders in such a short time. The loft was finished within the first few days and Jesse herself had worked a good part of the day sanding and putting a thick coat of wax onthe wood floor. Once it dried she wasted no time putting a bed up there and moved a few of her things in. The phone was hooked up and the electricians had laid wire and were waiting on the electric company to turn it on. The Kelly's were a bit apprehensive when she gave her notice but understood fully with everything that had gone on with Toni's death and with Jesse's career taking off. It was expected. Right now she was waiting on the last of her things from Nashville. Jackson and Bobby Jim were bringing a U-Haul truck loaded with everything that was left in the apartment. It was sad cause she really didn't have a lot of things to account for all the years she lived in Nashville. But money had always been tight. She had bought new furniture but it wouldn't be delivered until the living room was completed. This was her fresh start and Jesse now had the money to do it in her own style. She was a bit puzzled she couldn't find all of her pictures she kept on the mantle when she was packing. After Hank Moleson trashed the apartment he knocked it somewhere she couldn't find. Hopefully the guys might have found then when they moved her furniture. There was a lot of confusion that night of the break in and she cherished her memories of home. They helped her capture the years of her childhood and what she had loved dearly. A person never gets those times back nor the inspiration and determination she had at such a young age.

Norman found her staring out the huge picture window towards the mountains. "I want to reinforce these beams in the living room like we did in the loft. I noticed you moved some of your things in here. Does that mean you're occupying the place now?" He asked.

"Yes. I just couldn't stand the city any more." Jesse turned around to look at the progress this man had done in such a short time. "You have done an excellent job Norm but I have to know. You watched the movie didn't you." She grinned.

"Yea, but do me a favor and don't be tellin' everyone. I got a reputation you know." He returned the smile. "That Jane Wyman had some nice legs back then." He noticed Jesse roll her eyes.

"It wasn't her legs I wanted you to pay attention too." She commented.

"As you can tell I saw what you wanted." Norm would never admit to anyone that he had actually enjoyed the movie.

"I know but I have to give you a hard time. Because I like you, now how are you about Doris Day movies?"

159

"Uh huh, no way. My wife already thinks I'm gettin' sensitive and mushy. I just can't. But I'll tell you what. You watch the next Tennessee State football game and I might consider ol' Doris." He compromised.

"I get the point." Jesse replied. Suddenly her cell phone rang and she went over to the counter to answer it. The guys were probably lost. "Hello? Mom is that you?" She heard her mother's voice cackle with static on the other end. She wasn't prepared to hear the reason she for the call. Jesse braced herself against the kitchen counter as her mother told about the barn and about Nelly. Her knees started to buckle and she had to sit down. Her mother also told her about Riley's accident. How it was intentional and the police think who ever cut Riley's saddle strap was responsible for the fire. No one knew why but someone was terrorizing the town. "I'm coming home. I'll be there in a few hours. I don't care. Tell Dad I'll be there. I have a few things to take care of here." The tears stung at the corners of her eyes. Nelly her horse was dead. The horse she had raised from birth. The first thing that popped into her mind after she hung up was Hank Moleson.

"Are you all right?" Norman couldn't help but notice how suddenly Jesse became upset from the phone call.

"Some bad news from home." She dialed Wesley's cell phone. "I'm going to have to go back to Indiana for a few days."

"I understand. Don't worry about things here. We got it under control." He stood back. He never could deal with tragedies very well and from the look on Jesse's face it was bad.

"Wes, this is Jesse. I just got a call from home and I have to leave for a few days. I have a feeling I know where Hank Moleson has been hiding" She told him everything her mother related to her about the accident and the fire. Wes told her to hold tight. He was on his way. She went up to the loft and started to go through the boxes she had her clothes in. The first one she saw was a box she had packed months ago when she wanted to condense her wardrobe but wanted to keep a few things. Jesse tore open the packing tape across the top and dumped the contents onto the floor. A smaller package fell at her feet. She didn't recognize the large envelope as being hers. She sat down on the bed and carefully opened it not prepared to find the large bag of a white powder substance. Jesse thought better by touching it before dumping the contents out of the package onto her bed.

"Oh my God. This was what Moleson was after." She realized. "Toni must have been hiding her stash in Jesse's closet without her knowing about it. But why? Then it dawned on her. If this was the same stuff that was tainted then Moleson's finger prints would be all over the bag. That was the evidence needed linking him to Toni's death. He knew Toni had it and he was trying to find it so there wouldn't be any proof. She carefully scooted the bag back into the envelope. Threw some clothes in a bag and headed downstairs.

Jackson and Bobby Jim were waiting outside by the moving van when Jesse walked out the door. Norman was talking with them when she walked up.

"I have to go home for a few days." She replied sensing Norman had said something to them.

"What happened?" Jackson asked concerned.

"I just got a call from my mother. Apparently someone set their barn on fire last night. And a friend of mine was hurt in an accident." She was getting upset. "My horse died." Jesse knew it sounded childish but she couldn't help it. Jackson put his arms around her as she tried to push him away. Why? Why did Hank Moleson have to take this out on her family? How did he find out where her family lived? "Wes is meeting me here. I know it's Hank Moleson." Bobby Jim looked at her in disbelief.

"How and for what reason?" Jackson asked.

"I found this in a box that was stored in my closet back at the apartment." Jesse showed him the large envelope. "Jackson if that son of a bitch is responsible for this I swear to God I'm going to kill him."

"And go to jail? I don't think so." He stated sternly knowing very well what was in the package. "Let the police take care of this Jess. You have been through enough already. Don't lower yourself to that scum's level."

"Jackson he has found my family and is trying to destroy them. Not to mention Riley." She took a deep breath to calm her nerves.

"Who is Riley?" Bobby Jim asked.

"The best friend I have ever had. Just like Toni. And he tried to kill her also. "Now I know why. His finger prints are probably all over this stuff." Jesse was frustrated. "What is he going to do next?" She asked as she saw the car coming up the drive.

Wes jumped out from the driver's side just as Jesse met him at the car. "I found this." She handed him the package and watched as he opened it looking inside.

Wes understood now. Everything became crystal clear. "Where did you find it?" He asked.

"Stuffed in a box of old clothes I kept in my closet. Apparently Toni hid her drugs in my things I guess for this very reason." Jesse couldn't help the feeling that her friend had betrayed her. Toni knew how she felt about these kind of drugs. But apparently she didn't care.

Wes called Reed on his cell phone giving him directions out to Jesse's house and instructions on what to pick up. He informed his partner they had the evidence connecting Hank Moleson to Toni Griffin's death. He would leave it with Jackson. He'd call him when he got more information.

The trip to Indiana was quick as Wes kept his red light going all the way at ninety miles an hour. Jesse filled him in on everything her mother had told her about the rodeo and the fire. He had to agree it fit the profile of Moleson. But what he didn't understand was why Hank would go to the extreme lengths as to finding Jesse's family just to get even. He had to of known about the bag of heroin, which explained why he broke into Jesse's apartment. But why her family?

It took Huck, Dale, and Lucas to lift Nelly's lifeless body onto the bed of the wagon. The grave was near the pond at the base of a huge oak tree that Jesse's father had picked out. Everyone of them knew what this animal meant to Jesse and her final resting place had to be perfect and peaceful. Riley decided to pass on the burial. Instead her and Tess walked towards the Monroe house.

"This sure hasn't been much of a vacation for you." Riley looked over atTess wandering what she would have done if she hadn't been here to support her.

"I wouldn't say that." Tess looked away towards the charred remains what once was a barn. "I've gotten to know you a lot better than I ever imagined Riley. I understand why you came back to this place. People care about each other down here. I never saw that before in any place I have ever lived."

Riley smiled to herself. How she handled their relationship three years ago was wrong. They both had changed over the years. Last night when they made love it was as if it was for the first time. Most important was the fact when Riley needed her most Tess was there. Before she couldn't count on that. And neither could Tess. But that was in the past and now they had so much more to build on. If it were possible.

The Monroe's were standing by the sheriff's car when the two women approached. The State Police had already sent men up into the hills. Arson was a federal offense and it was as clear as day when the firemen pulled a charred gas can from the rubble. Roy had his cans and lawn equipment stored in his shed. He had no use for a gas can in the barn. The suspicion was on the terrorist. The police wasted no time putting men on the trail. "When Huck and Dale get back tell 'em we headed on out. We'll take the south side and work our way north. If they'll come up from the west then there's no way we could miss this guy." Wilbur started his engine. "Riley, I'm tellin' you two women tobe careful. This man ain't foolin' around." He stated sternly.

Riley just nodded.

"Jesse is on her way home." Roy informed her. "I'm sure she's going to want to see you. We told her about everything that's happened."

"I'm sorry about Nelly. I know how Jess felt about the horse. Hell, I think we all felt the same way." Riley commented. "I just don't understand why all this is happening. I have racked my brain and for the life of me I can't come up with anyone who hates me this much."

"Honey, I don't think anyone has a clue as to why. It just doesn't make sense. None of us has hurt anybody to deserve this. Especially that horse." Roy ran his dirty hand across his hair leaving a black smudge on his forehead.

"If you need anything let us know." Riley replied.

"Take care of yourself Riley. I don't want anymore bad news." Jesse's mother commented. Riley hugged her tightly before she went with Tess towards the Ford. She backed out and headed down the road back to her house. The ride was silent as both women were worn out from the lack of sleep and the excitement. It's almost as if she was waiting for the next move. Someone has got to stop this man and soon. The truck rattled over the bridge and Riley made the comment that she would have to fix it soon. A comment she always thought of when she went over it. Katie's truck was parked near the barn. "Looks like Katie has plans this afternoon since she is here early." Riley remarked. She also noticed the horses were out in the pasture and the chickens were in the yard pecking at the ground looking for food.

Tess got out of the truck and stretched. "I'm going to the barn and see if Katie needs any help. You look tired. Why don't you go lay down." Riley came up beside her and put her arm around Tess' waist. "Thank you." She whispered close to her ear.

"For what?" Tess asked a little bewildered.

"For just being there for me. You've been there a lot for me lately. Why is that?" Riley teased. Anything to lighten the moment. Both women were so worn out.

"You have to believe me when I tell you I wouldn't have wanted to be in any other place. Last night opened my eyes. You need me as much as I need you. I was hoping you would see it too and I guess you have." Tess looked at her in such a way Riley's heart swelled. Tess pulled her close and they shared the most intimate kiss either had shared since last night. Reluctantly Riley pulled away.

"Let me go give Katie a hand. I'll be up in a minute." Riley stepped back and headed towards the barn. Tess went up the walk and when she reached the porch steps she noticed the broken glass and the open space that used to be a window. Tess turned around yelling to get Riley's attention who noticed the alarm in Tess' voice and despite her sore leg she ran back to the porch.

When she reached the walk she saw the window. "What the hell?" Riley exclaimed.

"I found this in the glass." Tess showed her the picture. Riley's eyes widened in recognition and ran into the house with Tess at her heels. Right on the fireplace mantel where it has been for the last three years was the same photo of her and Jesse at the limestone quarry. The exact duplicate as the one she held in her hands. There were only two prints made and as far as she knew Jesse had the other.

Tess looked at the picture on the mantel. It seemed to fall into place. She suddenly remembered Katie out in the barn.

"Katie!" Tess shouted in alarm and both woman ran out the front door taking the steps at a jump. They raced to the barn.

"Katie? Katie?" Riley yelled as she ran up the ladder to the hayloft thinking she might have seen what happen to the house and would be hiding. No such luck.

"Riley look." Tess pointed to the two buckets lying in a pile of spilled oats by the tack room door. "There's two saddles missing also." Riley's heart began to beat fast. Katie had been here. Her truck was outside and she had been ready to feed the horses. Where in the hell was she?

"I don't have a good feeling about this." Tess could feel the chills run down her spine.

"Neither do I." Riley ran outside just as Huck's truck came over the bridge. She waved at him and Dale frantically. Before they could make it out of the truck she was on them. "Katie is missing. Her truck was here when we got home and the front window is smashed in. He was here and look what we found in the glass." Riley handed them the photo she realized was still in her hand. "As far as I remember there were only two prints made and the other is in a frame on my fireplace mantle."

"I get it now. It's your friend Jesse not you that he is after." Tess interrupted. Everyone turned to look at her. "Think about it. Maybe he's some crazed fan or something. Why else would he have that picture. Look on the back. Stanford, Indiana wrote right on the bottom. If there were only two prints then he's gotten that one from her." The whole scenario fit. The accident and Jesse's parents barn. The boys knew Tess was on to something from the looks on their faces. Riley turned suddenly.

"I'm saddling up Cherokee. I'm going up there. This time he's gone too far and I ain't waiting on any law to go find Katie. Tess there's a rifle behind the kitchen door. Please go get it for me." If this man wanted her that bad then he could have her. Not at the expense of Katie, Nelly or anyone else for that matter.

"Riley what in the hell are you going to prove by goin' up there?" Huck was at her heels. "What about Tess? Don't you care enough about her not to go gettin' yourself killed?" The words sunk in as making her stopped in her tracks. She hadn't thought that far ahead. Tess looked surprised at his comment. Huck understood more than Riley gave him credit for. He turned towards Dale. "Get the rifle out of the truck. We're going with her." He had seen the anger and fire in her eyes before and if anything would make any sense by her actions it would be for that love she had for the dark haired woman standing next to him.

"That man has been trying to destroy me or Jesse. Now he has taken Katie. I can't stand by and let her get hurt. I just won't do that Huck." Riley ran her hands through her hair out of frustration.

"I'll let the sheriff know which means Katie's parents will be showing up here also." Tess walked over to Riley. "I just found you again and I can't lose you now. Please be careful." She half pleaded.

"You're not going to. Not like this. I won't let it happen." Riley looked over her shoulder seeing the boys riding up on their horses leading Cherokee by the reins. "I love you Tess McGuire." She replied.

"I love you too. That's enough reason to use your head." Tess stood back as Riley mounted her horse before kicking his sides to take off into a canter. She looked back and saw the worried look on Tess' face. Once they were out of sight Tess went into the house and made the calls.

The police car turned the corner right outside of town and sped down the country road. Jesse glanced out the window noticing a few changes here and there in Stanford. The feed store and co-op were still in the same place. Bulls Gap still seemed bigger than home. As a child everything seemed so much larger and coming home for the first time in years more had changed than she even realized. Wes slowed down when Jesse informed him her parents drive was just up ahead. He turned and drove up the long lane. When Jesse saw the barn still smoldering she gasped. Wes placed his hand on hers for reassurance. He parked near the back door and Jesse got out going towards the charred remains. The screen door banged and she turned around to see her mother coming towards her.

"Jesse." Mrs. Monroe replied as mother and daughter embraced. "I'm so sorry about Nel." Jesse noticed the tears in her mother's at having to tell her the awful news. "Huck and Dale buried her by that old tree near the pond."

"Oh Mom, I can't believe this." Jesse glanced up as her father walked over and she went into his arms.

"You got here pretty quick." He noted. Jesse suddenly remembered Wes standing back by the car.

"Wes, these are my parents Roy and Laura." She turned to him as he approached. "This is Wesley Carson a police detective in Nashville."

He shook Roy's hand. "Nice to meet you both." Wes greeted. Jesse noticed a shyness about him that she hadn't seen before but then again she really hadn't known him very long. Everyday she learned something new about him that made her feelings grow.

"A detective. Seems like this town is full of your kind lately." Roy remarked.

"What happened here?" Wes asked.

"Arson. We got a kook amongst us. I told Jess about a friend of hers had an accident at the county rodeo. Her saddle had been tampered with. The horse damn near trampled her to death." Roy answered.

"Riley. How is she?" Jesse asked.

"She just left not too long ago. She's fine. Bruised up and got a concusion but you know her. Can't keep her down long."

"I think we have an idea who this guy might be. Is there a sheriff in town?" Wes was all business now.

"He went out to Riley's. The county and state police are searching up in the hills for the same man you're probably lookin' for." Roy mentioned.

"I need to get out there." Wesley commented.

"Jess remembers how to get to Riley's grandpa's place. Lord knows they spent a lot of time out there as kids." Roy smiled at his daughter. "Let us know what's going on."

Jesse instinctively hugged her father and went with Wes to the car. "Be back shortly." She replied as she got into the passenger side. Wes backed up and sped down the drive following Jesse's directions. The drive wound around the bend and the car hit the bridge with a thump. "Holy shit!" Jesse exclaimed chuckling. "I forgot about that." The police cars were parked along the drive. Wes hurried out making sure Jesse was close to him as they headed up to the porch. Something was wrong. The front window was busted out. Jesse's heart began to beat faster. She opened the door. "Hello?" She replied as she went in.

"Is anyone home?" Wes asked cautiously looking around. Then the dark haired woman appeared from the kitchen. Both women looked at each other. Jesse had never seen her before but from the look on the woman's face she saw recognition.

"Jesse?" The woman asked in disbelief.

"I know you're not Riley Jones." Jesse smiled.

"No. I'm Tess a friend of hers. There's been some excitement since we got back from your parents." Tess looked worn. Katie's parents were at the kitchen table with one of the police detectives. "I wish it were better circumstances but it's nice to finally meet you."

"What do you mean?" Jesse remembered the window.

"We came home and found the front window broken with this lying in the glass." She went over to the table and showed Jesse the photo.

Her face went white. This was the picture missing from her stuff and the exact one she had been looking for. She turned to Wesley. "It's him. This was on my fireplace mantle in the apartment. I hadn't seen it since the night he broke in. I thought it was just misplaced."

Wes looked closely at the picture. "This guy is cracked." He glanced at the others at the table.

"Katie, the girl that works for Riley is missing. These are her parents Barbara and Jim Wilson and Detective Williams from the State Police." Tess introduced.

"You know who's responsible?" The detective asked.

Wes pulled out his badge from his back pocket and showed it to the fellow officer. "I'm from the Nashville Police Department. I have very strong reasons to believe this man is Hank Moleson. A local thug but a dangerous one. You say he's taken this girl?"

"Hell yes. They're up in the holler somewhere and I am fixin' to go look up there myself." Jim interrupted. Katie's parent's nerves were on end. The waiting was worse than not knowing what was going on and if they had found their girl alive and safe. "I don't like not knowin' anythin'."

"Jim you're better off here. You can't do anything the police have the training. I couldn't stand it if I lost both of you." Barbara choked up. Tess put her hand on her shoulder for comfort but caught Jesse's eye who was motioning towards the living room.

"Any way for us to get up there without Katie's father seeing us leave?" Jesse asked.

"There's a few more horses in the barn. Riley runs a boarding business." Tess answered. "I could sneak off and saddle them up."

Jesse nodded and went over to get Wes while Tess headed outside. She made it to the barn and corralled the three mounts. By the time Jesse and Wes walked out from the back door Tess had the saddle blankets on all three. "We have to make this quick. Jess you know the holler better than anyone so you take the lead." They saddled up and headed quickly out to the pasture and found the trail. Tess rode up to her. "What the hell is all this about?"

"It's a long story. This guy Hank Moleson is a drug dealer in Nashville. My roommate Toni Griffin bought some heroin off him and it was tainted. The police found her washed up on the Columbia River." Jesse stated not wasting anytime with details. "I had an altercation with him and he's had this vendetta against me ever since. He broke into my apartment and trashed it and apparently he took that picture of Riley and me which had Stanford, Indiana written on the back. This morning I was going through some old boxes from my apartment and found a bag of dope buried in my things. I know Toni had placed it there." Jesse informed.

"I received a call on our way up here from my partner that the finger prints found on the plastic bag matched Hank Moleson's. This man is a psychopath in and out of prison. He will stop at nothing to get what he thinks he deserves. After he broke into Jess' apartment he disappeared. I can't say for sure that guy is Hank Moleson but it all fits. The photo proved that much." Wes situated himself in the saddle. It had been years since he had been on a horse.

"What happened to Riley? Dad said there was an accident." Jesse asked.

"She was a contestant at the county rodeo. The cinch strap on her saddle had been cut just enough so when pressure was applied it snapped. The saddle slipped off and Riley hit the ground hard. The horse kicked her on her right hip and again in the back of her head. She had a concussion. If the blow had been any harder she would of cracked her skull." Tess saw Jesse cringe as she continued. "Logan had just seen a man near the corral that she didn't recognize and he hadn't been seen since until last night. Somehow he made his way to Riley's and Katie came early to feed the animals. She probably didn't even know about the fire. The police have been searching the woods and when Katie came up missing Riley, Huck and Dale took off about an hour before you arrived. Do you think he will harm the girl?" Tess asked concerned. If this man was Hank Moleson then hard telling what type of danger Katie was in.

"I don't know." Wes replied.

They reached the old homesteader's place and saw a few horses tied near the chimney where the Sheriff and a few other men were. They turned around quickly when they heard the horses approaching. Wilbur looked hard at the riders recognizing Tess.

"What's up?" He asked as they rode up. Seeing Jesse up close clicked in his mind. "Oh my God. Is that you Jesse Monroe?" He smiled.

"I didn't think you would forget me Wilbur." Jesse remarked. "This is Detective Carson from Nashville Police Department. I think we can help you out with this investigation." She introduced Wes while he dismounted and shook Wilbur's hand before going into the scenario of Hank Moleson. Jesse and Tess sat on their mounts. Jesse looked up near the trail to the old woman's cabin she remembered going to as a kid.

"I wonder if Martha Cowan still lives up there?" She asded mostly to herself.

"She's the old woman Huck was talking about. Yes, they were just up here this week." Tess informed.

"You're kidding?" Jesse was surprised the woman has lived this long. She was old back when she and Riley used to ride up to visit with her. The old woman was tough. She should of known it would take more than old age to get Miss Martha.

"Riley and the boys went north to check on a woman living up there. Then they were going to backtrack towards the ridge. I haven't heard anything from them. We got men covering the southern base and working their way north. If he's out there we're going to find him." Wilbur commented.

170

"You better be looking high as well as on the ground. He has the reputation of being where no one can see him." Wes studied the map Wilbur had laid out on the fireplace hearth.

"We're going due east. Care to join us?" One of the other officers asked.

"Yea. That might be best." He turned around to let Jesse know. They had decided to go on up to Martha's place to make sure she was all right. Wilbur didn't see too much harm in it since that area had already been covered. "Be careful Wes." Jesse replied as she and Tess turned their mounts to the north.

"You both keep an eye out for this guy. I don't want any repeated incidents." Jesse knew he was referring to the night at Bogg's.

Chapter Eleven

High up in the trees on the ridge a flock of birds took off in sudden flight. Martha Cowen glanced up at the sky at the noise. Something must have scared them she thought to herself. The sun would be high in the sky by mid noon. A sign of a hot day. She finished hanging up her few pieces of wash. Picking up the basket she headed towards the front of the cabin. Whistling as she went. What was the saying her mama told her about a whistling girl and a cacklin' hen never 'mounts to much in the end. That never made much sense to her even now. When she turned the corner of the porch she never saw what hit her as she crumpled to the ground.

"You bastard!" Katie screamed as she tried desperately to get lose and go to the old woman. It took one backhanded slap to the mouth from Moleson that knock her down.

Hank went over to where she landed and yanked her up by the leather strap that tied her wrists. Katie winced in pain. He got into her face. "What the fuck did you call me?" He spat at her. "One more fucking word from you and I'll show you what a bastard really is." Katie never once looked away from his eyes. The dark color that seemed to have no pupils black as coal. "Now git your ass in there." He shoved her towards the cabin door. Once he secured her to a chair with piece of cloth he found laying on the table he went back out and dragged Martha inside. Moleson left her in a heap near the fireplace too far for the girl to reach her. This would be a good place to rest and get his thoughts in order. He knew the law was after him by now. Once he regained his barring they would head further south until they reached the lake. A lot of boats docked this time of year. He'd let the kid go after he got to a car safely. Then it didn't matter. They'd never find him then.

"Riley slow it down or we'll lose the tracks." Huck shouted from behind her. She wasn't paying any attention. Her heart was pounding hard in her chest. If anything happened to Katie she would kill him with her bare hands. "Take a look." Huck motioned at the tree branch hanging slightly over the trail. Part of stem was broken and just hanging. Dale was just up ahead near a briar bush where he found a piece of cloth.

"She's trying to leave a trail. From the broken stem and knowing if she leaned into this bush the thorns would tear her shirt. Smart gal." Dale remarked. "Looks like they're heading North."

Huck looked up ahead of the trail. He just had a feeling this guy was trying to throw them off. His gut told him they were going towards Martha Cowen's. Was Katie's life worth risking on a gut feeling?

Riley reined in her horse once she reached the ridge. From her position she could see for miles and miles. The only obstruction was the places the trees were so close together the naked eye couldn't see through. Every now and then she spotted a dark cap knowing it was the police. They were several miles away but from the pattern they were making their way towards where she was. It would take a good hour at their pace to reach the ridge. She backed up Cherokee and started down the incline.

Logan just finished the breakfast rush and was balancing the drawer when Mrs. Simms came running through the door. What customers were left all looked up when the heard her. "Logan have you heard what happened out at the Monroe farm?" She gasped for air without waiting for a reply she proceeded with the report. "Their barn caught fire early this mornin' and burnt clean down to nothin'." Logan looked at her in disbelief. "That ain't all honey. The man responsible took Katie Wilson."

173

"What?" Logan almost shouted. "When did this happen?"

"Early this mornin'. A big man hunt is going on up in the holler. Floyd Barker came in just a few minutes ago. He heard it on the scanner." Logan looked over at Sara who was listening.

"I need to get out there. Can you handle things?" Logan asked.

"Just go. Don't worry about this place. Keep me informed." Sara instructed as Logan rushed around to get her keys and was out the door. Mrs. Simms watched as she went.

"I don't know what is going on around here. First Riley's accident, Roy and Laura's barn and now Katie." She looked flabbergasted.

"I know what you mean. A bit much for a small town." Sara replied although her mind was elsewhere than on gossip. For the last few weeks she listened as the gossip flew around about Riley's accident. She kept quiet and tried to figure out herself why all this could happen to one person. Riley wasn't as much a mystery as people thought.

"It's those people from up north. They come down here thinking this is just a quaint little town and how they all would love to live here. They want to be apart of this little community. Can't happen. People here have built a trust and no stranger is going to fit in unless they earn it." Mrs. Simms was on a tangen. Sara tried to ignore her without being rude but the fact was Mrs. Simms was right. Sara wasn't one for relying on hearsay and she would just wait for Huck to fill her in.

Logan made good time getting to Riley's place. The drive was full of police cars and she had to park near the barn. She ran up to the porch where a group was waiting. She immediately saw Jim and Barbara and went up to them. "Has there been any word?"

"Not yet. Jesse Monroe and a detective friend of hers from Nashville were here. Something about this picture." Jim handed her the photo. He appeared to be at his breaking point. "No one knows a damn thing."

"Where's Jesse now?" She asked.

"Tess, her and the detective took off up into the holler." Barbara pointed behind her. The fact that this sort of man was at the mercy of her daughter made her stomach turn. She prayed that Katie would keep her wits about her. Maybe then he wouldn't harm her.

"All we can do is wait. From the looks of it the police have got a handle on it. You have to come to terms these people are professionals and they deal with situations like this on a daily basis. Kind of like Jim here who knows about farming. We just have to pray and let these people do their jobs." Logan comforted wishing she believed her own words. She had too for the sake of these two parents whose child had just been kidnapped.

Jesse raised her hand for Tess to stop. She wanted to go on silently. If her memory served her right then Martha Cowen's cabin was just up over the next hill. Tess leaned over and whispered. "Are we close?"

"I think so. It's been so long." She looked around getting her barrings. "We need to go in slow. I don't like the feeling I have. Let's tie the horses up here so they'll be out of sight and sound."

Tess followed as Jesse carefully walked towards the hill. Halfway up she crouched low motioning for Tess to do the same. One of the main instructions Mrs. Cowen had instilled in her mind was to always trust her gut feeling and her instincts. Right now they were screaming warnings at her. Near the top they lay down on their stomaches and looked down on the cabin. They were still a good distance away but they could see the two horses tied to the clothesline. Tess nodded at the questioning look Jesse gave her. Those were Riley's horses. Tess looked closely at the cabin. Something was wrong. She moved towards Jesse to whisper.

"It's ninety degrees out and the cabin door is shut. I don't think this woman has air conditioning." Jesse looked and sure enough Tess was right. "Let's move in closer."

Jesse backed down the hill with Tess so they could use the cover of the trees to move faster without being detected. From the clearing of trees they spotted the back of the cabin. There was no back door to the house. That was in their favor. Only one way out. Jesse pointed over towards the woodpile near the side of the house. They made a break for it and hid behind the stack. Tess took an extra few steps and found herself up against the wall and inched her way towards the window. Jesse sat back and watched. This woman had guts.

Tess carefully peaked in the window and saw Katie tied to a chair and a man standing at the door with his back towards her. He appeared to be looking out through the crack. Suddenly Katie glanced towards the window. Her eyebrows raised in recognition and she glanced away not to draw attention. Tess carefully backtracked to the woodpile. Once safely behind it she whispered. "Katie saw me. He's at the door looking out through a crack. He doesn't look armed but we're going to need a plan just in case." They both looked around trying to spot something to use as a weapon of sorts. Jesse spotted part of a dead tree limb lying near the edge of the pile where smaller sticks were piled. They devised a plan between them and Tess took the limb and went around to the other side of the cabin. Jesse counted and then walked out into the yard by the fire pit directly in front of the porch. She watched but the door didn't move. She was going to have to coax him out.

"Hey Moleson!" Jesse shouted. "I hear you've been looking for me. Are you too much of a chicken shit to show your face?" The door opened slightly.

He stared out in total disbelief. The bitch was standing right in front of him. All these weeks and she is not four feet from him now. He started to get confused. This wasn't the way it was supposed to be. She was to stay in Nashville so he could terrorize all that meant anything to her. She was ruining his plan. He would just have to finish what he started at the tavern. He jerked open the door and came out on the porch in a rage.

"You fucking whore!" Moleson yelled as he took a couple steps toward her in a fury of anger. Tess came from around the corner of the cabin and with all of her might hit the man on the side of his head breaking the limb in two. She heard a crack as he went down and didn't know if it was his skull or the limb itself. He started to get up but another blow put him out like a light.

Jesse ran into the cabin and found Katie tied to a chair with the rag still in her mouth livid with fear. Jesse pulled out the rag and Katie started to gag. "Miss Martha, he punched her in the face. She's over there." Katie motioned with her head towards the heap on the floor. A low groan crept from the old woman as she was beginning to come around.

Jesse hurriedly untied the girl and gave her the rope. "Go give this to Tess." She instructed as she went to the old woman who was now trying to sit up.

Outside Katie found Tess standing over the man who was laying face down in the dirt with blood oozing out from the cut above his ear. Tess looked over at Katie who rushed into her arms crying of exhaustion and relief. Tess stroked her hair. "It's all right honey. It's all overnow." She hoped Katie could believe it.

"I...I thought he had killed her." She sobbed into Tess' shirt. "I was so scared Tess." Katie tightened her grip around Tess' waist afraid to let go. Tess held her tight for comfort. No one would know the fear this child had gone through the last few hours.

"Let's get him tied up." Only then did she release her hold on Tess.

"Who is he?" Katie asked as she held his hands for Tess to wrap the rope around and tighten not caring if the blood was cut off or not.

"He's a drug dealer from Nashville that apparently has been terrorizing Jesse by going after her family and friends." She answered.

"That's Jesse Monroe?" Suddenly her spirits picked up. Tess pulled hard on the rope until she was convinced it would hold him. "I had no idea."

Jesse had helped Martha on to a chair and was applying cold water to the wound just below her eye, which was swelling up.

"Where's that youngin'?" Martha asked as her sight began to focus.

"She's alright. She's outside helping Tess tie up the son of a bitch who did this to you." Jesse assured her.

"Sucker punched me when I was hangin' out my wash. I..." She looked up at Jesse recognizing the voice. "Good Lord, I never expected to lay my eyes on you ever again chil'."

Jesse started to laugh. She was beginning to wonder if Martha Cowan was going to recognize her or not. "Keep this on your eye." She instructed. "How do you feel?"

"Like a fool." Martha retorted. They both heard the horses coming through the thicket at a high rate of speed. Dale shouted at them before reining in and dismounting.

"Looks like we're too late." He replied going over to where Tess and Katie stood. Riley wasted no time dismounting and running up to them.

177

"Katie!" She felt relieved as the girl ran into her arms. Riley looked up catching Tess' eye. There was no need for words as Tess saw the gratefulness on her lover's face. She felt the color rise in her cheeks. Riley stepped back to get a good look at Katie. She saw the bruise just below her left eye. "I am so sorry this happened to you." She pulled her close. "So sorry."

"I'm all right Riley. I don't think he had a chance." She turned to look at Tess and saw Jesse appear from the door onto the porch.

"You knocked him out?" Riley asked in disbelief but her eyes told more.

"She had a little help there." Jesse chimed in. Riley looked over on the porch where the voice had come from. The long curly reddish blond hair pulled back in a ponytail with that all too familiar teasing smirk on her face. "Again, you have missed all the excitement."

Riley had never been so glad to see her friend as at that moment. "Yea, and once again you stir up this whole mess and expect me to clean it all up. Just like old times." They went towards each other and embraced.

"It has been too long." Jesse replied. "I can't tell you how good it is to see you."

"Me too. Look at you." Riley let go and looked at her.

"You haven't changed a bit, jeans, sleeveless T-shirt and cowboy boots." Jesse took in the sight of her old friend.

"That reminds me." Riley walked over to where Hank Moleson lay still unconscious and with the all the strength in her leg she kicked him hard on the thigh. "I owe you that much. You piece of filth." Tess and Jesse started to laugh when Huck and Martha came out of the cabin.

"She's going to be all right but I'm going to stick around to make sure she doesn't start seeing double or nothin'." Huck glanced at Jesse before realizing who she was. "I should of known you had somethin' to do with all this." He smiled and gave her a bear hug.

Everyone jumped when Dale shot of three consecutive shots up into the air to notify the police the man had been caught. "I hate to break up this high school reunion but would someone like to tell me just who in the hell this guy is and why he did this?" Dale replied when he went over to greet his friend. Jesse was almost finished explaining whole thing when Wilbur, Wes and the rest of the police came riding up over the hill.

"How did you know he would be here? Huck and I had already been up this way this mornin'." Dale asked.

"Jesse had a gut feeling." Tess replied. She stood next to Riley who held her hand tightly. "I've learned a whole lot about intuition today."

"Then it all wasn't such a waste." Martha chimed in. "I have been teachin' these youngin's that all my life and I'm glad one of ya has listened."

Wesley jumped of his horse and Jesse went to him. He embraced her in his arms and kissed her. "I was worried about you when I heard those shots." He replied as though no one but the two of them were there.

"Tess here had more gumption than I think anyone has given her credit for." She smiled up at him.

"What the hell is going on here?" Wilbur replied as he went up to the man who was beginning to regain consciousness.

"That's your man Sheriff. Hank Moleson. The one I told you about.

"A mean son of a bitch. 'Cuse me ma'am." Wilbur looked towards Martha.

"Like I ain't heard or said it before myself." She retorted.

"Let's get him tied on the horse and get him into to town. I can guarantee he won't be seein' the light of day for a long time. I'll take your statements when we get off this hill." The other police officers helped get him tied into the saddle and started on down the hill towards Riley's place.

Riley went to the old woman and apologized for dragging her into all of this. Jesse intervened but the old woman wouldn't hear any of it. There are reasons and in time those will be known if it was meant to be. Martha told Riley sincerely.

Riley told Jesse to take Cherokee and she would walk down the hill where they had tied their mounts with Tess.

"You stop that nonsense that you have working inside of yourself." Martha instructed. "Don't be afraid of love. You have no control how it comes to you. Promise this old lady that much." She stated. Riley just looked at her before hugging her.

"I will. You are a wise woman Martha Cowen. I love you very much." Riley replied.

"Good. Now git that chil' to her parents." She turned to Huck. "I got some venison down in the root cellar. We can have us a celebration tonight." Huck just grinned back at her.

"I'll see you tomorrow. You can fill me in." He told Riley. Her and Tess walked up the slope towards where the horses were grazing. Once they were out of sight of the cabin Riley took her hand. "If I had any idea you were in the danger you were in I would have been out of my mind with worry."

Tess squeezed her hand and smiled in response. Riley didn't have to say it. She could see the feelings on her face. "What are we going to do about this?" Tess asked.

"I don't know. But right now all I want to do is get you home and into our bed." Riley remarked. Tess picked up on the mention of it being their bed. This was going to work. She felt it in her gut and according to the old woman it meant it was right. "And I don't ever want you to forget that it was I who took that guy out. Might be something to remember in the future." She grinned.

"I still can't believe it. Wait 'til I tell E.G. and Lynn. They're not going to believe this on either." She laughed. "You are full of surprises Ms. McGuire."

They took a short cut through the woods on their horses and caught up with the rest of the group making their way down the hill. At the clearing Riley saw the commotion going on around her house. "Katie, I think you caused a huge ruckus. Look at all those news people and the police cars."

Katie saw for herself. "Cool." She stood up in the saddle to get a better look. "All this for me?"

"Yea, think how popular you're going to be at school this year." Tess commented tenderly.

"I never thought. This is pretty cool. But I really wouldn't want to go through all that again." She replied.

"You are a very brave girl." Jesse praised.

"Does this mean I can have front row seats at one of your concerts?" Katie asked eagerly.

"Honey, you can have your own backstage pass. "You've earned that right by me." She grinned and looked over at Riley. "And for you, I swear I won't ever get you into any more situations."

"Jesse, I don't think you could make that promise and I wouldn't want it any other way. Tess, have I got some stories to tell you about this girl." They all laughed but the bond between these two childhood friends had become stronger than ever. "Now tell us about this detective." She noted when Wes turned around.

"Yea, Jess I'd like to hear this." He smiled.

When the posse made it to the barn the television cameras and news reporters swarmed in on them. Riley told them to leave the horses and she would take care of them. While they answered the questions and hurried Moleson to jail where he would stay for a very long time. Jim and Barbara ran from the house when they saw the group coming up through the pasture. Katie jumped down from her horse and fell into her father's arms. The emotions were so high it touched everyone around them. They thank everyone for their help and soon left to take her home. Katie was so excited she couldn't stop talking. Riley and Tess kept in the background while the media got their story from the detectives and once they recognized Jesse Monroe the scoop was greater than expected.

Logan came into the barn when they arrived and demanded to know the whole story which Jesse and Tess were glad to relate.

"I may have been a few years younger than you and Jess but your reputation has always preceded you both. So it was true that this was a vendetta against Jesse. That is so weird. To think a person can hate another so much to cause all this." Logan remarked. "That is something she's going to have to deal with being in the limelight."

"I think it mostly had to do with her roommate Toni. I guess she was an addict and it just filtered into Jesse's life. Her only fault was caring about another person. Jess has always been like that. It's over now and she as well as the rest of us have to move on." Riley commented.

"I love you." Logan replied out of the blue. "Don't get all jealous over it Tess not in the way you love her." She chuckled. "I just do. You worried me to death that something could happen to both of you. Don't put me through that again." Logan stated.

Riley and Tess just looked at each other and on instinct they both grabbed Logan into a bear hug. "We love you too, girlfriend."

"Stop it. I can't do all this mushy shit." Logan found herself laughing.

Later that evening when everything seemed to calm down Riley and Tess were sitting out on the porch with Logan, Jesse and Wes who filled everyone in on the story from the begining. Hank Moleson was in the Springdale Hospital under police lock up. He would be arraigned on the charge of kidnapping, arson, two counts of attempted murder and endangering livestock in Bradford County. After a trial he would then be extradited to Davidson County, Tennessee to face drug trafficking charges as well as breaking and entering and at least one homicide. It would be a long time before he would ever see the day light outside a prison wall.

"Stanford will be talking about this for a long time to come." Riley commented.

"So anything else shocking would be mild compared to this." Logan looked directly at Riley. It didn't take long for the meaning to register.

"And of course I'm the one once again." Riley shot a look right back at her.

"What does that mean?" Jesse asked. There was something going on by the way Riley reacted to her comment. Not only was she fidgeting but there was a redness in her neck that Jesse knew was from nerves.

"Too many years have gone by since we last talked. I suppose you were making a name for yourself in Nashville while my life was going through a lot of self awareness and through that I discovered something about my sexuality." Riley stated as if she had rehearsed those words a thousand times.

Wes shook his head trying to understand what it was that she meant by her evasiveness. Jesse stared at her wandering what the hell she meant. "So you're a lesbian? Is that what you're trying to say?" Riley nodded. "Then why in the hell didn't you just say, 'Jess, I'm a lesbian.' Instead of going through all of that?" She asked. A sigh of relief seemed to escape Riley's mouth when she started to laugh.

"It's not like something you could just say after not seeing you for over ten years. Like 'Hello Jesse by the way I'm a lesbian.' Just doesn't sound right." Everyone busted out laughing at the thought of her doing that.

"Is Tess your girlfriend cause if she isn't she ought to be to keep you in line. I saw first hand what she can do with a stick." Jesse looked over at her new friend.

"Yea, you just better do as I say or I just might take a stick to you." Tess began to playfully poke at Riley's arm.

"Hail Mary!" Logan exclaimed. "How hard was that?"

"You know something Logan you're about as subtle as a hooker goin' to a prayer meetin'." Riley retorted.

"Yea but don't you feel better?" She didn't wait for the answer, as she got up to leave. "Jesse it was nice seeing you again and meeting you Wes. Good luck with your record."

"Thank you. We'll stop in at Miss Mayme's before we head back to Nashville." Jesse offered. They watched as she got into her truck and sped off down the drive. "She's a character. I remember her now from school."

"She's been a friend. That I can say." Riley stated.

The rest of the evening Riley and Jesse got caught up on the missing years of their lives. Their struggles, dreams and what direction they were now headed. Wesley and Tess laughed at the stories that were told and a new level of friendship was made.

That night after everyone had left Riley and Tess were getting ready for bed. Tess noticed a change in Riley's attitude. She seemed distant. When she brought it to her attention Riley just shrugged it off saying it was just an emotional day. But Tess knew there was more to it. Riley stood at the window looking out over the farm and didn't hear Tess come up behind her.

"I know there is something wrong." Tess stated quietly resting her cheek against the good shoulder.

Riley took a deep breath and let it out slowly before finding the words she wanted to say. The past week and a half she and Tess had taken the time to really get to know one another. Something they didn't have the time for years ago. Riley couldn't deny that she was getting used to having her around. But in the back of her mind she also knew it would end. She just wasn't ready to hear it. Earlier Riley had walked in while Tess was on the phone to Lynn explaining a certain sale that was in question. The way she handled the call made

Riley feel like she couldn't ask her to stay and give up all Tess had worked her whole life for. That would be too selfish but then again Riley wasn't willing to give up all she had worked for either. She placed her hands on Tess' arms, which held her securely around her waist.

"You're leaving tomorrow aren't you." That was more of a statement than a question.

"I need to get back to the gallery." Tess was glad she couldn't see Riley's eyes. She wouldn't be able to handle the hurt. Together they had been through so much in this short time. Even for Tess she had found new things about herself that she would of never of found with anyone else.

"What's next for us?" Riley asked. A lump was forming in her throat. She swallowed hard. Tess kissed the side of Riley's neck working her way up to her ear.

"I was hoping you would know that answer." She breathed heavily as her tongue began to trace the contour of Riley's ear sending currents of arousal through her body. Tess let her hands roam up under Riley's shirt teasing her breast through the fabric of the bra. Riley slowly turned in her arms kissing Tess tenderly while untucking Tess' shirt from her jeans and lifting it up over her head letting it fall to the floor. She unhooked her bra releasing her breasts. Riley cupped each one in her hands with her thumb she gently rubbed at the nipples. The excitement growing inside of her resisting the urge to take her at that moment. Not tonight. Tonight they would go slow so she could savor and put to memory their last night together.

Tess removed Riley's shirt, and bra all the while teasing Riley with her mouth. Riley turned Tess around so her back was up against her chest. She placed her mouth where she knew Tess liked. Her hands slowly found their way to Tess' waistband and undid the button and unzipped her jeans placing her hand inside her panties. Riley gasped in pleasure feeling the moistness on her probing fingers. She rubbed her finger against Tess' clitoris very slowly establishing a rhythm. Arching her back Tess found Riley's mouth with her own. A groan escaped from her throat when their tongues met. Tess reached down and took Riley's hand from her now dripping pussy.

She turned around taking off the rest of their clothes Tess led her to the bed. Riley laid down against the pillows as Tess followed on top of her. She started with Riley's breast teasing the nipples working her way down to Riley's parted legs. Riley arched her back fighting to control her weakness. She ran her hands through Tess' hair feeling each stroke of her tongue. "Tess." She gasped and gave into to the desperately needed release. She quickly pulled Tess up to her and rolled her onto her back. Riley took her into her mouth savoring the taste and feel of her lover's body. Tess lay writhing in the pleasure Riley's mouth gave her bringing her to an exploding climax. Each time was better than the last. Riley lifted her head from between Tess' legs. She ran her hands up Tess' stomach to her breast. Kissing every inch of her body along the way to her taunt nipples. Both women were breathing hard and they wrapped their arms around each other. Riley pulled her on top of her and their faces were within inches.

"I love you." Riley whispered.

"I love you too." Tess answered before kissing her lips. Riley felt a tear drop onto her cheek from Tess' tightly closed eyes. Riley held her and vowed to never let go.

The interstate traffic was starting to get busy as rush hour was just starting. Tess knew it was late when she left Stanford. Riley had gotten up early to feed the animals and was just coming in the back door when Tess was at the counter making coffee. They looked at each other for a long time before either could find the strength to speak. Casual conversation and making plans to see each other the following weekend. This was now how it was going to be for them. Riley took her cup and sat down at the table stirring sugar into the steamy liquid. The sight of Tess standing there in just an old flannel shirt two sizes too big was arousing with last night still fresh in her mind. "What time are you leaving?" She asked.

"Are you trying to get rid of me?" Tess teased to ease up the tension. She went over and sat down on Riley's lap. Riley breathed in her scent mixed with the aroma of the coffee.

"Never." She answered. "Never again." She tilted her head up to see Tess' face. Those crystal blue eyes starring down at her with a mischievous spark. Riley stood up letting Tess slide against her leg and led her back to bed.

A horn blew snapping Tess back into reality before the Jaguar merged into the flow of traffic. The car swerved just in time to let her in and the driver gave her a dirty look. The exit was coming up and she signaled to get over. No one was going to let her in. Figures. She was back in the city. A sudden surge of homesickness overcame her once she got on the off ramp. The familiar sights should say welcome home but instead it offered her loneliness and longing. She had to get her mind back on work. There would be a lot to catch up on since she'd been gone for a week and a half. The Jag swung into her parking spot in the back of the gallery. Tess didn't have but a small bag and her briefcase to carry since her trip was only planned for a day when she left. The back door was locked and instead of trying to find the key she went around to the front.

The bell above the door went off and Lynn looked up from the desk. Her eyes grew wide in shock. "You are alive!" Lynn exclaimed in greeting. "I expected you earlier."

"The traffic slowed me down." Tess walked around to the other side of the desk where the stack of mail was.

"Look at you." Lynn was referring to the cowboy boots Riley had given her the first day she worked in the barn. "The Marlboro Woman has worn off on you." Tess couldn't help but smile at that remark. "First tell me what in the hell happened down there? It was all over the news last night." A sudden commotion at the top of the stairs caught her attention.

"Miss Thang, you come back from the wilderness!" Fernando exclaimed from the top of the stairs. "Did you tame that wild beast down there?" Fernando was the last person she had expected to see. It had been months since he made his rounds through the art circuit and ending up through Albany.

"When did you get into town?" Tess asked surprised.

"The day after you left so Lynn says. She tell me the whole truth." He started to check her out as he strolled down the stairs. Fernando never did anything including walk without his usual flamboyant affair. "Hmmm, I love the look. The tan and the dark hair so Native American. You have the blood, no?" He turned her around slowly checking out her backside. "Last night we sit and eat popcorn while the news comes on and there you are on a horse being so John Wayne butch. I tell Lynn, she so John Wayne butch."

"You both are something else." Tess tried to ignore her Latino friend as she sorted through the bills and the party invitations. There seemed very little to do other than answer the mail. Lynn was so sufficient she never did worry about the gallery the whole time she was gone. Obviously she smiled inwardly.

"Let's go get Java and you can tell me everythin' that happened." Fernando took her hand and headed for the door.

Lynn looked up and shouted before the door closed. "Carmel latte skim!" She hoped they heard. Fernando knew what she liked since the day Tess left every morning he went to the coffeehouse across the street to get them cappuccinos.

Once outside Fernando let go of her hand. He took a cigarette out and lit it. "Okay, the whole story. How is Riley?"

"She's great." They ordered their drinks from outside at the table they sat at.

"That good. Now tell me what happened and why was you chasing a criminal?" He took a sip of his coffee.

"I don't think even I believe the whole week and a half I was there. When I first arrived in Stanford there was this town rodeo that everyone was at. So I went there first. I arrived just as Riley was getting into the chute with this wild horse. The next thing I knew she fell and landed under the horse, which kicked her a couple times. She received a concussion and a bruised hip. I decided to stay when I saw her in the hospital. It was as tho' it was meant for me too. You know when you get those feelings. We spent the time really getting to know each other." She paused to make sure she had his attention and from the look on his face of total disbelief Tess was convinced. "When I saw that horse kick her into the dirt I felt the blow in my stomach. I thought I had lost her before I could make amends. It was then I realized I never stopped loving her. Getting Riley convinced was not that easy."

"How did you do it?" Fernando was deep into the story. He noticed the light that seemed to glow around his friend from the smile on her face.

"We got to know each other. We went swimming in the crick as she calls it. We sat on the front porch at night and told stories about our pasts. We started becoming friends. I realize now that was what was missing in the relationship before. We never took the time to

187

really get to know each other. We hit the sheets that first night we went out. Remember?"

"Yes, I am responsible for this one. What next?" He asked.

"Apparently Riley's childhood friend is a recording artist in Nashville, Jesse Monroe. Her roommate had gotten involved in drugs and this man Hank Moleson sold her drugs. She ended up injecting tainted heroine and died. For some reason he went after Jesse and found out where her family lived and terrorized them. He cut the cinch strap on Riley's saddle at the rodeo, which snapped causing the accident. Then he burned Jesse's parent's barn killing her horse. It was Jesse and I who found him up in the woods at a cabin where an old wise woman lived. Very primitive. He had taken a girl who works for Riley hostage and this woman. Jesse lured him out and I hit him over the head with a big stick. It wasn't long before the police found us. It was the most amazing thing I have ever been through. I would of never of thought a small town such as Stanford could produce such excitement. The whole town is like this huge family. Outsiders have to prove themselves worthy." Tess felt the pull in her chest. Stanford had a grip on her emotions and she knew it. Fernando just looked at her oddly. As though he knew exactly what was going on inside of her and couldn't believe it himself.

"What's going to happen to you and Riley?" As if Fernando really had to ask.

"I don't know. I love her that much I do know. But I haven't a clue what to do about it." She leaned back in the chair and watched the people walking by. Everyone was so proper when they walked. As if they knew they were being filmed on camera. Very few of them didn't care how they walked down the street.

"You do what makes you happy. It will come to you darling." Fernando took her hand. "We have parties to go to now that you are home. I have found the Latino wonder of the art world. He was hiding from culture in a loft in New York City in the village. Locked in his studio throwing paint on canvases and inscribing his talent with each stroke of the brush. A magnificent genius." He exclaimed. "He will be arriving in Albany tomorrow and I have a reception here for him at nine o'clock in the evening."

"At the gallery? Fernando there is no way I can be ready for that." Tess exclaimed. Nor was she in any mood for a party.

"You have been gone too long. All arrangements have been made. Lynn is a very efficient woman." He noted. Tess had already realized that fact. There would of never been a trip to in the first place had she not been able to put her complete trust in Lynn's capabilities. Lynn could be aloof and demanding but E.G. seemed to be influencing her away from certain attitudes.

"Let me get her latte and we can get back." Fernando motioned for the waitress.

The rest of the next day Tess and Lynn worked diligently through to the evening getting ready for Fernando's latest find. The Latino's pieces of art started arriving early that morning. Fernando was in his element as he arranged the displays in the back room, which was used for showings. The lighting was perfect to capture the pain and anguish thrown upon each canvas. The choice of colors expressed the emotion and mood of the artist. It was almost five thirty when the phone rang upstairs. Tess' private line. She hurried up the stairs and managed to answer on the fourth ring. "Hello?" She replied out of breath.

"Now that's how to answer the phone." She heard Riley's voice on the other end. "I couldn't wait 'til tonight."

"I know what you mean." Tess lay back against the pillows on the sofa. "I missed you last night when I fell asleep."

"I almost called you then." Riley admitted.

In the background Tess heard a howling sound like a coyote in the distance. "What is that noise?" She asked.

"That I probably need to explain." Riley just started doing so when the sound grew louder. "Hold on." The receiver was placed down and she could hear a ruckus then more howling. What on earth has Riley gotten herself into now? She had only been gone one day.

"Okay, I'm back. That was Duke." She was playing with Tess.

"Duke? Who is Duke?" Tess asked.

"Duke is a dog. I found him yesterday wandering down by the road. We chatted for awhile and he followed me up to the house. Every thing was cool until he decided to go sniff out Percy. Remember the rooster? Well, Percy didn't take to Duke's sniffin' and turned on him pecking at his nose. Now he won't leave Duke alone and he's retaliating by howlin'." Riley heard the laughter on the other end.

189

Tess knew first hand nothing was to be expected from her girlfriend. This was just another incident of many. "What kind of dog is this Duke?"

"A cross between an Australian Shepherd and a Beagle with a bit of chow thrown in. He is so cute and still young." Riley had been going over the idea of getting a dog for the ranch. She could use the company.

"You just found him?" It wasn't as though there were a lot of houses around Riley's place where dog's could just run off.

"People drive all the way out to the country to dump off their pets they don't want anymore. Duke was just lucky I was out fixin" the bridge when he came along. When you live in the country its good to have a dog around to watch over things."

"Sounds to me he has taken Percy's job." Tess was shocked to hear that Riley was finally giving some attention to the bridge everyone feared driving over. The thought of people would actually just dump their animals off cause they didn't want them anymore irritated her. But it was probably better for the animals than staying where they weren't wanted and being abused.

"You're just going to love him. Oh, before I forget everyone says to tell you hey. Katie hasn't stopped talking about you. Jess and Wes went back to Nashville this mornin'. I'm sure we'll be hearin' weddin' bells shortly from those two." Riley had met the couple at Miss Mayme's for coffee the morning they left.

Tess closed her eyes and pictured everyone Riley was talking about in her mind. She saw Katie as she worked at cleaning the stall. Just like she was there helping her again. Logan was dragging Riley out to an auction later in the week in Waynesboro. A town just due east. Tess visualized it all in her mind.

"When would you like to get together again?" Riley almost whispered.

"Right now." Tess replied as her heart sank knowing it couldn't be. "I want to see you right this instant." She could feel the smile come across the line. "Tonight Fernando and Lynn have a showing/reception at nine."

"How is Fernando?" Riley asked. "Has his English gotten any better?" That brought a laugh from Tess. They talked on the phone close to an hour when Tess had to start getting ready for the showing.

Tess told Riley she would call her tomorow and said her goodngihts. When she hung up Tess went to run the bath. Fernando and Lynn could do all the work this was their event and she was going to give it to them. A hostess she would be for the evening.

Promptly at nine a small crowd of people gathered in the reception area of the gallery. Lynn was making sure the champagne was chilled and instructed the caterers when to bring it out to serve. The Latino boy wonder was in the office with Fernando and Tess. When she was introduced to him he gave her the once over declaring her beauty and how he would love to put her on canvas. Normally Tess wouldn't give much thought to those remarks as she was used to them but now things were different. She informed him although as tempting the offer was there just wasn't enough interest on her part. She noticed the look and shrugged it off. Fernando also saw it and mad mental note.

They made their entrance into the showroom and everyone turned at the sight of the artist Julio Romez as he walked towards his paintings. A small round of applause went around the room while the guest studied, criticized and praised his talent. Lynn was in her element and Tess caught sight of E.G. standing alone with a drink over by the sculptures. Their eyes met and Tess went over to join her.

"I see Lynn has managed to drag you here tonight." Tess remarked warmly. She had always liked E.G. but never took the time to get to know her other than that she was a friend of Riley's.

"Yea, now she has to go to the police department's annual Christmas party with me this year. A trade off of sorts." E.G. welcomed a friendly face.

"I need to thank you." Tess tipped her glass of champagne towards her glass of beer.

E.G. shook her head and smiled. "No need. I'm just glad it has worked out. I talked to Riley last night." She leaned closer to lower her voice. "You know Lynn was right all along about you two. She was the one who actually put this all together. Don't let her know I told you and please don't tell Riley." She rolled her eyes for effect.

"So Lynn wrote the letter. We were convinced it was you." Tess was surprised.

"What letter?" E.G. was confused. "Oh the one I gave Riley." She remembered. But Lynn said Tess had given it to her to give to Riley and Lynn thought it would be received if it came from E.G.

Tess looked at her strangely. "You don't have a clue do you?"

"Yea, I think I do. Lynn had given me the letter on the way down to Riley's. I was under the impression it came from you. I saw the hand writing on the front of the envelope." E.G. saw the scenario dawn on Tess. "How did she get you to sign Riley's name?"

"I can't remember. But I obviously did." Tess thought now the attempt seemed hilarious. "I guess she knew something we didn't."

"Lynn has been telling me for years that you both belonged together and you had never gotten over Riley's leaving. I on the other hand knew for a fact that Riley had never been able to do the same with you. No matter how far she ran. It would never be far enough. Sometimes a good kick in the ass is needed to get the ball rolling." E.G. "Of course I didn't count on it being a kick from a horse to do it. But it worked." They both laughed at the irony. "So how are you guys going to work out the distance?"

"We haven't thought that far ahead yet. We'll work it out. I love her so much E.G." Tess confessed. "The country kind of grows on you. Did Riley tell you she has a dog now?"

E.G. raised her eyebrows. "Why wouldn't that surprise me? I also heard about you capturing a criminal. That surprised me more. Is she wearing off on you already?" E.G. noticed Lynn was trying to get her attention. "Guess I best see what she wants."

"If you get too bored you're more than welcome to go upstairs and catch the game." Tess offered.

"Thanks. I may take you up on that." E.G. remarked heading across the room. Tess went over towards the door. She glanced in the full-length wall mirror next to the coatroom. She styled her hair in a French twist with wisps of hair falling at the sides. The black silk suit with the white chamois under the sheer black shirt emphasizing her figure. The small diamond stud earrings complimented her tan skin. Tess looked like everyone else in the room but felt like an outsider. She remembered what she said to E.G. about the country life growing on you. The town of Stanford had gradually seeped into her blood. That was the feeling she couldn't quite put her finger on. She not only missed Riley but the town of Stanford that gave her the feeling that she belonged. Tess had never experienced that in any other place she lived.

She stood back and watched the people mingling about the room. Important people who held a certain status in the community. People she hadn't seen in months and some for years. She found herself wishing she was somewhere else.

As the evening grew longer Julio Romez was now the art world's newest find. The receipts started coming in rapidly as his work was selling quickly. Lynn was calculating and arranging the final sale dates for the new owners to pick up their pieces. Tess watched as she took total control of everything. She didn't notice when Fernando came up behind her startling her.

"Ah, my Tessy. You are someplace else eh? This showing is a fabulous success. Julio has sold many pieces yes." He replied as he placed his hands on her shoulders from behind.

"He is superb." Tess had looked at several paintings noticing the detail was defyingly correct. The shades of colors chosen to make the impact were spectacular. Fernando had been correct about the talent of this young artist. "Why did you choose Albany to have his first showing when New York or even Chicago would give him the exposure he deserves?" She asked.

"I should of but this way we first have to see if he is liked. And he is definitely liked." He gestured with his free hand. Tess chuckled. She knew the real reason. She just liked to give her friend a hard time. "I must now go mingle. You need to mingle too sister. Come now." He led her over to a group of people and interrupted their conversation.

The night seemed to drag on and before midnight the last of the guest had left. Tess was with Lynn in the office tallying up the receipts while Fernando seemed to have disappeared with the guest of honor.

"Look at this." Lynn showed her the balance. "We did quite well with our percentage."

"I'd say." Tess looked at the five figure amount at the bottom. The gallery was showing quite the profit. More of these showings might put them on a higher level in the art society. She didn't notice the way Lynn was looking at her. E.G. had long ago went up to the loft to watch the end of a basketball game while she waited for Lynn to finish up.

"So where were you tonight?" Lynn asked.

Tess looked up from the receipts. "What do you mean?" She retorted with her own question. She was too tired to get into an analytical conversation with her friend tonight.

"You were more distant than usual." She got up from the sofa careful not to knock over the champagne glass on the table. "Have you ever thought of taking a more permanent vacation?"

Tess narrowed her eyes. She knew what she was getting at. Lynn had proven herself in managing the gallery and tonight she proved it beyond anyone's expectations. Lynn had managed to pull off one of the most influential and profitable showing they had in a long time. Now was not the time though to make a decision of that importance. To answer her question, yes she had thought about nothing else since she returned. But her friend didn't need to know that. "What you're saying is my mind can't do two things at once." Tess stated the question.

"What I'm saying is you're not here anymore and you don't want to be. So why torture yourself with it any more. That's the problem with lesbians of your statute. When did the business start running you?" Lynn looked at her directly while standing in the doorway. "Let me answer that for you. When did you put down your own paint brushes?" She shot her a look before backing out the door. Let Tess think about that for awhile. Tess knew she was right. She sat there dumbfounded. Of all people it had to be Lynn who knew her better than most. She heard E.G. shout her good byes as Lynn rushed her out the door.

Tess sat there at her desk looking at the four walls, a door and several pieces of her personal artwork scattered about. The sculpture of the Frightened Indian she named was perched on the shelf behind her. She took it down handling it carefully. She absently rubbed the fine texture remember how long ago it had been when she made it. She was in college and a group of art students went to the Grand Canyon. They walked the trails and at night when the campfire was low she found herself staring alone out into the night. It was then Tess spotted an old Indian peering from the top of a boulder in the distance. The image was so intense Tess kept it in her mind until she was back at the studio on campus and she closed her eyes and molded the figure from memory. This was her most treasured piece she had ever made. Sometimes just before falling asleep she could see the Indian once again as clear to her as that night. A friend had told Tess of the spiritual guides that are around to keep people on track with their destiny. Funny that in times of despair she always sought out this statue for some kind of comfort it brought her. Like tonight. Maybe Lynn was right and it was time to rethink her ambitions.

The thought of Jesse leaving her roots in a small town to go after her own dream of fortune in Nashville. What made her stand out from the rest? Talent? Determination? All factors in achieving a goal or dream. What was Riley's dream and ambitions? The ranch and the peace that came with it. But was it enough to fulfill her completely as a person. That was exactly how Tess was feeling now. She was not completed as a person. The success of the gallery was not enough. The challenge was gone and the business was running itself. Maybe it was time to hand off the responsibilities of managing it to someone else.

She gently replaced the statue back on the shelf and turned off the lamp on her desk. Once upstairs Tess undressed, took off her make up that she despised putting on in the first place and went to bed. The clock on the nightstand told her it was almost one in the morning. Riley would be fast asleep by now since she had to get up so early. She closed her eyes and tried in vain to block everything out of her mind.

Huck parked his truck up under the tree nearest the creek and got out. "I don't believe it!" He exclaimed going over to the bridge that Riley had just put in the reinforcement beams on. "That horse must of kicked some sense into you." He started to laugh. Riley shot him a look. She was up to her knees in creek water. "Need any help?"

"Take a look at the beams and make sure I did 'em right." She waited while Huck lay down on his stomache to look under the planks at the beams.

"Looks fine to me. At least you know what you're doin'." He commented.

"I've never braced a bridge before. Test it out and drive your truck over it." Riley challenged.

"Those are words of confidence." He chuckled going back to his truck. Riley waded through the water to the embankment and watched as Huck slowly drove the truck over the bridge. No swaying. A good sign. She looked closely at the joices and saw the bolts had reinforced the beams. It would be awhile before she would have to worry again about loosing a vehicle in the creek. Huck parked on the other side and got out. "So?"

"I think it'll work for another twenty years or so." She smiled up at him as he helped her with the toolbox. "What brings you out?"

"Nothin' really. How's your leg?" He asked as they walked back to his truck.

"Pretty good. I declared myself healed." Riley raised the hammer for emphasis.

"Hell, you done declared that the day after you got out of the hospital." He teased. "Logan said your friend went back home a couple days ago." Huck noticed her change in attitude.

"Yes she did." Was her reply.

He pushed his hat back on his head. A sign he was trying to be serious."I also talked to Doc Garvey. He said you both had a talk. I kind of figured from the way he looked you had told him about Tess."

Riley turned around and leaned against the tailgate. "I had too. I didn't want him to end up getting hurt. I think he thought there was a chance for us and I couldn't lie. I am who I am and for the last few years I tried being someone I wasn't."

"You don't have to convince me." He looked over at her. "How did you meet Tess?"

"I was remodeling an art gallery and the owner at the time brought his friend over to check the place out. Tess was the friend." Riley was a bit confused at the suddenness of the conversation. "Tess ended up buying the gallery and that's where she is now."

"And you're all the way down here. Doesn't seem right."

"I know but what kind of life could Stanford offer her?" She had asked herself that over and over trying to convince herself they could make a long distance relationship work.

"A person never knows with other people. You think you know someone pretty well but there's always that one side no one will ever get in. No matter what." Huck seemed to be talking from experience. "Well I think you deserve a lot more." He didn't finish once the dog

196

rounded the corner of trees and bounded towards them. Riley backed off as Duke jumped into the truck bed going up to her with a dripping tongue to which he proceeded to wipe her face with.

"Down Duke." She tried to sound stern. The dog wasn't listening.

"Now where on earth did you get this mutt?" Huck asked as Duke started licking his face affectionately.

"He just showed up when I was working on the bridge. Came out of the woods. I think he was dumped." She replied. Duke was all up in Huck's business.

"He's a playful pup. There boy, down. Get down. That a boy." Huck rubbed the dog's head. "He minds." He picked up a stick and threw it into the grass and watched as the dog went after it. "I best get goin'. Just thought I'd come out and see how things were goin' now that the excitement has calmed down around town."

"Thanks. It's back to normal I guess." Riley commented and took her toolbox down from the tailgate.

"You know Riley, if Tess comes down here permanently I really don't think its gonna matter. I just don't want you to be unhappy." Huck stated. Riley put down the toolbox and went up to her friend putting her arms around his broad shoulders.

"You've done so much for me Huck. A true friend to your word." She noticed the redness creep up into his face from embarrassment. It took a lot for Huck to express his feelings. He always has watched out for her. And from the looks of things he always will. He waved from the window as the truck backed slowly over the bridge. Riley waved back.

"Come on Duke let's go up to the house." The dog started running ahead as Riley walked slowly enjoying the evening. Once on the back porch she glanced at the tools and the memories swept over her. Everything was reminding her of Tess McGuire. Will this be another episode in her life that she had to get over? Riley asked herself. The last couple of weeks when Tess was here everything felt so good. Waking up in the morning next to her in bed and falling asleep at night in her arms. The thought made her shiver with desire. Maybe this weekend Tess would come down for a visit. A visit. She repeated the word over and over in her mind. A visit. A short time of seeing someone before they left to go home. That was how it was going to be from now on. Visits. In a perfect world...she started to say but the ruckus outside drew her attention as Percy the rooster was teasing Duke again.

Early Saturday morning Tess got up to the sound of birds singing outside her window. A sound she never paid attention to before. The clock said it was ten minutes after six. She had gone to bed after midnight as she put the finishing touches to the contract she had drawn up yesterday with her attorney. In less than two hours she would be on her way. Lynn and Fernando were due in at seven thirty to sign the final draft. Lynn would then be the new manager of the Florence Street Art Gallery. Tess would still hold the deed but the full reins were being passed. The decision was not made in haste but it was all Tess could do to keep her sanity. She no longer wanted her old life back in Albany without Riley. If this were a mistake she would still have an income and now was the time for changes. The past month taught her a lot about herself and what she deserved and wanted out of life. The people in Stanford all had their dreams and if they didn't find them at home then they went elsewhere. Just as Jesse did. Tess hadn't even told Riley of her plans. Riley knew she was coming down for the weekend but she didn't have a clue how long a visit it would be. There were chances that Tess just had to take.

She got up from the table and showered before making sure everything was packed in her suitcases. Later she would worry about the rest of her things in the loft. Lynn had mentioned that she and E.G. might be interested in taking up residency here to save some money. Tess heard the bell on the door go off downstairs letting her know Lynn had arrived. The excitement started to grow. "I'll be down in a second." She shouted from the top of the stairs. She hurriedly dried her hair deciding to leave it down and went over to the bed to put on her boots. This was her style now. A lot of changes were in store for her and it made her even more excited.

"Hey girl." Lynn appeared at the top step. "Are you having second thoughts?"

Tess looked over her shoulder at her and grinned. "Are you kidding?" This was a huge step for Lynn but one Tess knew she was more than capable of handling. Or she wouldn't have even thought of doing this in the first place.

"I don't know. Do you think life in the boonies will make you happy?' She tested.

"I'm getting back to painting, drawing, sculpting and anything else I can do with my hands. I need to get back to who I was before this business consumed me." Tess remarked.

"I know what you plan on doing with your hands and your Marlboro Woman." Lynn teased. She was going to really miss her friend.

"Yea, that too." Tess replied with a mischievous grin on her face.

"I think you're crazy but I understand." Lynn heard Fernando downstairs. He must of came in the backdoor. "Let's go do this so you can be on your way."

Tess followed her down the stairs and into the office where Fernando was waiting on them. She went around to sit for the last time behind her desk and took out the folder containing the contract. In a few quick strokes of the pen Lynn was now the manager of the gallery and she was just a silent partner. Lynn couldn't control her excitement. She finally had something to build, grow and respectfully call her own. Fernando popped a cork on a bottle of champagne.

"To Lynn with her fiery attitude congratulations. I help you sister." He whispered even though both women could hear him. "And to you my flower." He gazed into Tess' eyes noticing the happiness that radiated towards him. "You go find your dreams. You have searched so long. Now you go. Bye bye." Their glasses clinked together in the toast and the deal was sealed. Tess emptied her glass in one gulp. She turned around to pick up the Indian statute on the shelf.

"You know you're not getting rid of me that easily." Tess suddenly felt the impact of leaving all of this behind. But the pull on her heart was greater.

"You go play on the farm and we take everything here, okay? " Fernando replied. "I'm going to miss you sister." He opened his arms and tearfully hugged Tess goodbye. Lynn joined in until all three started to laugh through their tears. Tess broke free and went back upstairs to get her luggage loaded into the Jag. Fernando and Lynn helped. One last hug goodbye with promises that they would come down to Stanford to visit and she was on her way south.

Saturday was the only day Riley spent alone on the ranch. Katie didn't work on the weekends as it was filled with teenage stuff to do. The 4-H Club was getting ready for the end of summer carnival at the fairgrounds. Fall would be setting in soon although the heat of mid-day gave no hints that would happen anytime soon. The garden was harvesting and Riley had bushels of tomatoes she planned on canning after the weekend. Tess would be here sometime this afternoon. When she talked to her last night she said she had an early meeting and would head down afterwards. Riley remembered those kinds of meetings and didn't expect her until later in the day. She couldn't help the excitement that overcame her at the thought of seeing her again. It had only been a little over a week but in their situation that was a lifetime.

The stalls in the barn had been swept out and Riley piled the dirty straw and manure in the bed of the truck. She was starting a compost pile near the garden so when the last of the vegetables were picked she'd spread it on the dirt for fertilizer. She was up in the hayloft throwing down bales of straw when she saw the black car making its way over the bridge heading for the house. Riley stood at the hayloft door and watched as Tess got out and looked around.

"Up here!" Riley shouted and Tess turned placing her hand over her eyes to shield the sun. Riley waved to her to come up. This was a surprise she thought to herself. Maybe the meeting wasn't as long as she thought.

Tess climbed the ladder quickly leading up to the loft. and saw Riley throw down another straw bale before she turned around. "I didn't expect you 'til later this afternoon." She smiled. Tess looked good. Riley noticed the cowboy boots and jeans and the swell of her breast from the neck of her tank top. Riley felt the tingling in the lower part of her stomach.

"The meeting was brief." Tess replied seductively. She had envisioned this encounter for the last couple hours on the road. She moved in closer. "There have been new developments at the gallery you should be aware of." Tess hooked her finger in the waistband of Riley's jeans and pulled her towards her.

"Really? And what is that?" Riley put her hands on Tess' waist. She could feel Tess' hot breath against her mouth when Tess started planting small biting kisses on her lips. This was more than Riley could stand. Tess was seducing her and Riley let her have her fun until she couldn't stand it any longer.

"Well first." She started between kisses. "Hmmm, I'm no longer managing the Florence Street Art Gallery." Riley pulled back in surprise. "I still own it but this morning I made Lynn the new manager and Fernando her consultant." She waited to see the impact the news had on Riley. She was shocked and a bit bewildered. That gallery meant everything to Tess.

"I don't understand?" She questioned.

"I don't either. All I know is how much I love you Riley Jones. My life has changed because of it. I feel like I've come home. And I'm here to stay." Tess looked into Riley's green eyes for any signs of hesitation. But there was only love staring back at her. A deep honest feeling for the woman she held in her arms. Riley lowered her head her lips finding Tess'. Their tongues touched sending ripples of desire through their bodies. Riley took her hand and led her over to the clean pile of straw in the corner.

"What are you doing?" Tess asked though hestitating at the gesture.

"I'm goin' to make a proper country gal out of you yet." Riley stated pulling a horse blanket off of the wall spreading it over the straw.

"And how are you going to do that?" Tess asked.

"For starters," Riley gently pulled Tess down to the blanket next to her before placing her hands under Tess' shirt softly caressing her breast covered by the soft silky material of her bra. Riley kissed her soundly then leaving little kissed down to the soft hollow spot of her neck. She breathed in the scent of Tess' perfume that only identified Tess.

"Hmm," Tess groaned. "And then what?"

Riley unbuttoned her jeans and ran her hand down Tess' stomache then under the elastic band of her panties. She slid her fingers along the wetness between Tess' legs and began to rub gently. Tess raised her hips and aided in the process of getting rid of her jeans. Within seconds their clothes were off and they lay began to explore each other's body. The feel of the rough material beneath her gave more excitement to Tess. She had never made love in a barn loft before. A first of so many firsts.

201

Jennifer Baylor

Riley kissed the inside of Tess' thigh feeling her shudder against the touch. She ran her tounge along her lower stomach until it was buried between the moist folds of skin. She tasted Tess' excitement and drove her tongue deep creating a moan from Tess' lips.

Tess placed her hand on the back of Riley's head as her hips came off the blanket. Her legs spreading wide to allow the sensations to blend with heated passion. Riley never let up on the pressure of her tongue until Tess couldn't stand it and came in an exploded orgasm. Riley lifted her head. Her mouth wet from Tess' juices. She propped herself up on her hands laying her body against Tess'.

She brushed back the strands of wet hair from Tess' forehead picking out the pieces of straw. "I love you so much." Riley kissed the tip of Tess' nose.

"Oh Riley." Tess sighed contentedly. "I hope we can make this work." She started to say before a sudden racket from outside drew their attention to the loft door.

"Ugh. I don't even have to look to know what that commotion is." Riley reluctantly raised herself up and put on her t-shirt and jeans before looking out the loft door. Sure enough there was Percy giving chase to Duke who was bewildered as to why this animal tormented him so much. Riley glanced back at Tess who was dressing and joined her. "That is Duke." She pointed to the dog who was sniffing out his enemy and receiving a few pecks on his nose in response making him howl.

Tess threw her head back and laughed. Not once had she regretted her decision that it was time to go home. And this farm would be just that for her and Riley, their home.

202

About the Author

I was seventeen years old when my parents informed my siblings and me that we would be moving from our small farm in rural Monroe County. Devastated, I walked out of the house and began walking down the road. I had no destination in mind but the need to be surrounded by everything that I grew to love about my home. I walked about three miles that day ending up at the limestone quarry at the end of the road. I was in mourning for the home I was going to lose. I memorized every detail I could that day. How the sun shone on the water between slabs of rock. How the trees seemed to sing a tune every time the wind blew through the leaves. I knew Stanford would always be my home even though I can never go back to recapture my youth that still resides there through memories.

I currently reside in Anderson, Indiana with my partner of five years and together trying our best at raising two girls in hopes that some day they will look back on their childhood with the same found memories that we have had.

Printed in the United States
1049400005B